Steel in the Morning

DJ Cockburn

DJ Cockburn's has been pursuing writing for some years, during which time his successful pursuit of form rejections has been interrupted by the occasional publication and winning the 2014 James White Award. He has supported his unfortunate writing habit by working as a scientist, initially in zoology and more recently in medical research.

He lurks on the internet at Cockburn's Eclectics (http://cockburndj.wordpress.com/).

The cover was designed by Manda Benson, (http://www.tangentrine.com/).

Contents

Cassandra's Cargo

George Harding lay in his hammock and closed his eyes. He knew the gloomy room he found himself in was a delusion of the malaria that chilled his blood, but it felt so real he could smell the bodies pressed against his.

Boots echoed on stone and stopped beside him. Rough hands pulled manacles off his ankles and hauled him to his feet. His legs quivered as though unused to carrying him, which was a familiar sensation because George Harding's flaccid muscles often protested at his weight. He looked down to see not the pale paunch that he was accustomed to, but the contours of a muscular African half his age. His head recoiled upward. The rows of prone Africans that he had been pulled out of stretched into the gloom. The sight drove out all thought of a comfortable hammock because he simply couldn't imagine the terror screaming through him.

He wrenched an arm free and drove his elbow into a face, his fist into another. The hands holding him slackened just enough. Shouts chased him into the gloom, but he was already at a wall at the end of the rows of bodies. A ladder gave him the choice of up or down. He climbed up for no reason he could name.

Another wall in front of him. He turned and ran between more rows of chained men. A man in trousers swung a staff at him. It was aimed at his face and the joy of ducking under it and hurling the man to the floor was as real as the terror that flung him at the next ladder. There was light shining above it. The light of the sun. The light of hope that caressed his shoulders as he climbed and dazzled his eyes so he did not see what hit his head and dashed him back to the floor below.

He had no doubt that the boots thudding around him were real, and so was the burning pain they crunched into him. He wrapped his arms around his head, not to protect himself so much as to hide from the nightmare that consumed him. The kicks stopped and it took him a moment to recall the shout that had stopped them. His arms were wrenched away from his head, and he found himself looking upon the most blessed sight he could have dreamed.

A white man.

A white man, who had the authority to give orders. An angelic sight from his tattered shoes to his yellow teeth. The appraising look in the man's eyes belonged less to an angel than to a farmer sizing up cattle at a market. The angel barked an order in a language that George Harding felt he should understand but didn't. Iron fingers prized his mouth open and the angel rolled back his lips and nodded approvingly.

No rescue would come from this man. Manacles clamped George Harding's ankles again, and he was bundled down several ladders to be dragged back into the light. He was not even surprised to find himself shoved into a line of similarly manacled and naked Africans, shuffling out of the fort toward the masts of a ship. Knowing there would be no rescue did not stop him shouting "I am George Harding" over and over again, but his mouth would not form the words so nobody listened.

~~~~~~

"Bugger."

George Harding heard his own voice with relief. There were no manacles, no ships, and his hand was still white and plump when he managed to focus his eyes on it. He was still George Harding, His Britannic Majesty's agent in Bathurst. Still trying not to die of malaria before somebody in Whitehall remembered to give him a pension. His worst tribulation was not that he had been sold into slavery, but the salty taste that told him his throbbing gums were bleeding again. He tried not to think about how much he had paid that surgeon for his new set of teeth, and concentrated on thinking about what he would do to the man with his own tooth extractors when he next saw London. They hurt more than the rotten set they replaced.

He swung himself out of his hammock and yelped at a stab of protest from his ankles. It was only gout, not manacles. Stupid thought. He pulled off his clammy shirt and flung it on the floor for the houseboy to pick up. He opened the drinks cabinet and found a bottle of brandy and a glass. The malaria surprised him with a last tremor, splashing the brandy over the papers strewn across his desk.

"Bugger."

He opened another bottle and measured out fifty drops of laudanum. His head stopped spinning, and he could even read the label on the bottle. He could also see how little was left in it, and he formed an almost coherent prayer that the mail packet would arrive soon. The replenishment of laudanum would more than make up for the lack of mail.

He drank brandy from the bottle and grimaced when it was so hot it almost burned his tongue, but it was worth it for the calm that it brought. He'd feel up to looking at some paperwork in a minute.

"Please Massa!" Harding turned round to see the middle-aged houseboy in the doorway. Harding grunted.

"Boat come, Massa."

"Boat? What boat? Packet's not due for another week and the buggers are always late."

The boy's forehead furrowed. "Boat come, Massa."

Why couldn't someone teach these buggers to speak the King's English? Then again, Harding was uncertain that King George himself could understand him through these teeth, whichever King George it was that wore the silk stockings at the moment. He elbowed past the houseboy and stepped outside. The sun flayed at his bare back, adding its share of discomfort to the steam bath of Bathurst in October. The tangle of mangrove surrounded what his documents of appointment called his 'residence' and the garrison officers called 'Harding's Hovel', except where the liquid mud of the River Gambia provided the anchorage that got the navy excited about the place. Then they needed a battery and a dockyard and a poor bloody acting-governor to make sure the Union Flag went up and down the pole every day. Too much to expect the Navy to think about the miasma that would rise up from the swamp and give the poor bloody acting-governor three bouts of malaria for every hoist of the flag.

"Typical bloody Navy," he muttered to himself, as he waddled to the edge of the river.

The boy was wrong. There was not a boat coming in, but two ships. The first was a three-master with the narrow sails of a merchantman. He saw the name *Cassandra* embossed on her stern as she hove to. The second was coming round Banjul Point, and the rake of her two masts identified her as a man-of-war long before Harding made out the White Ensign. The merchantman was wearing the same ensign, which Harding could not understand until he realized that the smell assailing his nostrils was far more acrid than the usual stink of the swamp. There was only one sort of ship that smelled like that and only one reason why it would be coming into a British port with a Royal Navy flag at her mast. Some busybody had caught a slaver, which would mean that the smell was only the first sighting of a fleet of vexations bearing down on him.

A third vessel appeared from behind the merchantman, under every sail that her single mast could carry. She flew the Fleur-de-Lys of France, which told Harding that his papers would be waiting a little longer.

"Bugger."

He trudged back to the residence to throw some water over himself and find a shirt. Wouldn't do to meet whoever was in that cutter without one, even if it was probably some frog pirate.

Armand de Valois's neat frock coat and powdered queue would not have looked out of place in the Tuileries, and Harding wondered how he could look so well groomed when he must have been at sea for weeks in that little cutter. Harding had met de Valois a few times and knew that he made his first fortune from his privateers, which he'd converted into slavers when Bonaparte's exile brought peace. He decided he had been right to expect a frog pirate.

Harding was pleased with his own appearance as he pushed himself to his feet against his desk. He hoped that his uncombed hair and bloodshot eyes would pierce the dapper Frenchman's veneer, but de Valois's smile lost none of its charm as he wrung Harding's hand. "Ah, Governor 'Arding, it is an honor to meet you again."

"Your servant," grunted Harding. He was not a governor because Bathurst was not a colony in its own right, but de Valois could call him one if he pleased. He made the title sound so apt that Harding even forgot to be irritated by the consonant de Valois's accent deducted from his name.

Harding waved a hand at a chair. De Valois settled into the sagging wickerwork as though it was an emperor's throne.

Diplomatic etiquette dictated that Harding, as the host, should open the conversation.

Bugger diplomatic etiquette.

He glowered at de Valois, who smiled politely back. Harding allowed his eyelids to droop, as though he were falling asleep. De Valois raised his chin with an expression of sudden interest. "Forgive me, Governor 'Arding, but I cannot help but observe your very fine teeth. Surely those dentures must be ivory?"

Last time Harding had seen de Valois, he had still had the rotten remains of the teeth nature gave him, which had not been very pleasant for either him or anyone facing him. Now he had a set that would be as fine as any in London society, if only they had not cost so much that he had been forced to accept a posting nobody else would take to pay them off.

"Not ivory," he said. "Genuine Waterloo teeth."

"Excuse me?"

"Waterloo. The battle. When we sent the crapauds packing." Harding could not resist trying to provoke the Frenchman, but de Valois just nodded with the perfect blend of interest and deference. The man was insufferable.

"I needed new teeth but I didn't want them from some bugger who'd been scraped out of the gutter when he'd died of the French disease. These came from a soldier killed at Waterloo. Proper English teeth, these."

De Valois nodded again. The man was impervious to insult. Whatever he wanted, he wanted it badly.

"I 'ear Waterloo teeth are the talk of London. I congratulate you on acquiring a set," said de Valois.

Harding noted de Valois had not known what Waterloo teeth were when he thought describing them would appeal to Harding's self-importance. He grunted to avoid having to say anything polite.

"Governor 'Arding, may I come straight to the point?" said de Valois, now that he had prevaricated for five minutes.

Harding grunted again.

"I fear there has been a grave misunderstanding, and I came here aboard my own yacht to rectify it. I am afraid that it may even threaten the peace that your nation and the United States of America have enjoyed these three years."

Harding raised his eyebrows. "The United States?"

A crash shook the bungalow. Harding nearly fell out of his chair. His skull had barely stopped ringing when it echoed with a second crash, and he recognized it as the man-of-war announcing her arrival with a salute. Couldn't the bloody Navy do anything quietly?

The two men regarded each other as the cannonade rolled over Bathurst, de Valois with his polite smile and Harding wincing as the explosions rattled his teeth.

"As I was saying," said de Valois after the last sledge-hammer blow to Harding's mind, "a grave incident has occurred. The captain of that man-of-war has, with intentions that were no doubt excellent, unlawfully seized a merchant ship of the United States."

"You mean that slaver?"

"It is true that the ship was carrying a cargo that your government would not approve of..."

"Slaves?"

"But as I said, there has been a terrible misunderstanding. Governor 'Arding, we are men of the world and I need not tell you how the best of reasons may seduce a young man into error. The captain of that man-of-war would no doubt have distinguished himself at Trafalgar, but several days ago, his zeal led him to seize that ship in the belief that she was a Frenchman, when in fact she wears the flag of the United States."

De Valois was talking fast and no wonder, thought Harding. The salute announced that the man-of-war had dropped her anchor and her captain was probably stepping into a boat at this very moment. "I presume we're talking about one of your own slavers?"

De Valois gave a look of such mortification that Harding would have had to stifle a laugh if his teeth had not hurt so much.

"No, of course not. My ships are registered in France and so the Royal Navy would have every right to seize them if they found slaves aboard, which of course they would not."

"Because France signed the Treaty of Vienna after we got Boney where he couldn't do any more damage."

Harding could not resist the opportunity to rub salt into a wound that must still be fresh.

De Valois showed no sign of bleeding. "Indeed. I was pursuing my entirely legitimate trading interests when I became aware of your countryman's mistake. Naturally, I came here as fast as I could because it is the plain duty of men of good sense, such as ourselves, to avert the consequences of such a misunderstanding. It does, after all, amount to an act of war against the United States and I am sure we can agree that neither of us wants to see the Royal Navy lose any more frigates. "

Harding hid his satisfaction. He must have nettled the frog if he felt the need to mention the poor performance of the Royal Navy against the Americans. De Valois could not know how much Harding detested the Royal Navy. "Your point, Monsieur?"

"I have no doubt that your good sense will prevail when the captain presents his log book, which will presumably say that the ship was wearing a French flag when she was sighted. I assure you that he will be mistaken, which I will prove in time. It is easy to make a mistake when it is dawn and you are looking through a telescope..." de Valois spread his hands in a disgustingly Gallic expression of helplessness.

Tongue enough for two sets of teeth, thought Harding. He scratched his crotch. "What's your proof?"

"You 'ave my word that I will provide it in time. The problem is that we do not have time. The cargo of the ship that has been seized is, shall we say, perishable? It will lose much of its value while we send for the documentation. I entreat you to take my word and release that ship immediately."

"Your word?" Harding didn't try to keep the amusement out of his voice.

"The word of a Frenchman. Naturally, I appreciate that there are certain expenses involved. There are five hundred gold guineas aboard my yacht, and I will gladly place them at your disposal to avert the crisis."

Harding's eyes snapped open. He could pay off his teeth and return to London with five hundred guineas, and the hell with the service.

It was not difficult to guess what had happened. De Valois had been using the cutter to make arrangements before he committed the larger merchantman to an anchorage that would leave it trapped by a navy patrol, and he could not be arrested because his yacht carried no slaves. The captain of the slaver had thrown all evidence of French registration over the side before she was taken and de Valois was willing to spend some of his capital to preserve his cargo and his ship.

Harding assumed a contemplative frown. Who really cared where the slaver was registered? Ten years ago, Harding's duty would have been to welcome a slaver as an honored guest and assist him with his legal trade, and damned if he'd see five hundred gold guineas for his trouble. Unfortunate for the slaves of course, but then nobody ever asked Harding if he'd wanted to go to Bathurst.

But he'd never breached his trust before. The odd grease for certain administrative wheels was one thing, but to pretend a French ship was American was something else. Then again, how much was a flag worth in the balance with five hundred gold guineas? He winced as his teeth started throbbing again. "I'll think about it."

He stood up to end the interview, and de Valois stood with him and extended his hand. Etiquette demanded that Harding should offer de Valois a room in the residence, but de Valois said that he would be aboard his cutter before Harding got the chance to pointedly withhold an invitation. He saw de Valois to the door and watched him stroll back to the wharf, as though he were ambling down the Champs Elysée instead of through the ankle-deep mud of Bathurst.

A flock of brown birds burred over his head and landed in a tree. Ha-ha-ha-ha, they babbled. A bomb of fury exploded in Harding's breast. They were laughing at him!

He dashed back to his desk and pulled a pistol out of a drawer. Tears of rage blurred his sight and his shaking hands scattered more powder over his desk than he got into the pan, but eventually he got it loaded and dashed outside. He pointed it at the tree, but the birds had gone.

The pistol sank back to his side, and he waited for his breathing to slow down and his jaw to stop quivering. A chill marched up his spine. Surely he couldn't be about to have another bout of fever so soon after the last one? "Bugger."

~~~~~~

George Harding was running. He didn't know where he was or where he was going, but the barking dogs behind him left him in no doubt of what he was running from. Branches whipped out of the night and slashed across his body. There was no help for it except keep running on his shredded feet, turning every aching breath of fetid air into a few more paces between him and the plantation.

Plantation?

The question stirred a dispassionate part of his mind. Fever had brought strange visions before, especially since he had discovered how quickly laudanum helped him to recover from them, but they had never been more than disconnected impressions. Now he knew that he was in Jamaica, running from a sugar plantation, far more clearly than he knew that he was shivering in a hammock in Bathurst. He even knew he had had hit a slave-driver, and would be flogged to death if he stopped running.

His legs plunged into warm mud, and he got a mouthful of foul water from a creek he had not seen. He could not see the other side, so he had no chance of swimming to it before the dogs led their handlers to the bank.

There was a light on the water. He blinked mud out of his eyes. It was a fishing lantern in a boat, no more than a stone's throw away. He threw himself forward and swam. He expected the boatman to row away from a fugitive, but the man just watched him approach. He placed his hand on the gunwale, and hands of the same dark shade hauled him over it, pushed him down in the bow and motioned him to silence. He struggled to stifle the breaths tearing at his chest. The sounds of the dogs were no longer muffled by undergrowth, so they had found the place where he fell into the water. He had only seen one boat, so there was only one place where he could be. He closed his eyes and commended his soul to Allah to do with it as He would.

Where had that idea come from? The dispassionate part of George Harding's mind reasserted itself. He was a Presbyterian, damn it! Even if he'd almost forgotten what churches look like from the inside, he didn't go around commending his soul to Allah. He still cowered in the boat when he heard a slave-catcher's voice calling to the boatman.

"I no see 'um, Massa," said the boatman.

Harding had never been to the West Indies, let alone run away from a plantation. All he really knew, as he lay there biting his fist to keep from gagging on the salt clinging to the back of his mouth, was that he wanted the slave-driver to believe the boatman more than he had ever wanted anything in his life.

The boatman said "I no see 'um, Massa" again. This time, the only answer was splashing and curses. There was a gentle creaking and rocking. Whether or not George Harding had been to the West Indies, he had no qualms in silently giving thanks to Allah when he realized the boatman was rowing away while the slave catchers searched the bank. He even savored the pain of his scratches, because noticing them meant that he was no longer running for his life.

The rowing stopped. The change of motion reminded him of the thanks he owed the boatman. He opened his eyes just in time to see an oar slashing toward him. A flash of light, then darkness.

Darkness was an improvement on dogs. Hopefully, it meant he was coming out of the fever. He could not endure many more dreams like this. He would have to increase the dose of laudanum.

A sensation of cold seized him as though in a claw, and he writhed in a pool of water on a dirt floor. His head felt as if there was an axe in it, and a scythe-fingered demon wrung out his guts until he vomited.

"Ah Christ!"

He looked up to see a man wearing the red coat of the men who carried long guns. The three stripes on the sleeve belonged to someone who shouted a lot rather than someone who was usually shouted at. The empty bucket in the man's fist told him where the water had come from.

"You'll clean that up if I have to make you lick it up," said the man in a language that George Harding recognized as English. It sounded strange, as though it was a language that he had recently learned.

"Now get up off that floor, Lord Sambo! You ain't the colonel's daughter so you ain't gonna lie there all day."

He could not find a grain of strength in his body, but he still got to his feet when the red man started toward him. Somehow, he had learned what happened when he did not do what men who spoke English told him to.

"That's better. Now come 'ere." The red man waved at a window. More red men stood in lines, with straight backs and their hands straight down by their sides. They stared at a man tied to a wooden triangle while another man whipped him. George Harding had seen many floggings, but his astonishment almost overcame his nausea when he saw that what was left of the skin of the flogged man was white.

"See that, Lord Sambo?" barked the red man into his ear. "Now I don't give five minutes with a poxed sailor's whore what you done. The army paid good money for you, so you do what I tell you and no one will want to know. But you give me any trouble, an' you know how you'll end up, an' I promise you you'll give your black arse to get back wherever you run away from. Now fall in, Private Sambo!"

~~~~~~

Harding was unsure whether his teeth or his ankles hurt more when he lurched out of the hammock. A hundred drops of laudanum helped, and so did what was left of the brandy. He fingered another bottle, thinking that he should delay opening it in case he ran out before the mail packet arrived, but he knew it would be empty by dawn tomorrow.

"Please Massa?"

Harding didn't take his eyes off the bottle. "Yes boy?"

"Blue-blue man come, Massa."

"Blue-blue man? What the devil d'you mean...oh!" A man in the blue coat of a naval officer was standing behind the houseboy. The officer's fingers drummed on the hilt of his sword. He looked every inch the sort of fighting captain that England had been so besotted with since Nelson toadied his way into that tomb in St. Paul's. Harding disliked him on sight.

"Come in." Harding sank into the chair behind his desk without offering to shake hands.

The officer stepped into the room and removed his hat. "Matthew Cooper, Master and Commander of His Britannic Majesty's brig-sloop *Electra*, at your service sir."

Not only was he bloody navy, he was a bloody Yorkshireman. Harding raised an eyebrow. "George Harding at yours."

The houseboy scurried in to retrieve the latest shirt that Harding had thrown on the floor. If a succession of dandies insisted on inflicting themselves on him, he could at least make them feel overdressed.

Harding made no move to invite Cooper to sit down, hoping to force him into the gaffe of sitting uninvited. Cooper seemed happy for his broad shoulders to loom over Harding. Harding wanted to pretend to fall asleep, but he could not stop himself looking up at eyes that should have belonged to a leopard deciding whether a mouse was worth the effort of pouncing on.

"Been waiting long?" Harding could play the game no longer.

"About half an hour." Cooper's tone added that it had been half an hour too long.

"Touch of fever." Harding heard the conciliation in his own voice and disliked Cooper even more.

Cooper glanced at the brandy-stained papers and spilt powder on Harding's desk. "I see."

"Won't you sit down, Commander?" A commander carried the courtesy title of captain, and Harding smiled inwardly when Cooper's eyes narrowed with irritation.

"I prefer to stand, sir. May I come straight to the point?"

Harding waved a hand expansively.

"Five days ago, we found that abomination slipping out of the Akokra River." Cooper jerked his head at the wall that hid the *Cassandra*. "We chased her for three days and it's taken two to get here. The poor souls aboard are starving and some of them already have fever. I request permission to land them immediately, and send them proper food and a surgeon."

Harding hid a smile. Cooper had handed him the perfect excuse to refuse. Best not to say so straight away, especially when he could irritate the man. "You've unchained the poor souls of course?"

Cooper looked satisfyingly uncomfortable. "Well no, of course not..."

Harding raised his eyebrows. "Why on earth not? What the devil do you mean by keeping your poor souls in chains?"

Cooper's knuckles were white as he crumpled his hat. "I couldn't.

There are scores of them and they don't know the difference between us and the slavers. They'd tear us apart..."

"How can I explain to them that you rescued them by keeping them in chains?" Now would be a good time to get up and stroll to the window, but Harding was afraid he would pass out if he tried. Not that it really mattered because the anguish in Cooper's eyes showed Harding that he had won the point. Five hundred guineas, he thought.

"I can't land them if they've got fever. Half the garrison is sick as it is, without a new contagion in the middle of Bathurst."

Cooper looked as though he'd been struck. "Sir, five hundred souls are in your hands. I demand that you write an order to land them immediately!"

Harding sighed and folded his hands across his stomach, trying to assume the image of the wisdom of age faced with impetuous youth. He hoped Cooper did not notice the empty bottle rolling on the floor. He stared at the epaulette on Cooper's shoulder, where the veneer of gold had worn off to expose the lead beneath and reveal that Cooper was not a wealthy man.

"You fellows get prize money for taking blackbirders, don't you? Quite a lot for a beauty like that, I'd say."

"Prize money be damned!"

Harding cringed back.

"You may throw my share of the prize money into the sea for all I care," barked Cooper, "but I'll not see those poor wretches suffer more than they already have for want of a few strokes of your pen!"

Harding found his voice. "You an abolitionist, Commander?"

Cooper stepped back, pitifully easy to confuse.

"Proud to be. What's that got to do with it?"

"You may see it as your duty to chase slavers, but I'd like to remind you that you're a King's officer." The force he put into those last words recoiled into his molars, and he closed his eyes while the pain receded. "While you wear that uniform, you'll remember your oath to the King, which unless I'm very much mistaken, does not include decimating any of his outposts by filling them with fever."

Cooper turned a delightful shade of red. He looked ready to tear his hat in half.

Harding pushed on relentlessly. "Whatever your politics, Commander, no man can serve two masters. Good day to you."

Harding fidgeted with some papers on his desk, trying to get rid of Cooper before he calmed down enough to form an argument. Cooper turned on his heel and walked out. Pity the next defaulter on his ship.

Harding leaned back. Five hundred gold guineas, and a cottage in…Devon? Dorset? Maybe not a cottage, he would be able to afford an inn, which would provide him with as much brandy as he could drink. He took a deep breath, and nearly retched at the smell from the slaver.

Chained to the floor, rolling in excrement, nothing to look forward to but the lash.

Five hundred gold guineas, he told himself firmly. Perhaps his teeth wouldn't ache like this in England. Perhaps that familiar chill wouldn't march up and down his spine.

"Oh Christ, not again."

~~~~~~

Running again. Running faster than his ruined body ever could. Faster than this dream self had run before, because he was on an open field. Nothing to bar his way but a haze of powder smoke that stung his throat. Not looking back because he did not need to see Napoleon's cavalry behind him when the ground quaked and thundered with their hooves. No need to see the forest of lances when his back tingled as though they were already stabbing through his red coat. No desire to look back when the smear of scarlet ahead was made of men in the coats that had once meant imprisonment, but today meant the only hope he had.

The redcoats were in a line two deep, the front row on one knee. Their muskets pointed straight at him. He knew that the muskets were aimed at the cavalry behind him, just as the cavalry's lances were pointed at the infantry in front, but none of that would matter if the cavalry caught him or the muskets fired before he reached that red line of hope.

Close now. So close he could see the grime on the coats and the gritted teeth behind the muskets.

Hear the fear in a sergeant's shout. "Wait! Waaaaiiiiit!"

Close enough to meet the eyes of a mounted officer behind the muskets of hope, see the decision in them when the officer saw the color of his face, see his sword drop. See hope vanish behind stabbing flames and more smoke.

George Harding told himself, yet again, that he had not left his hammock, but damn it he *felt* lead slam into him. He *saw* iron-shod hooves hammer into the grass around his fragile head. He *heard* the screams of men and horses and musket balls blend into a diabolic crescendo. He even found himself retreating into memories that weren't his, of the scorching heat of the island where he first put on a red coat; of the endless days of sweating with the Brown Bess muskets that tore the air above him. He remembered the day when the sergeant finally nodded his approval. "Not bad, Private Sambo. We'll make a major of you yet."

He had laughed with the rest of his platoon at the twin absurdities of a Major Sambo, and any officer handling a musket. He drifted away into those memories while mosquitoes whined around his ears, and the future of a foreign continent was decided in death piling up around him.

Fingers glided across his body. The shooting had stopped, leaving only groans that sounded as though they came from the ground itself. The weight of the purse of coins around his neck was missing. Hands were under his coat now, tugging at the juju belt he wore around his waist. A woman's voice grunted with bemusement when she pulled it free but the hands came back, into his mouth this time. Something pricked his gums. His eyes snapped open to see a woman's smooth face bathed in moonlight. Her hair brushed his cheeks with a silken caress. He was still trying to smile for her when her knife flashed out of his mouth and into his throat.

~~~~~~~

George Harding rolled away from her and fell out of the hammock. He sat up cautiously. His head was clear and he felt no sign of fever. He had not felt this healthy since he arrived in Bathurst. He stood up without any complaint from his gout, and almost felt as though he could do without a drink.

Almost.

A man was sitting behind his desk. He blinked and shook his head, but there was still a black man wearing a red coat in his chair. Harding was furious. Whatever reason he might have for being in the room, he had no business in Harding's chair.

"Who the hell do you think you are?"

The man replied with a tight-lipped frown.

"Boy!"

The soldier was wearing an infantryman's coat, although there were only artillerymen and engineers in Bathurst. Not that being a visitor gave him any more right to act as though he owned the place.

"Massa?" The houseboy appeared at the door.

"What's this damned impudence?" He waved a hand at his chair.

"Massa?" The boy looked confused.

Harding made a great effort to speak slowly. "What. Is. This. Man. Doing. In. My. Bloody. Chair. Damn your eyes!"

"What man, Massa?"

Harding's face burned and he felt as though an anchor chain was crushing his chest. He tried to remember if he'd left that pistol loaded.

"This bastard! Here! You make game of me, boy, and by God I'll see your black arse flogged off!"

The boy looked at the chair, then back at Harding. His perplexity faded to an understanding that belied the only name that Harding had ever used for him. "I get Massa Chaplain, Massa."

The boy disappeared, leaving Harding's mouth working to form words that would not come.

"He can't see me, you know," said the soldier behind the desk.

"What?"

"Your boy. He can't see me, so you might as well let him be."

Harding was as startled by the accent as the words. He'd never met an African who could speak more than a few words of pidgin, but this voice belonged on Wapping docks. "Just as well he's gone. You and me got things to talk about."

"What things? I don't know you."

"Not exactly, but we're close acquaintances. You got my word on that." The soldier rolled back his lips to reveal torn, toothless gums.

Harding's teeth unleashed a gale of pain that almost blinded him. "Oh my God!"

The soldier smiled and nodded. Harding sat down heavily. "It's not true. I'm imagining you. You're a fever dream. Just need a stiff drink."

Harding reached for his brandy. The soldier smiled again. "If you could see the state of your liver, you'd see fever's the least of your problems."

Harding's hand flew to his chest, where he thought his liver probably was. He could feel it swelling like a filling wineskin, shoving aside stomach, lungs, heart, anything in the way of its conquest. That was ridiculous, his chest had felt fine all day. It was the only thing that had. "A drink."

"Won't help. Nothing will."

Harding gave up trying to push himself upright. "Is that why you're here?"

The soldier stopped smiling. "Dunno why I'm here. I mean, I know you got my teeth, but I dunno much else."

"Oh God."

"Maybe. I know I weren't very good to Him. I'm sure He knows that slave drivers and sergeants don't let you stop what you're doing to pray, and He knows the army don't give you nothing to drink except rum, but perhaps that just means Muslims should avoid slavers and stay out of the army."

Harding felt a chasm open up inside him. He was used to thinking of death as an end to be delayed for as long as possible, but now the end had come and this man was saying that it wasn't even an end. Saliva ran down his chin and his nose filled. "What will happen to me?"

The soldier stood and took Harding's hands. There was real compassion in his voice. "I don't know."

Vicars liked to preach about conscience. Perhaps that was what

Harding needed now. He rifled through the broken bottles and lost paperwork of his soul, knowing he had hidden from his life's frustrations by bullying others and blinding himself with drunkenness. That gave him no claim to clemency, but there was nothing he could do about it now.

Nothing? He looked up. The soldier helped Harding to stand. Harding took his seat behind his desk, and managed to keep his hand steady enough to write an order to land the *Cassandra's* slaves, and provide them with whatever food and physic they needed. He looked at the tear-stained paper in front of him and wondered whether it would count for anything in a few minutes time. Still, something in his chest felt a little lighter for writing it. He blew his nose and wrote another letter, commending Commander Cooper for his zeal and humanity for his representation on behalf of the souls he had liberated. That made him feel better too, though two pages of blotted ink were little enough to apologies for a life as miserable as his. He hoped the houseboy would spare him a kind thought when he and the chaplain found him.

The soldier took his hand. "Come on. There's something else we both need to do."

Harding stood unaided, and let the soldier lead him outside. They stood, side by side, with their backs to the setting sun. The soldier knelt and touched his head to the ground. Harding knelt beside him, and he knew he would not be getting up.

The Endocrine Tyranny

Gareth stared out of his kitchen window. He didn't pretend to be riveted by the pigeons bustling between Nottingham's rooftops. He knew their only attraction was being at the opposite end of his flat to the bedroom. He cursed himself for a fool and poured some orange juice into a glass.

It took almost as much courage to slide back the bolt he'd crudely installed as to open the door. Mary turned her head to look at him and he looked back at the five-foot-two, ginger-haired woman. He looked for the fear or accusation he would expect in any other woman he'd handcuffed to a bed, but her face remained as devoid of expression as when he brought her here three days before. She turned her gaze to the ceiling.

Gareth sat on the bed and tried to smile. *What the hell am I doing*? he asked himself for the hundredth time that day.

"I brought you some orange juice," he said.

Her eyes flicked to the glass, then back to the ceiling.

"You used to like it."

He held the glass close to her hand, but she made no move to take it. Gareth had never been into bondage, and asking the retail assistant in the sex shop for the handcuffs with the longest chains had been excruciating. They needed to be long enough so Mary would be able to feed herself, but she'd refused everything but the occasional sip of water.

Gareth put the juice on the bedside table. "Are there any books you'd like?"

The pile of books on the table lay as he'd left it. He'd bought some of her old favourites like Richard Dawkins and Jared Diamond, but perhaps she now found Dawkins and Diamond as far beneath her as she used to find his own favourites like Nick Hornby and David Brin.

"Need the bathroom?"

He took her lack of response to mean no. He lifted her left forearm and checked that the cuff was not painfully tight.

"Not hurting you?" He knelt to check her left arm. She didn't answer.

Mary sat up and snatched the glass from the bedside table by its base. Gareth looked up, startled at how fast she'd shed her torpor. She smashed the glass against the table and thrust the jagged edge at her throat. Gareth threw himself across the bed and caught her wrist. Mary strained against his hand.

Gareth was in an awkward position, and he struggled to hold her with both hands. She tilted her head back and inched her throat closer to the glass. Her arm quivered. She went limp so suddenly that Gareth fell off the bed and the glass thumped to the floor. Mary slumped back on the pillow.

"You stupid…" Gareth took a deep breath to control his temper. "Why'd you do that?"

"Why did you stop it?"

Gareth's eyes snapped to her face but she was back to staring at the ceiling, her expression as blank as when he came in. He bit off the response that she knew very well. Her understanding of sarcasm was gone with the rest of the personality he remembered. The important thing was that she'd spoken to him at all.

"I'll answer your question if you answer mine," he said.

He wasn't sure whether he imagined the slight twitch of her mouth that used to signal impatience, but she replied.

"Death is preferable to life without access to the serum."

Her days of silence had given Gareth time to forget how unsettling it was that she didn't speak in the first person.

"I liked you the way you were."

"Emotions induce stupidity."

"There are compensations for stupidity."

"Perhaps, if the emotions do not lead inevitably to depression. Yet you cannot be persuaded to allow the rational choice between access to the serum or death. You make your decisions by emotion and then defend them with arguments invented to avoid considering the possibility that you may be wrong."

Gareth was unsure whether she meant him in particular or the whole human race. He could think of no answer so he started gathering broken glass.

"Now you answer," she said.

Gareth tried to remember her question. Her face was still blank. She wasn't testing him; she'd simply forgotten how other people lost the thread of a conversation.

"Why did I stop you?" He remembered. "I could tell you I was saving the world, or that I'm afraid of what you might do to yourself. But you'd know I'd be lying. The truth, Mary, is that I love you and I think you're still in there somewhere. That's why we're both going to wait for you to come back."

He forced himself to look into her eyes. They revealed as much as a pair of marbles.

"Love is a metaphor for addiction to endorphins that are mistakenly associated with a particular person."

Gareth straightened.

"Perhaps. But here's another question. Isn't what I'm doing what you really wanted when you had that implant fitted?"

Mary stared at the ceiling. Gareth checked there was no broken glass where she could reach it. He'd have to get her a neck brace in case she found something else to jam into her throat.

When he'd cleaned up the rest of the spilled juice and broken glass, he found himself at the kitchen window again. The five o'clock traffic jam under the Nottingham rain was almost hypnotic, but couldn't push the thought of the woman in the bedroom out of his mind. Then again, she'd rarely been out of his mind since the day two nineteen-year-old biology students happened to sit next to each other in a basic genetics lecture.

Gareth found himself thinking of his Uncle William, who had been struggling to break his alcoholism for as long as Gareth could remember. He would stay dry for months at a time, going to AA meetings, holding down a job and telling everyone how much better he felt about himself. Yet even as he said it, the wistful tone of his voice told of something missing from his life. Something he feared for what it would do to him, yet something he was not complete without. Last time Gareth had seen him, the man ranted for an hour about how much he hated what he was doing to himself, punctuating the conversation with whiskey shots. Sincere as William's self-loathing was, Gareth had seen the man as oddly content, as though he'd found his true niche.

He presumed that William remembered his first drink as Gareth remembered that genetics lecture.

Now, ten years later, Gareth's hand closed into a fist at the knowledge that he'd spent nearly all his adult life addicted — Mary had chosen the best word for it — to being alternately disparaged and desperately needed by her.

Once he thought he'd untangled himself. Two years after she dumped him, he had his own life two hundred and eighty-six miles from her, though he'd recognised that he only knew the length of the leash because he hadn't managed to slip it. He wondered now whether part of the reason Mary had jerked the leash tight with a late night phone call was to reassure herself he was still at the other end.

~~~~~~

Several weeks of dating had culminated in the first time Gareth hadn't slept alone since the split with Mary, so his sleep had been fitful and he'd woken immediately when his phone crashed into *Sultans of Swing*. Radhika had groaned beside him as he fumbled for it.

He flipped the phone open. "Mm?"

"Gareth?"

The one word swept away sleep like a bucket of cold water. "Mary?"

He felt Radhika stir.

"There's something I need you to know, Gareth," said Mary.

He recognised the hesitation in her voice. Mary was at her most vulnerable, needing approval from the one person who would always give it. But, he reminded himself, she could not depend on him anymore because he'd vowed to break his dependency on her. That decision had begun his claw back to sanity after the break-up.

"Mary, it's, uh, half past three in the morning and I've got work tomorrow."

"Please, Gareth."

Gareth's thumb caressed the button that would cut the call. He clung to the idea that he might actually press it for a moment, before moving his thumb away.

"OK, I'm listening."

"I can't tell you on the phone."

Gareth knew nobody else who would call in the middle of the night to say they didn't want to talk on the phone. In the two years away from Mary, Gareth had spent an unhealthy amount of time reflecting on their relationship. He felt he had a much better understanding of what made her tick than he ever had while they were together. He'd begun to understand her need to reassure herself of his devotion, and her inability to see her own need for herself. If he'd tried to point it out to her, he could imagine the impeccably reasoned arguments she would use to dismiss the idea, and her scornful remarks about 'soft sciences like psychology distilled to the lowest denominator by daytime television.'

Gareth took a deep breath. "Mary, what's going on?"

"I've got a, well, a *procedure* today. I'd like…I *need*…you to be here."

"What do you mean, a procedure?"

"I…it's hard to talk about it on the phone. I'll tell you when you get here."

"Here? Where's here? Edinburgh?"

"Yes. I'm sorry," she said, "I know I should have called you before. I wasn't going to bother you with it but I haven't slept all night and all I can think is that…that I need you here."

"What time is this procedure?"

"Nine this morning."

"Nine? I can't be in Edinburgh by nine."

"You can. If you start now…I need you. Gareth? Gareth, are you there? You'll be here, won't you?"

Gareth ended the call. The best thing to do would be to put an arm around Radhika and go back to sleep. He was as likely to do that as Uncle William was likely to take one drink and pour the rest of the bottle down the drain.

"Where are you going?" Radhika's voice was dangerously calm.

"Edinburgh."

Her silence spoke louder than any words as he dressed. He found his keys and paused at the door. She was sitting up with the duvet pulled to her chin.

"Something you want to tell me?" she asked.

He tried to etch every line of her face into his memory, even the angry crease down the middle of her forehead. The last image of a happy time.

"I'll let myself out, then," she said.

He closed the door, wondering what Mary meant by a procedure.

The U2 CD he'd left in his car's player alternately caressed and pummelled his ears as he drove through Nottingham and on to the M1. Three lanes of empty tarmac left his mind free to wander, but the only direction it could go was back to the eight years of Mary. For the first six months they had felt perfect for each other, although Gareth now recognised that if they hadn't sat next to each other that day, it would only have been a matter of time before they each sat next to someone else.

Mary surprised nobody by graduating at the top of their class. She moved on to a virology PhD at Oxford, which she accepted as her just due. "Some of us have it, Gareth, and some of us just don't." They moved into an flat together and Gareth gave up on biology to separate his career from hers. Not that she appreciated his reasons. "*Retail,* Gareth? Couldn't you find anything more constructive than that? There's no reason you couldn't at least be a technician."

He did the cooking and cleaning while she worked seven

fourteen-hour days a week and came home tired and short-tempered. "Gareth, how many times have I told you I can't eat eggs with rice?"

Even then, he'd known he was her pressure valve, though he was never sure how much of that pressure came from her supervisor and how much from herself. He hoped it would get better when she moved on to a postdoctoral position in Edinburgh but the end was inevitable and looking back, Gareth was surprised that it didn't come earlier.

"Gareth, you're driving me up the wall. I think it would be best if you just move out."

Discotheque segued to *One* and Gareth realised he was pushing his VW Golf along at ninety-five miles per hour with his hands tight on the wheel. He eased back to seventy, not wanting to catch the attention of a bored speed cop. There had been some good times, hadn't there? Yes, he remembered, the days when she would just want to be held because an experiment hadn't worked or because her results had been criticised. Her need for him would soothe the running sore her sarcasm kept open and give him a reason to stay when she threw herself back into her work. Tonight she'd shown that, contrary to the excellent advice Bono poured out of the speakers, it was not too late to drag the past into the light.

One segued to *Electrical Storm* and Gareth realised how foolish it was to be smiling.

It was only when he turned off the M6 that Gareth remembered he hadn't asked Mary if she was living in the same flat, but then it would take more than the memories of a broken relationship to drive her to the trouble of moving. An earthquake or an offer of a more prestigious post might do it, but nothing less. He couldn't decide how he'd react if Mary had only weeks or months to live. What frightened him most was that he might be relieved at having his fixation placed beyond reach.

By the time he parked at half past eight, Radhika was already a distant memory. He took a moment to call his line manager and report sick and forced himself out of the car and up to the flat.

He bit his lip as he knocked on her door. Whatever was about to happen would confirm he was still at her beck and call. Or perhaps she'd moved away and he was about to make a prize prat of himself with someone in a hurry to get to work.

Mary opened the door. There were new wrinkles around her eyes and her hair was lank and unwashed. She looked as if she hadn't eaten or slept properly in weeks. Gareth started to speak but she rocked forward and somehow he was leaning down to hold her and her arms circled his waist and *damn* it felt good.

A neighbour walked past. They broke apart and shared an embarrassed smile. She led him inside and they sat on the same sofa he remembered hauling up the stairs by himself. She snuggled against him. "Thank you for coming, Gareth. I wasn't sure you would."

Gareth had nurtured the rational part of his mind since he'd last seen Mary. Now it was in full retreat, but it still managed to yell "bollocks she wasn't" from over the horizon. It would be so easy to close his eyes and give himself over to the warmth of her, but it was already twenty to nine. "Mary, what exactly is this all about?"

"I can't handle my emotions."

That was not news. "Mm?"

"So I've decided to get rid of them."

"What?"

"Look, I've been clinically depressed for the last two years. I couldn't cope without you but I was always anxious and unhappy when you were here."

"I remember."

"I've tried four different antidepressants, but nothing worked. If this goes on, I'm going to end up killing myself."

Gareth didn't doubt she was telling the truth. It must have been bad for her to admit a need for help, even to herself.

"Then I ran into an old friend from Oxford. A neuroendocrinologist."

"A what?"

"Neuroendocrinologist," she said as though talking to a child, the familiar impatience in her tone. "He's got a technique for excising emotions at the source. He'll be here in a minute."

Something tightened in the pit of Gareth's stomach. From anyone else, he might have expected a harmless piece of quackery but Mary would sneer at anything lacking a mechanistic foundation that she could thoroughly research.

The knock came before Gareth could frame a pertinent question. Mary opened the door to a gangling man in his mid-forties. Gareth eyed his briefcase nervously. The man looked startled when he saw Gareth.

"Gareth Forrest, this is Stephen Underbird," said Mary.

"I thought you'd be alone." Underbird spoke with the expensive accent that Gareth recognised from a lot of Oxford academics.

"Gareth's an old friend," said Mary. "He'll understand and don't worry, he won't recognise your name."

Mary had never learned tact. An alarm bell rang in Gareth's head because there *was* something familiar about the name, although he couldn't remember what.

Underbird shook Gareth's hand as though it was a rotting fish.

"Stephen," said Mary as they sat down, "could you explain this to Gareth? You'll put it much more simply than me and it's important he understands."

"You haven't told him?" Underbird looked ready to bolt for the door.

"Gareth won't make trouble, will you?" said Mary.

"Uh, no." Gareth suspected he should be throwing Underbird out of the window, but there was no arguing with Mary.

"Well," Underbird still looked doubtful, "if you say so. Mary's told you about her depression?"

Gareth nodded.

"My research has shown that chronic depression comes about in individuals whose emotions overwhelm them. The same people may have periods of happiness, even euphoria. They may distract themselves by immersion in achievement through work or sport, or in relationships, but the negative emotions always prevail in the end and the result, in layman's terms, is what we call depression."

Gareth nodded again. It sounded like a fair description of Mary.

"The solution is to remove the hormones that drive the emotions." Underbird might have been talking about clipping toenails. "It's a simple procedure. I insert an implant into the lower spine. Then, every day Mary will inject herself with serum containing a cocktail of antibodies against hormonal receptors in the brain. The implant transfers the antibodies to the cerebro-spinal fluid…"

"Hang on a minute!" Gareth found himself on his feet. "You're saying you switch off emotions by making the brain unable to respond to hormones?"

"That's a reasonably accurate synthesis, yes."

Something was falling into place in Gareth's mind. "And you've done this to how many people, precisely?"

Underbird's mouth opened but he didn't speak.

Mary cut in. "I told you I can't go on being who I am, but think about the potential for a moment. Reproductive hormones won't be distracting me with sexual urges. Adrenaline and cortisol won't be making me afraid of failure. All these hormones that have been holding me back will be gone and I'll be able to *concentrate* in a way that nobody ever has before...."

"How many?" Gareth had never cut Mary off like that before.

"I'll be the first." She spoke as though it was a privilege.

"Perhaps I could..." Underbird broke in. "I've done this extensively on monkeys and though their behaviour changed, they lived longer and suffered no ill effects. Yes, it's a radical procedure that I wouldn't do lightly, but Mary is capable of understanding the procedure as well as anyone and would certainly benefit from it."

Gareth remembered where he'd heard Underbird's name. "But you never had approval to do it to the monkeys, did you? Nobody would support your mad ideas, so you diverted funding earmarked for something else and bypassed the ethics committee to hide it. How could I forget a name like Underbird? You were struck off the medical register when they caught you, weren't you?"

"That was an exaggeration by the press. I was asked to resign from the university. I returned to neurosurgery and I've been practicing ever since."

Gareth felt adrenaline overwhelming him. He couldn't restrain himself from shouting. "That's why you're doing it in Mary's flat, isn't it? You *would* be struck off if anyone knew about it."

Underbird stood up. "I think I'd better go..."

"*No!*"

Both men turned to Mary.

"No," she repeated. "Gareth, this is the only chance I have to be someone I can stand to be. Please don't block my way. It's really no different than Prozac. It's all about regulating the neurochemistry, but this has so much more potential."

"Bollocks! This bastard," Gareth waved at Underbird, "just wants a successful experiment so he can try out his pet theories. He's taking advantage of you because you're in no state to make your own decisions."

"Gareth." Mary used her conversation-over voice. "Please."

The hard line of Mary's mouth told of the same decision as when she announced they were moving to Edinburgh, and again on the day she told him to move out. He recognised the taste of futility as his objections shrivelled and died on his tongue. Three strides took him out of the door and he didn't stop until he was back in his empty flat in Nottingham.

~~~~~~

"Gareth!"

Mary's shriek cut into Gareth's sleep like a whip. He jerked awake and fell off the sofa.

"Gareth you bastard!"

Four days of silence had come to an end. He scrambled to his feet and burst into the bedroom, the room lit by the low-wattage lamp he left on for her. She was sitting up, straining against the cuffs, her teeth bared in pure rage.

"There you are! I'm going to kill you, you bastard! You *kidnapped* me! You're going to jail for the rest of your life!"

Words stumbled into each other until Gareth couldn't understand what she was saying, but there was no mistaking the meaning. Emotion had returned to Mary, if only the emotion of anger. She ran out of breath and lay back panting.

"They'll come for you." Her voice was lower but pregnant with malice. "You'll go to jail and they'll gang rape you every day and I'll visit you just to laugh in your face."

Gareth was more startled by the use of the first person than by what she said.

"Nobody's coming," he said. "There's been nothing in the papers about you going missing."

"They'll come."

"Not unless someone reports you missing, and I'm guessing you've become so reclusive that nobody knows what you're doing from one day to the next. They probably assume you're at home writing a paper or something. Am I right?"

He was going to add that if anyone had reported her missing, a quick review of security camera tapes would have led the police straight to his door by now. Mary cut him off by lunging at him so hard the bed moved forward.

Gareth changed tack. "If they do come and they find out what you've been doing, think about what they'll do to you?"

"You're still stupid. You destroyed the evidence."

"They'll have your notes, and do you think they'll let you have your serum back while they're working out whether you're a bioterrorist or not? That'll take months."

Her face contorted.

"Bastard! Bastard! Bastard!"

Gareth lost track of how long she ranted, shrieking threats and obscenities. Her abuse had never been such a blunt instrument before. He stood in the doorway and soaked it all up.

Eventually she slumped on the bed from sheer exhaustion. Tremors of rage quivered through her body, but subsided as he watched. The defeat on her face was harder to take than the hatred. He fetched her

some water in a plastic cup he'd used since her suicide attempt. He
expected her to throw it at him or turn away, but she let him hold her
head up while she drank.

She slumped back and blinked away the tears in her eyes. She
turned to him with no sign of anger. "You were right, weren't you?"

"What?"

"When they find out what I did, they will call me a terrorist.
They'll never let me out."

Gareth clung to the word 'I'.

"You were right too," he said. "I destroyed the evidence."

"But my laptop, my notes, it's all there..." Her face was pale
with an expression that Gareth suddenly recognised as terror.

"I'm not going to tell anyone and nobody else knows. I'll get
everything for you."

Her fear was unchecked. It occurred to Gareth that he was trying
to reassure her with reasoned words, but no words could help. The cause
of her fear was a deluge of hormones that her brain had become unused
to, and the only way to counter it was with another hormone. He'd read
everything he could find on endocrinology recently, and the word
'oxytocin' sprang to mind. A hormone released by touch that engenders
trust.

He slipped his hand into hers, expecting her to pull away. She
seized it as though it was a lifeline. Gareth felt himself returning her grip
with equal strength. A warm glow spread up his arm. Oxytocin, he
thought, but knowing the name made the feeling no less real.

He rolled on to the bed and gathered her in his arms. Her body
was rigid and trembling, and he felt her try to embrace him but she
couldn't hold him properly because of the cuffs. He tried to sit up but she
clung to his T-shirt.

"I'm going to get the keys," he said, thinking even as he said it that perhaps oxytocin engendered too much trust.

"No, no, don't leave me alone, Gareth. Just hold me. Hold me. Don't let me go."

"I won't," he said. "Never."

He held her, feeling her tension drain away. He revelled in the sensation of her, even as he held himself ready to jump clear at the first sign of another mood swing. As the grey Midlands dawn drowned the electric light, he heard her breathing assume the rhythm of sleep.

Perhaps, just perhaps, he was doing the right thing.

~~~~~~~

A few days ago, his biggest problem had been an irate customer who was convinced there was something wrong with a television because it wouldn't pick up channels he hadn't subscribed to. Gareth had retreated to the back office to wonder whether his promotion to department manager had been a blessing or a curse.

His phone vibrated.

"Hello?"

"Gareth?" The voice was female, but so devoid of inflection that he couldn't place it.

"Speaking."

"It's Mary Bellard."

"Mary?" He hadn't heard from her for a year, since what he'd come to think of as the Day of the Underbugger.

"There's something you should know."

"Look Mary, I am *not* racing up to Edinburgh again just because you call me out of the blue."

Gareth wished he sounded more convincing, if only to himself.

"You can hear it on the phone."

"How long will this take?" he asked.

"It depends on the number of questions."

Gareth felt the sting of Mary's tongue, but there was no sarcasm in her tone. He had the sense that she was reacting like the department's accounting database when he forgot to fill in a column of data. He told her to wait a moment, and went into the staff toilet to avoid being seen taking a personal call at work.

"OK, let's start when the Underbugger did his experiment on you."

"Underbird."

"Underbird, then. What happened?"

"You can't understand it. The best way to put it is being able to think clearly. The mind could operate without the hormonal distractions that had slowed it down before."

That was when Gareth noticed she'd stopped using the first person.

"You mean your depression?"

"That cleared immediately, but there's no way to explain how the mind improves when it is not distracted by the endocrine system."

"You're going to start preaching about freedom next."

Gareth was rarely sarcastic, but he wanted her to snap at him to show she was still Mary.

"Yes, freedom is a reasonably precise metaphor."

Gareth took a deep breath. "Mary, is that all you had to tell me?"

"No. You should know that the freedom will soon become general."

Gareth felt icy prickles in his spine. "What does that mean?"

"The freedom will be given to everyone."

"Yes, I got that, but how? Tell me in metaphor if you think I can't understand it."

Mary was quiet for a moment. He guessed she was thinking of the best analogy to communicate her 'free' thoughts to a traditionally wired brain.

"Stephen Underbird worked out how to prevent hormones influencing the brain, but his system is inefficient. Constant re-administration of antibodies is expensive, and most peoples' hormones would make them afraid to use it. I spliced the receptor proteins into a rhinovirus. That is, a common cold virus…"

"Jesus Christ!"

"You understand?" Mary's voice conveyed surprise in spite of her monotone.

"You mean you and the Underbugger are planning to release a highly infectious virus that will switch off people's emotions?"

"No. Stephen Underbird was unable to comprehend the results of his procedure and has abandoned it as a failure. The virus was developed without his involvement."

"That's…"

Gareth bit off the word 'insane' as it would be stating the obvious. What Mary had done to herself made her insane by any definition.

"How?" he asked.

"By self-infection and frequenting public places in the subsequent days. The process will begin tomorrow."

Gareth rubbed a hand over his eyes. It just didn't make sense that he was standing in the staff toilet while his ex-girlfriend told him she was about to free humanity from emotion. Mary must be either deluding herself or inventing the whole thing for some esoteric reason of her own.

"Haven't your colleagues had something to say about this?" he asked.

"With sleep requirement reduced to two hours in twenty-four, it is possible to pursue several projects at once. Also, emotions make people easily distracted from matters beyond their immediate understanding."

There was a ring of truth to that. Mary had always been a workaholic and had few friends even before the Underbugger.

"Mary, this isn't exactly *ethical*, is it? Don't you think most people would prefer to keep their emotions?"

"Hence the preparations were kept secret and the reason freedom will be imposed rather than offered."

She seemed to have fixated on the metaphor of freedom.

"Isn't it their right to choose freedom or not to?"

"A minor issue. People would choose freedom if they had experienced it. A broader issue is that the hormonal drive to procreate is depleting natural resources to the extent that for most, there will soon be little choice but misery."

"Oh spare me the try at a bleeding heart. You mean that without emotions, people will be happy to stay at home and stare at the wall."

"That metaphor is poor. Experience shows that most people will exercise their intellects and wish to occupy themselves productively. Sufficient resources are available to support people alive today for the remainder of their lives."

Mary's intellect had always dominated her personality and she'd never shown any interest in having children, and he was about to point out that she had no insight into how less cerebral people would respond to losing emotions. Then he saw the implication. It knocked him down on the toilet seat like a blow to the solar plexus.

"So humanity goes peacefully to its grave because everybody's lost interest in sex."

"It is the greatest benefit for the It was his own endocrine-dominated emotions that made the idea so repellent.

"Mary," he struggled for something that might persuade her. "*I* don't want to lose my emotions."

"Would you describe yourself as content?"

That was the wrong question for a man who recently spent his thirtieth birthday with a bottle of wine and a James Bond box set for company. "I'd say so, yes."

"The tone of your voice indicates the contrary."

"You're pretty good at decoding emotions for someone who doesn't have any." Gareth was on his feet again.

"You can assess the mood of a dog. It does not mean that you think like one."

"So we're all dogs to you, is that it?"

"It was merely a metaphor."

Gareth took a deep breath. He was being drawn into an argument he was not going to win. He needed to focus on the obvious point.

"Mary, why are you telling me this? Why not just set me free with everyone else?"

There was silence from the phone.

"Mary?"

She cut the call.

He sagged against the wall.

"Mad," he said aloud. "She's gone completely round the bend."

She must be delusional, he told himself. He should not take her too seriously or he would find himself acting on the silly, probably illegal ideas that were forming in the back of his mind. Mary must have lost her job long ago if she'd taken to spouting nonsense like that.

"She's not my responsibility." He marched back to his desk. "I have my own life."

His words reminded him that the nearest thing he had to a life was a twice-weekly trip to the gym. He found himself bringing up the Edinburgh University website and plugging 'Mary Bellard' into the staff directory. She was still listed as a postdoctoral researcher with a long string of publications to her name. There were eleven in the last year alone, and Gareth knew enough about research to recognise an extraordinary level of productivity. It also suggested that since her work was surviving peer review, it was lucid.

"No," he said. "I am not going to…"

He was already on his feet and heading for his Golf.

He started up and the CD player crashed into the middle of *Hotel California*.

"I know the feeling." Gareth wondered how many times he'd checked out of Mary's life as he flicked the player off. He had no plan beyond getting to Edinburgh and he needed to formulate one without having his mood jerked around by the Eagles. It wasn't until he passed Newcastle that he acknowledged he'd had a plan in mind before Mary ended the call. The difficult part would be keeping his nerve to do it.

He stopped at a service station to buy a T-shirt, a denim jacket, a toolbox and a roll of duct tape.

He parked outside Edinburgh University's virology building in the long Scottish twilight, and blinked back memories of the days when he'd come here to bring Mary a snack or a drink when she worked late.

There were a few lights on and he could see figures through the windows, but he couldn't get in without a swipe card. He stripped off his white shirt and replaced it with the T-shirt and jacket. He forced himself to sit and wait while his stomach felt as though it was trying to force its way up his gullet. Knowing it was the combined effect of cortisol and adrenaline made the mix no less potent.

He saw a young woman heading to the door. He got out of the car and jogged to intercept her.

"Excuse me!" His voice sounded almost steady. The activity was clearing his mind

She looked up from her handbag, where he presumed she was looking for her swipe card.

"Hi there," said Gareth. "I'm from MacAllan Electrical. I got a call because a freezer's broken down but I can't get into the bloody building."

The woman's eyes flicked to the toolbox and Gareth tried not to hold his breath. He was counting on the virologist's perpetual fear of a freezer breakdown destroying collections that took years to assemble. Hopefully a postgraduate student, as he guessed she was from her pierced lip, would not know who serviced the freezers. He'd invented MacAllan Electrical on the spur of the moment.

"Which lab?" she asked.

"Professor Hillman." Gareth named the head of Mary's research group.

The woman looked relieved and swiped her card. Her question had been born not of suspicion but fear that it was her samples thawing out.

"Second floor, last on the right," she said. "Good luck."

"Thanks." Gareth climbed the stairs and paused at the lab door to check there was no one inside. He closed the door behind him and switched on the lights. He started with the nearest incubator, working through the stacks of flasks filled with rose-coloured medium until he found some labelled with Mary's meticulous handwriting.

He traced her initials with a finger.

"Oh, Mary."

The sound of his voice broke his reverie. His lapse of concentration seemed absurdly funny and he had to force down a fit of giggles. He really wasn't cut out to be a burglar.

He worked through every incubator, piling up Mary's flasks on a bench. He'd spent enough time in labs to know there would be a bottle of bleach powder somewhere and he found it under the sink. He put a pinch of into every flask he could find with Mary's initials.

He visualised the bleach ripping through cell membranes and viral envelopes, but instead of relief, a sense of guilt welled up. He was committing an act of violence directed at Mary's work, the most important thing in her life since long before the Underbugger. He forced himself to finish the job and dump the flasks in the incineration bin. Mary would have some virus in cryostorage, but his next stop would be Mary's flat.

The lab door clicked open. Mary stepped through it. She gave him a glance and strode to one of the incubators. She jerked open the door to reveal the spaces where her flasks had been. She found them in the bin and looked at Gareth again. He searched for any sign of surprise or anger in her unblinking stare, but saw nothing he recognised.

"You are very attached to your emotions," was all she said.

"Call it force of habit."

"An accurate metaphor. It was a mistake to tell you."

Gareth stepped toward her, as though his plan had taken control of his body while his conscious mind looked on.

"It's only a setback of a few days. More can be cultured." She looked up at Gareth standing over her. "Unless the habit is strong enough to kill for."

Gareth paused. There was no fear in her voice or her expression. His hands fastened around her throat. His brain became a forum for debate. Emotion screamed in horror while reason pointed out what Mary would do if he left her to do it. His hands held their grip. She pulled at his wrists, but moved him no more than a child could. She reached for his face. He held her at arm's length and she clawed at empty air. He closed his eyes to hide from the pallor of asphyxia in Mary's face.

Her hands fell away. Gareth found himself holding her up rather than holding her back. He shifted his grip and pulled her to him. Her head rolled back and she drew breath with an almighty gasp. Gareth almost collapsed with relief that he hadn't overdone it, but he guessed he had no more than a minute or two before she regained consciousness.

He scooped her up and ran for the door, ready to tell anyone he saw that he'd found her unconscious and was taking her to the hospital, but they encountered no one.

He tilted the passenger seat back, then took off his jacket, rolled it and put it under her neck to open her airway, something he remembered from a department first aid course. She moaned softly. He longed to put his foot down and roar out of the car park, but it would attract too much attention so he kept his speed down.

Her hands were twitching as he pulled into the quietest street he could find and stopped in the middle of the road. He saw no faces in any of the house windows, so he got the roll of duct tape from the back seat, passed a length behind the small of her back and pulled the roll around her wrist and around the back of the seat. He taped down her other arm in the same way, and taped her ankles to the seat runners. He had no idea how Mary would react when she came to, but he didn't want her attacking him or jumping out of the door at seventy miles an hour.

Her eyes fluttered open.

"I'm sorry, Mary." He engaged the clutch. "I'm sorry."

His shoulders tightened, ready for the weight of rage or hysteria that his whole experience warned him to expect, but Mary sat in silence all the way back to Nottingham.

~~~~~~

Even oxytocin could not keep hunger at bay forever. Gareth slipped his arms from under Mary without waking her, and went to the kitchen for some breakfast. He brushed his teeth afterward, smiling at the irony of preserving mundane routines.

He opened the door to check on her and found her leaning toward a cuffed hand to rub her eyes. Gareth sidled in, looking for a clue to her mood. It felt like a first date.

"How are you feeling this morning?" he asked.

She looked at him. A spasm ran up her back. "Uh, I'm fine."

Gareth looked closely at her face. Was she blushing?

"Are you sure?"

"Yes, I'm…Um, Gareth? I think another set of hormones just found its way through."

"What do you…" Mary's hips writhed. "Oh!"

"Gareth?"

Gareth had never imagined his name could contain such a mix of invitation and urgency.

"I'll get the keys."

"Be quick."

When he released her, she attacked him with such energy that for a moment, he was afraid she'd been bluffing. She dragged him on top of her and Gareth gave up thinking for quite some time.

Afterward, they lay together without speaking. Gareth felt the full weight of the last few days as the adrenaline that had carried him through them ebbed away. It was dangerous to trust Mary. Her oxytocin smile might not survive another set of receptors being reintroduced to their hormones, but he was too tired to care. He watched her drift into sleep and could not help but follow her.

He woke after a few hours, but Mary was still asleep. He decided he didn't want to be lying naked next to her when her next mood woke her up. He kissed her forehead, rose and dressed. He found nothing to do after that, so he ended up in front of the television with the volume turned down. He was almost asleep again when Mary appeared in the doorway, wearing one of the t-shirts he'd brought. It fell to below her knees.

Gareth turned off the television and she sat down. He studied her face for clues but she just looked lost. Perhaps she was, he thought; adrift on a sea of hormones without chart or compass.

"Is there anything to eat?" she asked.

"Is that the latest…I mean, are you *very* hungry?"

"No Gareth, it's not a mood swing, it's the inevitable consequence of being chained up without food for a week."

Gareth felt the scourge in a familiar place.

"Four days actually," he said.

Mary's head sank into her hands.

"I guess that's me back to normal. It feels so horribly familiar. Like there's something about to boil over just here." She tapped a fist against her chest.

"That was almost an apology."

She looked up.

"Yes it was, wasn't it? Well, you've shown more backbone than I've ever given you credit for. I must be reacting to it."

Gareth didn't know how to answer that, so he got up and went to the kitchen. Mary followed him.

"French toast with maple syrup?"

Mary had always liked that.

"Sounds good," she said

Gareth cracked the eggs. Somehow it felt right to be cooking for Mary again. Not good exactly, because sooner or later whatever it was behind her breastbone would boil over and scald both of them. Just *right*, in a way Gareth didn't remember feeling since they broke up four years ago.

"Mary," he said. "I need to know. That virus of yours. Would it actually have worked?"

Her brow creased in thought.

"I don't know," she said at last. "I can't seem to think like I did. I doubt I could even understand my notes, but I'm not going to try. I'm going to destroy everything related to that project as soon as I get back to the lab."

Gareth whisked sugar and cinnamon into the eggs and dipped the bread in them.

"Gareth?"

"Mm?"

"What you did…bringing me here. I should be grateful, but you know what I'm like. I'll bring it up and hold it against you, so I'll say this now. Don't let me. You're stronger than I imagined and the best thing you can do for me is to stand up to me."

"Does that mean we're back together?"

"Of course."

"Thanks for asking."

She looked as though he'd slapped her.

"I mean, if you'll have me. Obviously."

Gareth thought about whether he could spend the rest of his life standing up to Mary. He was certainly stronger than he'd been, but was he strong enough?

"Of course I'll have you. I love you."

She looked at her feet. "You're addicted. We both are. That's why I called you, you know. Whatever I did to myself didn't cure the addiction. Even after the treatment, I was still following the plan to get your attention. To feed my need."

The hell with right, that felt *good* to hear. He'd assumed the connection between them had survived when she called to tell him her plans, but he'd never been sure until she said it. And perhaps she was right and he was strong enough for her now.

And perhaps Uncle William told himself he was strong enough to stop at one drink every time he opened a bottle.

None of those thoughts stopped the grin spreading across his face. "So you're addicted to me and I love you. What, precisely, is the difference?"

He left the stove and kissed her. The French toast slowly turned black.

Coldwater Cottage

"Don't." Ian was tense, and he wanted Jakki to know it.

Jakki sighed and tucked the cigarette packet back into her cagoule. "It's not dope, Big Brother, it's just a fag."

Ian waved at the can connected to the outboard motor. "This is just a tank of petrol. It doesn't know the difference."

Jakki gave him a look he'd seen a thousand times on the faces of the teenage runaways, prostitutes and drug addicts he spent his weekdays trying to turn into something other than human detritus. The look said, 'I know you mean well, but what you're saying has nothing to do with me'. Seeing it on his sister's face hurt him in ways he doubted she could imagine.

"Here, zip me up will you?" He said.

Jakki half crouched and half crawled over to him, unused to the motion of the small boat. He showed her how to close the zip across his shoulders and seal him into his drysuit. He attached the buoyancy jacket to the scuba tank and checked the regulators. Two hundred bars of air should give him plenty of time, but making the checks alone left him feeling naked. He was breaking the first rule of diving by going alone, and his club only let him hire the equipment because he said he was meeting a friend from another club.

"You know there probably won't be a thing down there but a pile of boulders?"

"You'll find the cottage. Mum will help you."

It was like trying to persuade an addict to clean up. Their mother had died in a car crash eighteen years ago, when he'd been six and she was two. Ian could see how she'd built her hazy memories into a guide and guardian angel over the years they'd been apart, but that didn't make it any more likely he'd find a house that had fallen off the edge of a cliff. He looked at the fortnight-old scar in the chalk where several hundred tons of rock had crumbled beneath their childhood home and dropped it into the English Channel, probably crushing and burying it in the process. It was eleven years since Ian promised himself he would never set eyes on Coldwater Cottage again. He didn't think he was likely to break the promise today. "You know what to do when I come up?"

"If you do nothing, I do nothing. If you wave, I turn the clutch," she fingered the lever on the outboard, "and drive over to you." Ian heard indulgence in her tone as she repeated what he'd said to keep him happy. He hadn't used the word 'drive'.

He pulled on his neoprene gloves, reducing his sense of touch to degrees of sponginess. The rubber gunwale felt very spongy as he lowered himself on to it. The edge of his mask was less spongy as he pulled it over his eyes and nose.

"You look like James Bond." Jakki's voice was muffled by his hood, as though she was a long way away. "You know what you're looking for?"

Ian felt as Jakki must have done when he repeated his questions. The hood made it difficult to say 'a silver brooch in the shape of a Celtic cross', so he just nodded.

"And Ian? Thank you. For trusting me this far."

He nodded again, glad he didn't have to say anything. He glanced at his dive computer, seeking refuge in technicalities. It was twenty minutes before low tide, which would minimise both depth and current. He put the regulator in his mouth and rolled back off the side of the boat. Silver bubbles tussled before his eyes as he bobbed to the surface. He waved to Jakki and emptied the air from his buoyancy jacket.

The waterline slid up his mask and knew it would be closing over his head, but he couldn't feel it through the hood.

Silence. Ian never noticed the perpetual noise of human existence until the sea took it away. Even on the boat, there had been the lap of water against the hull and the murmur of the wind. And Jakki. He let out his breath and broke the silence with a roar of bubbles.

He glanced at his dive computer. Six meters. The boat had already disappeared. The vermilion sleeve of his drysuit faded to grey as the sea drained the red from the light reaching him. He could be anywhere, going anywhere or nowhere. No, that wasn't true, he thought, irritated with himself. His bubbles showed him which way was up and the depth gauge on his dive computer told him he was going down. There were plenty of ways to know where he was and where he was going, and forgetting them was exactly the sort of thing that could make diving dangerous. Another thing being equipment failure, which was why you didn't dive alone.

So why was he diving alone? The reasons had made sense when he was on the boat. There was nothing in the PADI course about what to do when the sister you left behind eleven years ago appears on your doorstep, demanding a token of a mother she thinks she remembers and insisting you'll only find it if you go alone.

He remembered opening the door to her and trying to work out which of his runaways and tearaways had adopted a new look of cropped blonde hair, black eye shadow and pierced tongue and eyebrow. Her intertwined hands rose in front of her mouth as he looked at her. "It's me, Ian. It's Jack."

"Jack?" Her eyes met his, and he knew her. He just didn't believe it yet.

"Jack. Your sister. Only it's Jakki now."

"*Jack!*"

"So I can come in then?"

Thirteen meters. Ian saw ripples in the gloom before him, then shapes. He allowed himself a sense of relief. The deeper he went, the faster he would use up air. With the bottom at twenty meters, he should be able to stay down for a good half hour. Long enough to persuade Jakki he'd made a proper search when he told her he couldn't find the house.

The ripples solidified into bare boulders as he dropped closer to them. In a year they'd be covered in weed. Darting fish would be hunting snails and dodging larger fish, but now the debris of the landslide was as barren as the surface of the moon.

One of the shapes below him had unnaturally straight lines. Straight lines belonged to artificial objects like wrecks, not to boulders. He heard his breathing quicken and felt the pressure in his chest as the regulator's diaphragm refused to move far enough to give his body the air it demanded. It felt like the beginning of suffocation, and it could start a vicious cycle in which his demand for air would increase as he felt he wasn't getting enough. The greater his demand, the less it would be satisfied. He forced himself to slow his breathing and to ignore the protest from his lungs. They would find relief if they would just wait for the airflow to catch up with what they thought they needed.

Which left his mind free to contemplate the block he was sinking toward. He let some air into his drysuit to slow his descent and put out his fingertips to touch the block. Hard sponginess through the gloves. Something grey thudded into his mask and he jerked his head back. He looked around to see what it was. It hit him again, knocking his regulator. A trickle of salt water stung his tongue. He worked his jaw to reposition the regulator. He threw a hand in front of his face as his assailant came back.

"What the hell?" The words were a mumble in his regulator, but he'd got a clear look at the fish before it batted into his hand. He'd seen plenty of ballan wrasses before. Every one of them had thrashed their tails to put as much distance as they could between themselves and him, which was a prudent reaction from a fish no larger than his forearm. Could he have been mistaken? He lowered his hand and the white spots were unmistakable, even if the wrasse's true colour was reduced to shades of grey at this depth. The wrasse rammed his mask again and knocked his head back. He felt his fins scrape something solid, which seemed to infuriate the fish. It thumped against Ian's head again and again. It was like being swatted with a magazine, harmless in itself but he couldn't orientate himself and fend off the wrasse at the same time.

He flicked on the torch clipped to his jacket. The wrasse flashed into iridescent red and green in the light, then it was gone with a flick of its tail. Ian played the light on the straight edges in front of him. Flaking paint that had once been white glowed back at him. The glare blinded him to anything outside the beam, so he switched it off. The frame of a roof reached upward from the block. Slate tiles lay scattered beneath him. A knot of nausea tied itself into the pit of his stomach. He finned around the house, taking in cracked window panes that still held unbroken glass and the door he ran out of eleven years ago and swore never to pass through again. The door he'd promised Jakki he would pass through if, by some impossible chance, it was still there.

Because it *was* impossible. There was no way a ramshackle cottage could fall off the top of a cliff without being ground into fragments. Yet here it was, not quite level but still standing on what looked like a layer of soil that must have come down from the cliff, right below where he'd started his dive.

Ian stared back at the door, shut as it so often had been while a fire burned inside and rain fell outside.

"You're not coming in until you've chopped that wood!" The unshaven head disappeared as the window slammed shut.

"You'll stay outside until you've caught us a couple of rabbits. It'll be good for you!" Jack's face appeared at her bedroom window, her palms pressed to the glass as though reaching out for him.

Dad had been determined to be *self-sufficient*. It was a favourite word of his, like *manly* and *deadweight*.

"You'll learn to be manly if it kills the pair of us," to Ian.

"I never wanted a girl! You're just a deadweight," to Jack.

Ian's hand drifted through the soil, feeling no more than a slight resistance through the glove. A mist of fine particles rose before him. He remembered bunching his fists in that soil and watching blood drip on to the grass from his lip or nose after one of Dad's attempts at homeschooling. Dad's gifts as a teacher had been as meagre as Ian's as a pupil, and frustration was never more than one step away from flying fists. Ian never cried. He'd learned not to make that mistake at an early age. He'd clench his fingers into the soil as though trying to pull it out from under Dad, the house and his entire life. "Bastard," he'd say, "bastard, bastard, bastard."

Ian jerked his head, annoyed he'd let his thoughts wander. Forget 'manly' and 'self-sufficient'. The word he needed to remember now was 'narcosis'. Before his first training dive below eighteen meters, the instructor had told him to write his phone number backwards. He'd done it without hesitation, but when she handed him a pad on the bottom, he'd had to wring the digits out of his memory, and even then he'd mixed two of them up. It was as clear a demonstration of the effect of nitrogen under pressure on the human brain as he could have asked for. Yet here he was drifting through memories he'd spent half his life trying to forget instead of keeping an eye on his air. A hundred and fifty bars left, and he'd only been down for fourteen minutes. He shouldn't have let his breathing run away with him.

He noticed that the door wasn't shut as he had first thought, but slightly ajar. Strange, he could have sworn...but he hadn't looked that closely. He could just swim round in circles and tell Jakki that there was no house. He remembered the face at the window he left behind when he ran away, and knew he had to go inside.

He flicked his fins and bumped a hand against the door. It didn't move. Years of cold and damp had made it a poor fit for the frame long before he'd left.

"Don't bang the bleeding door, you little turd!"

Ian braced a hand against the frame and pushed. It ground across the slate floor, but it gave way and his momentum carried him through it. Into darkness. He couldn't see his hands. He felt his anxiety as he fumbled for his torch. It was only anxiety, he told himself, a long way from panic. This was not the time for panic.

The torch clicked on. Ian blinked in the sudden glare even as he saw the wall at the end of the living room. He threw his arms in front of his head before he gently collided with it. He felt the torch knocked out of his hand and opened his eyes to see the beam wandering around the room. The worn paint and bare floorboards were so familiar he felt sick. His repeat offenders must feel like this when they go back to prison, he thought. He retrieved the torch and the beam swept across the door to the kitchen. He saw a quick movement and refused to believe what had just appeared, because there couldn't be a human figure in the room and it just couldn't be "Dad!"

Ian kicked his fins and tried to twist his body toward the door he'd come in through. The door itself appeared in the torch beam, and he heard as much as felt his head thud into it. The sea exploded into pinpoints of light. He felt salt water in his nose and mouth as his mask and regulator shifted. He flailed his arms, feeling for the doorway, and somehow he was outside. He shoved the regulator back into place and found himself staring up at soil and boulders as the air in his drysuit rushed to his feet. Bubbles roared past his ears as he breathed in great retching sobs.

The image of that figure shimmered in his mind. A spasm of shivers shook him. Just as suddenly, he was furious with himself. It was stupid to be down here alone to start with, but he'd committed the cardinal sin of panic. Now he was out of control and drifting toward the surface when he knew perfectly well that a simple forward roll like *that* would get the air out of his boots and into his sleeves so he could release it through the wrist valve like *that*. Uncontrolled ascent turned into a gentle descent, and he landed on his knees on top of a boulder. He needed the feel of firm ground while he got his breathing under control. He pressed his hand to his ringing head, though he could feel nothing but the texture of neoprene covering a solid object. The boulder beneath him would feel the same.

He glanced at his air gauge. A hundred and twenty bars left after seventeen minutes. He was ripping through his air, seeing things and now he'd banged his head. This was the right time to return to the surface. And explain to Jakki that he hadn't found the brooch. He could see her face as he told her, a veneer of sympathy over her implacable conviction that he would go back. Her conviction would be justified because as hopeless as the quest was, he'd left her alone with Dad and would do whatever she asked until he atoned for it.

He looked back to the house. There was another reason why he'd go back in. He refused to accept he'd seen Dad in that room because it simply couldn't have happened. He made himself go over the scene in his mind and think about what he'd actually seen. The torch beam flicking around the room, sending shadows cavorting in all directions. A movement out of the kitchen. Or was it into the kitchen? A dark figure with no features. Could he have imagined it? It had looked so human. So *real*.

He had to know. He kicked back toward the house before he had time to frighten himself. He panned the torch around the living room. The same two armchairs he remembered lay toppled on their sides. The bookshelves were still screwed to the wall, although the books were reduced to lumps of pulp scattered across the floor. Ian remembered titles like *SAS Survival Manual* and *Bravo Two Zero*, but little of the words inside them. Instructions on butchering rabbits blended with tales of hard-jawed men slaughtering men with softer and darker features who never had names. Ian had always identified more with the slaughtered than the slaughterers. It wasn't until years after he ran away that he understood what an impossible dream those hard men had been for Dad, and understood Dad's rage that his son showed so little aptitude for becoming what he never became himself.

Yet the memory of Dad was all that was left of him in the room. There was no sign of Dad himself, though there was a faint haze in the room. Ian saw that it was made up of dark tendrils that diffused and dissolved as he peered at them. He finned into the kitchen. Something darted through the torch beam. Ian caught his breath as he recognised the same movement that had preceded Dad's appearance. He followed it with the torch and found himself looking at a cuttlefish. It hovered about two meters away, its crown of tentacles aimed at the torch, ready to defend itself. Waves of brown pigment chased each other across the striped body. It took Ian a moment to make the connection, then a gust of laughter swept through him. It was all he could do to keep his mouth closed on the regulator, and he knew he was close to hysteria, but a sodding cuttlefish for Christ's sake! It was so obvious. He'd startled it, and it had released a cloud of ink and dived into the kitchen. A predator would see what predators were most afraid of in the cloud: a larger predator. Ian had seen Dad. The haze in the living room was the remains of the ink cloud, which he must have been dispersed by his frantic exit.

Yet the cuttlefish wasn't throwing out ink clouds now. It was doing what cuttlefish usually did when they saw divers, which was to withdraw to a safe distance and have a look at the noisy, clumsy creature invading its realm. Ian occasionally wondered who was more interested in whom when exchanging stares with cuttlefish, but now he wondered why it had reacted so violently. He must have startled it, he thought, or perhaps the ink was from an octopus that was still hiding somewhere. It didn't matter. What mattered was that he'd seen Dad in an ink cloud, and now needed to search Dad's bedroom before he gave himself any more scares.

He inhaled and used the air in his lungs to carry him up, over the stone stairs. They were as bare as they always had been, but they wouldn't stay bare for much longer. After a few months, they'd be scattered with the dark brown sausages of cotton-spinner sea cucumbers and the grey coral claws of dead men's fingers that turned red in electric light.

Ian reached the top of the stairs and found himself between two doors. Dad's on one side, his and Jakki's on the other. He turned toward Dad's door.

"You ever come in here, boy, and I'll thrash your arse so you'll be sleeping on your belly for a month!"

Ian rotated slowly until he was facing the room he'd slept in until he was fourteen. He opened the door before he realised he'd decided to do it.

There had been two camp beds and nothing else in there when he left. Now there was a bare frame on Jack's side of the room and a space where his bed had been. Dad probably threw it out in fury when he found him gone. He remembered a night when he did have to sleep on his belly. Jack had burned the dinner, and Ian had deflected Dad's anger by saying he had broken a fishing rod. Jack had crawled into his bed and they kept each other awake while Dad drank in the living room, waiting for the bang of his bedroom door and the snores that would announce that he'd passed out, so Ian could slip down to the garage and actually break a fishing rod. Nine-year-old Jack ran her fingers over the welts on his back, and Ian felt the warmth of her tears on his shoulder. "I'll always protect you from him," he had said. At thirteen, he'd believed he meant it. Now he felt the void that eleven years of broken promise had opened in him.

A hundred bars. Twenty-two minutes. Ian was procrastinating, putting off entering Dad's bedroom. A new thought crossed his mind. Could Dad still be in there? The cliff had collapsed at night, so he'd probably been in bed. He could be behind that door, under a herd of crabs jostling each other for the last morsels of flesh. Ian had been so convinced he wouldn't find the house that he had not even thought about finding Dad's body. It was about the only thing he hadn't got round to being afraid of since he got down here.

If Dad's body was in there, it couldn't be helped. He had to search that room. And whatever happened, he wasn't going to panic. He turned the handle and opened the door.

Ian had a brief impression of a camp bed frame on its side,

clothes floating in the torch beam and the mattress trapped against the ceiling by its own buoyancy. Flailing limbs and armoured claws lunged at his face. He heard a click as something chitinous hit his mask. Pointed legs scratched his cheeks where the hood didn't cover them. He recognised the swimming crab as much by its aggression as by its shape, but it was the first one that had attached itself to his face. They went for the torch. Every time.

He fumbled for the crab's body and tried to feel the shape of it through his gloves. He tugged and the legs left his cheeks. His regulator shifted in his mouth as he pulled. He pushed it back into place with his left hand. The crab must have got hold of the air hose. He clenched his teeth and pulled hard. The crab didn't move.

He felt laughter simmering inside him, ready to boil up and overwhelm him. It was absurd to have a crab stuck to his face. It wasn't strong enough to cut through the hose, but he couldn't search the room while he was wrestling it.

Ian settled on his knees and took the regulator out of his mouth. The crab gripped the air hose with both pincers. Ian twisted the regulator around and pressed the purge button. A deluge of air bubbles sent the crab flying off the hose, all ten limbs flapping wildly. Ian replaced his regulator as the crab recovered and lunged back at his face. He caught it and flung it outside the room, then braced a hand against the wall and pulled the door closed. Ian passed a hand over his still throbbing head. What was making the wildlife so aggressive? First the wrasse and now the crab.

He was shut in Dad's room. Sharper, colder feet than the crab's scuttled up his spine at the thought.

He was procrastinating again. Ninety bars, twenty-four minutes. A pair of combat trousers floated in front of him, as though on an invisible hanger. He panned the light around the thick walls that were pierced only by a small window, designed to allow in a little light without making a larger gap than necessary in the insulation of the walls. Columns of bubbles glinted silver as the air he'd exhaled in the living room below filtered through the floor. Ian looked up to see the bubble of air he'd already exhaled spreading across the ceiling like a glass tomb for the mattress and a few cans that still held a little air.

The tools of Dad's obsession were strewn across the floor. A compass, a gas stove, a few shotgun cartridges. All that was left of a lifelong quest to become a man he could never have been. The beam caught the etched sides of a silver box that did not belong in Dad's macho dream. Ian flinched when he saw he hadn't been mistaken. It was a jewellery box. He shoved the handle of the torch into his buoyancy jacket and picked it up. He turned it around, and the glare of the torch faded from a glass cover over a miniature photograph. He hadn't seen that face since he was six years old, but his mother's smile stabbed like a knife. His eyes stung as he searched for a memory of her smiling like that. It didn't come. Her smiles had been rare and fearful, smuggled beneath the radar of Dad's disapproval of everything from coddled children to living in Didcot and working in a department store.

Dad must have brought the box with him after she died in the car crash. All that time he'd forbidden Ian and Jack to mention her. Ian had thought Dad had erased every trace of her from his life. He'd thought Mum's death had been a dream come true for Dad, as he'd been able to buy Coldwater Cottage cheaply and play at self-sufficiency between trips to buy booze. Yet what was this box if not proof that he'd never escaped the memory of her? Proof that he had loved her even if he'd never known how to show it? Ian's eyes stung, and not from sea salt. Dad, you *bastard*!

The catch on the box was tiny and it took Ian several attempts to get it open. There wasn't much inside. A pair of pearl ear-rings, a gold necklace, and pinned to the velvet under the lid, a silver brooch in the shape of a Celtic cross.

The torch went out.

That was odd. He'd charged the battery and the bulb was new. No need to panic. There was a light on his buoyancy jacket. Not as powerful as the torch, but it would give him enough light to get out of here. There was no need to panic. The fingers of his left hand closed, and Ian knew he had dropped the box. His right hand found the large switch on the spare light, which had been thoughtfully designed so Ian could find it in the dark while wearing gloves. He felt the switch click. Nothing. He jerked the switch back and forth but the light was dead. He felt the check of the regulator as his breathing threatened to accelerate out of control.

Calm down, he told himself. Think. There should be a faint light from the window, but Ian's eyes were still too used to the torch to make it out. Not that he could get through the window with the tank on his back. That left the door he had so carefully closed, which was behind him and to his right. Or was it to his left? If he could find the wall behind him, he could grope for the handle. He flicked a fin. His co-ordination betrayed him and his shoulder bumped the wall - or was it the floor or ceiling? - against his shoulder. He was disorientated, and now he'd have to search the whole room. He angled the backlit face of his dive computer toward his air gauge. It gave him just enough light to see the needle. Seventy bars wasn't much to get out of this room, get out of the house and ascend twenty meters slowly enough to avoid the bends, but it was possible if he kept his breathing under control and didn't panic.

The dive computer went out.

"Can't you take a hint?"

Ian froze and pressed his hand to the ache in his head. The voice had sounded as though it came from inside his skull, as if he'd spoken himself.

"I warned you, but still you had to go straight for the box. It's *hers*."

The hiss and roar of his breathing told Ian that he was still alive, but he wouldn't be for much longer. He was hallucinating when his life depended on clear thinking.

"Like I said, I warned you."

The voice sounded exactly like his own. He railed silently for it to shut up.

"I'll shut up when I want to shut up. This is my house now."

Ian felt his arms wrap themselves around his knees. He thought of Jakki adrift in the boat, waiting for him to come back up. What if no one saw her and called the coastguard? She'd never be able to steer the boat back to land. He was abandoning her for a second time. The thought sank into his stomach like a lead weight.

"What's that?"

A torrent of memories surged through Ian's mind. Of him and Jack clinging to each other while Dad raged through the living room. Of the trust in her face when he said he'd never leave her. Of the day he broke his promise and walked for miles to the nearest town, only to get collared stealing a Mars bar from a newsagent. Memories of the image of her that he'd conjured up to give him the courage to keep his mouth shut when the social services asked where he'd come from, convinced they'd send him back to Dad if they knew. Then the years of foster homes and college as he trained as a social worker. He'd wanted to help people like himself and Jack, but every lost soul was a poor substitute for the one he'd left behind.

"It's *you*?"

He ignored the voice this time, as his memories brought him back to Jakki, alone in the boat above him.

"She's up there?"

Yes damn it, she's up there, Ian thought. Happy now?

The voice was silent, and Ian began to think the hallucination had passed. He felt sick when he wondered how long he'd spent debating with himself. He had to concentrate. He had to get out of here.

"You really think I'm a hallucination, don't you?"

Ian groaned without opening his mouth. There was something hypnotic about the voice, something that commanded Ian's full attention.

"Close your left hand."

Ian stared at nothing, unsure whether his eyes were open or closed.

"I said close your left hand."

Ian's fingers closed on something flat and solid, about the size of his palm. He ran his thumb along the back of it and felt the pin of the brooch. How had it got into his hand?

He must have blinked because suddenly the room was lit before him, but something was wrong. The mattress was on the camp bed, and there was a sleeping bag thrown over it. The door opened and a girl sidled in. Ian recognised Jack, but she was older than when he'd left, perhaps thirteen or fourteen. She turned and whispered to him. "Where's Dad now, Ian?"

Dad must be out of the house, or she'd never dare to come in here. Jack nodded as though it was a reassuring answer and opened a cupboard. She pulled out the silver jewellery box and lingered over Mum's picture. She opened it and held the brooch up to the window. Ian's throat was tight with fear for her. He couldn't bear to think what might happen if Dad found her. He imagined Dad trudging home after a search through a dozen empty rabbit traps, and silently begged her to get out of the room. Jack looked up as though she heard him and replaced the brooch in the box. She closed the box with a precision that told Ian that she'd done the same thing many times before and knew how to get away with it. She closed the cupboard, left the room and closed the door without making a sound.

The room faded to darkness. Ian was sitting in the dark, waiting for his air to run out.

"I've seen your memories. Now I've shown you one of mine."

Part of Ian's mind refused to believe it, but the knowledge of how little air he had left was more powerful. It didn't matter whether the voice was real or not, only whether it could get him out of here.

"Look up."

Ian looked up and saw a rectangle of grey light that could only be the front door and was Ian's whole life as soon as he saw it. All he had to do was kick his fins and he'd be in the light with nothing between him and the surface.

"Do you understand who I am?"

It didn't matter who the voice was. Nothing mattered but light and air, but Ian found himself hesitating.

"Don't you remember the promise you made to Jack? Over and over?"

That wasn't fair, Ian screamed at himself. To bring up the one thing that would hold him here.

"She believed you, so she made it true. She kept something of you with her."

Ian thought again about how similar the voice sounded to his own.

"She kept believing you till she was sixteen. It took that long to realise she was depending on a shadow of you. So she left to build another shadow out of Mum."

Ian couldn't help but phrase his thought as a question. You're the shadow of me that she built? That makes no sense.

"You're in the *sea*. How can you hope to understand it when you don't understand your own sister. Now go to her before you join me."

Ian flicked his fins and wondered how he was going to explain the voice to Jakki, or even to himself once the reality had become a memory.

"You'll manage. You've banged your head and maybe got a touch of narcosis. Your conscious mind didn't know how to get you out, so it gave up and let your instincts take over. You'll half believe it by the time you get to the surface."

Surface. Light. Air. Life. The ideas flooded Ian's mind, and with it came another thought. He hadn't seen Dad, so where was he?

"He was in the garage when the cliff collapsed. Now get the hell out of here."

Ian shot through the door and blinked at the grey light bathing the boulders below him. He grabbed his air gauge and lifted it in front of his eyes. Twenty bars. Not much, but enough to get to the surface. He turned to face the house as he kicked upward, and perhaps he heard a distant voice say, "she was never really alone here," but he wasn't sure.

Back in the eternal grey between the surface and the bottom, eyes darting between the depth gauge and the Celtic cross in his hand. The cross glinted as red seeped back into the colour of his drysuit. Ian looked up to see the sparkle of sunlight on the surface above him. His head burst into the air, and he took the sweetest breath he'd ever tasted, for all the salt he inhaled with it.

He opened the valve into his buoyancy jacket, but the sigh of air died from the moment it started. It was enough to keep him on the surface, but Ian shuddered at the thought that he'd surfaced with less than one more breath in his tank.

The boat bobbed about fifty meters away. He could see Jakki's blonde head as she lay against the rubber side. He was only ten meters away by the time she saw him. She leapt to her feet, but staggered and lost her balance as the boat rolled.

"Ian!" Her voice was muffled by his hood, but he could hear the joy in it.

Ian slipped his mask down around his neck and threw his arms over the side of the boat. He opened his left hand and expected Jakki to grab the brooch. She glanced at it, looked at him and time stood still as he saw that old look of trust return to her face.

Jakki sprang forward, leaning over the side to throw her arms around his neck. "I knew you'd find it."

Ian pressed his face into her shoulder. "Yes," he said. "I found it."

Perchance to Dream

Pongo Ponsonby thought he was dead, but he wasn't sure. He decided to ask his flight leader. "Blue three to blue leader, blue three to blue leader..."

The flat sound of his voice stopped him. What was he going to say next? He'd have to buy drinks for every officer in the mess if he asked if he was dead. Besides, he couldn't feel the transmit button under his finger, so no one would hear him. Now he thought about it, he couldn't feel anything in his hands. Just something under his back. And someone patting his chest. Someone who breathed heavily.

He groaned. The last thing he remembered was cannon shells from a Messerschmitt he hadn't even seen, tearing his Spitfire apart around him. He must have bailed out. He'd been over France when he was shot down, so whoever was patting him was probably a German taking him prisoner. Damn.

The hands fumbled along his belt. He opened his eyes to a sky heavy with mist, and saw that he was lying on the bank of a still, dark river. This wasn't a hospital, and the hands belonged to a wizened old man whose loincloth didn't look like it was issued by a Wehrmacht quartermaster.

The old man gave a satisfied grunt and undid Pongo's belt buckle. Pongo remembered the gold coins sewn into it, standard issue for operations over occupied territory.

He sat up sharply. "Hey! Stop that! *Arrêtez-vous*!"

The old man scuttled backward.

"You - you old," Pongo stifled the word that sprang to his lips. He'd never be able to look the vicar in the eye if he swore at an old man.

A deep growl in his right ear filled Pongo's nostrils with the smell of recently eaten meat. Pongo's shoulders tensed. He'd never been fond of dogs, and that didn't sound like a small one.

He turned toward the growl. He found himself looking into the jaws of a dog the size of a carthorse with a set of teeth that would make a tiger envious. What made Pongo leap to his feet were the two other identical heads attached to the same body.

Pongo looked around to see if the old man had any idea how to cope with the monster, but he was paying no attention to the dog. He was haranguing Pongo in a language that sounded vaguely familiar, but wasn't French or German.

The man said something that sounded less guttural, and Pongo thought he caught a word, '*aurum*'. Then another one: '*doné*'. A memory of school surfaced, in which he was bent over Old Cribb's desk with his trousers around his ankles, answering Old Cribb's questions in that same language and making sure he got it right because the cane wasn't slow to point out any mistakes. The language was Latin, and the more guttural language had been ancient Greek. So he wasn't in France. He was dead after all, and Cerberus the hellhound was going to have some more meat to foul his breath if Pongo didn't pay the ferryman.

He found his pocket knife, cut through the seam of his belt, and handed the old man a coin. The dog stopped growling, but the string of saliva that fell from the middle mouth didn't look friendly.

The old man was frowning at the coin. "This coin is not Greek or Roman," he said, still in Latin.

Pongo blessed Old Cribb, cane and all, when he understood. "It's a coin of Britannia."

"Then the price is two coins."

Pongo recalled the song that advised, 'you can't take your dough when you go go go.' The lyricist would have to think again when he discovered that not only money but also inflation had preceded him. A look at Cerberus convinced him to hand over another coin.

The old man pointed across a field covered by a web of mist. "Go there for judgment, and if they send you back, tell whoever buries you to put the coin in your mouth next time. It makes my job much easier."

He waddled away, giving Cerberus an absent-minded pat in passing. Cerberus lay down and closed all six eyes.

Pongo found himself alone by the river, wondering why he'd spent every Sunday morning of his nineteen years being told what to do to get to a heaven that didn't extend invitations to three-headed dogs or septuagenarian extortionists. He wanted to sit down and wrap his arms around his knees until someone came to tell him that it was all right. He'd done that when he was twelve, and had been winded on the rugby field. The only person who came was the divinity master, who dragged him to his feet and told him that Waterloo wasn't won by crying. Not even the divinity master would come for him here.

At least it had been quick. Not like Harry, whose Spitfire had burned all the way down from ten thousand feet.

Poor Harry had been the only constant in Pongo's life since they met amid the genteel brutality of boarding school. They had somehow managed to stay together until they ended up in the same squadron. Then they'd both been killed in action, which meant that Harry would be here.

The thought focused Pongo's eyes in the direction the old man had pointed. He could just make out a pool through the mist, with three figures beside it. If that was where he'd been sent, it was probably where Harry had been sent. Pongo strode toward the pool, through the knee-high asphodels that splashed him with dew.

The three figures were all young men, dressed in splendid purple robes. They were all staring at him in open-mouthed amazement.

"*Salveté*, patricians," said Pongo as cheerfully as he could.

For a moment, none of them moved, then the one in the middle replied. "Oh, er, yes, *salvé*."

The man on the left kicked the speaker's shin and glared at him. All three made a visible effort to throw back their shoulders and arrange their features into expressions of grim dignity. They reminded Pongo of the school chaplain when he and Harry had chanced upon him urinating behind a hedge.

The one in the middle spoke again, employing the same grave tone that the chaplain had used on that unfortunate day. "Welcome, shade, to the Pool of Memory, where we shall judge your conduct in the Middle World and decide your fate in the Underworld."

Pongo found the idea of being judged something of a relief. He'd expected to be judged. He moistened his lips and startled himself by saying "jolly good," in English.

The speaker frowned. "I am King Aeacus. This is King Rhadamanthys and King Minos. We shall decide your doom."

He glared at Pongo, who put his hands behind his back and stared straight ahead. Headmasters and wing commanders appreciated that pose, so perhaps judges of the dead did too. The deepening furrows on Aeacus's brow suggested otherwise.

"His name," hissed Rhadamanthys.

Aeacus looked relieved. "Speak your name, shade."

Pongo felt like a new recruit, and he knew how recruits were supposed to behave. He snapped to attention. "Ponsonby! WR! Pilot Officer! Five-oh-nine-two-one-oh! *Sir*!"

That sounded rather formal so he added, "Most people call me

Pongo."

The three judges exchanged glances. Pongo wondered if he'd said something wrong, but he could hardly be blamed for his name, could he?

Aeacus was glaring again.

"His land," hissed Rhadamanthys.

Aeacus nodded. "What land do you owe your fealty, shade?"

"Britannia."

Aeacus started. Rhadamanthys and Minos looked as though their eyes were about to leap from their heads, but managed to retain their dignified poses.

"There are those in Britannia who follow the Olympians?" asked Minos. "After all these centuries?"

"I'm sorry?" said Pongo.

"Perhaps we should explain our confusion," said Minos. "No shades have arrived here for more than a thousand years. Now you arrive, dressed..." he waved a hand at Pongo's Irvine jacket and Mae West life jacket. They made a shabby contrast to the judges' regalia.

"Your name makes no sense in any civilised language," said Minos. "You say you're from an island that has hardly sent us anyone since the Romans left. What are you doing here?"

Pongo's shoulders sagged. They wouldn't be so surprised if Harry had come this way. "I'm sorry. I don't know why I'm here either."

Rhadamanthys sniffed. "Of course he doesn't know. Why bother asking a mortal?"

"It might be important," said Minos. "If there's been a resurgence of the old religion, we'll need more space down here and I'd bet my minotaur that they'll forget to tell us."

"Of course they will," said Aeacus. "Remember when Alexander started converting the Persians? No one warned us, and they were queuing up to their waists in the Styx while we looked for somewhere to put them."

"Then we'd better ask the appropriate authorities," Rhadamanthys glanced upward. "The shade knows nothing."

Pongo was used to feeling overlooked, but he had hoped that whoever was supposed to be judging his immortal soul would at least remember he was there. "Excuse me, but I'm Christian. Church of England."

The glare of the judges reminded him that recruits didn't speak until they were spoken to.

"Let us get the judgment out of the way, then we can discuss the important matters," said Rhadamanthys.

Minos and Aeacus nodded, and all three resumed their stern expressions.

"What was your profession, shade?" asked Aeacus.

That was a difficult question. Pongo didn't know the Latin for 'Spitfire pilot', and Icarus probably hadn't set a very good precedent. "I'm a warrior."

Aeacus snorted. "A warrior indeed! Then why are you wearing fancy dress? A young warrior like you should die in battle, not at a masque."

"I did die in battle. This is my uniform."

"Then where is your weapon? Why were you not clutching it at the end? Did you throw it down and run?"

A weapon that weighed two tons and carried you along at three-hundred-and-fifty knots would be outside Aeacus's experience. "My weapon was destroyed."

"Very well. Have you seen much battle in your short life?"

Pongo hadn't seen much else since he and Harry got off the train at Biggin Hill, two lifetimes ago. "Six months of constant fighting."

"How many enemies have you bested?"

Pongo swallowed. He'd known they'd have to get round to that, and lying wouldn't help. His voice faltered as he admitted his only cardinal sin. "Four confirmed kills, two probables."

He was about to beg their forgiveness, but all three were nodding with what looked like approval.

"Four dead enemies is a good epitaph for such a young man," said Minos. "Very good indeed."

"That alone qualifies him for Elysium," said Rhadamanthys. "Whatever else he may have done."

"I don't think we need to know anything else," said Aeacus, "and we need to find out if we're going to get a sudden rush. Go through that, young man. They'll find you some proper clothes when you get there."

Pongo looked around to see a rectangular hole in whatever reality he had fallen into. It seemed to be standing on the ground but as Pongo got closer, he saw that it was not a hole but something dark that looked as solid as glass but neither revealed anything on the other side nor reflected Pongo as he approached it. He squinted at it until it filled his vision. He felt a lurch like looping the loop after six pints.

Sunlight burst on his face and the chords of a lyre caressed his ear. He shaded his eyes against the light, and found himself in a field of deep green grass. Bearded men in leather armour surrounded him, lying against cypress trees or dancing to the lyre music.

Then he saw the girl playing the lyre, and forgot everything else. It wasn't just that she had the sort of lissom beauty he associated with the novels of Sir Walter Scott, but that her gown was cut below her breasts. Pongo had never seen real breasts before, although he'd stared at plenty of blouses and tried to divine the shapes concealed beneath. Harry once said that he'd seen Madame Brennier's breasts when she fell off her bicycle and her blouse split, and she hadn't been wearing a bra because everyone knew that French women didn't. Pongo wasn't sure if he believed it, but then it didn't really count because Madame Brennier was nearly sixty.

"I'd never seen a pair like that 'til I got here either!" shouted a particularly large man.

The lyre player's breasts shook as she joined the laughter sweeping through the glade. Pongo's face burned. "*Salveté*, sirs."

"Don't mind Achilles," shouted a man wearing the horsehair helmet of a Roman legionary. "He wouldn't have looked twice if he had!"

The large man laughed and threw an arm around the man next to him, who rested his bronze helmet on Achilles's shoulder.

"Give me a bedfellow like Patroclus any day," said Achilles. "He didn't hide from me for four days a month when we were alive, and joined me in Elysium now that we're dead. Show me the woman who could match that. But our new friend's gone purple!"

Achilles jumped to his feet and advanced on Pongo. "I'm not surprised you're a funny colour under all that leather. Get rid of it, the sun never stops shining here."

Achilles grabbed Pongo's Mae West. Pongo flinched, but Achilles was undeterred. "What sort of armour is this? It's as soft as an empress's skirt! No wonder you joined us so young. What land are you from, young warrior?"

Pongo's buttocks clenched reflexively. "Britannia."

He unclipped his harness and dropped his parachute, dinghy and Mae West to the ground. Achilles was right about the heat, and Pongo didn't want his help to undress.

The legionary leapt to his feet. "Britannia! I spent six years stuck on that pile of donkey droppings! We get no one new for a thousand years and now a Britaniculus! What next? A dog? A German?"

Pongo turned to the Roman's sneer. Anger burned away his embarrassment, and he wished Old Cribb had taught him some Latin expressions a bit more colourful than 'veni vidi vici'.

"You impertinent man!" was the best he could do. He tried to bellow like the flight sergeant who'd taught him to march. It sounded more like what happened when the music master assigned him to sing the bass part of Bach's *Requiem* and his voice kept reverting to soprano.

The Roman was not intimidated. "Call me impertinent? I, a citizen of the greatest empire the world ever saw, am called impertinent by a tribe that paints itself blue?"

The insult to his country was the first thing that Pongo had understood since he died. The wave of fury that swept through him brought the relief of a cold beer on a hot day. "Your little empire could fit into one little corner of His Britannic Majesty's! Look at a map of India some time!"

"Nonsense the pair of you," growled Achilles. "There was never an empire that could stand against my Myrmidons of Phthiotis."

"And all Greece was no more than a beetle's garden," Pongo delighted to hear his Latin getting more creative. "Glare at me if you like, you hairy tunic-lifter, but my king wouldn't use your kingdom as his lavatory!"

Pongo savoured the awed expressions that surrounded him. People were actually backing away from his eloquence. That would teach them to remember they were only foreigners, heroes of the Trojan wars or not.

Achilles put out a hand and Patroclus placed a spear in it. Pongo's anger fell away as quickly as his parachute had. Achilles's eyes seized Pongo's as Patroclus buckled a shield on to his left arm.

Achilles advanced. Pongo backed away. It just wasn't fair that you could bring a spear with you but not a Spitfire. His foot caught on a Cypress root and he fell on his back. Achilles put a foot on Pongo's parachute pack and raised his spear. "Now then boy, which of us pays homage to a piss-pot?" Achilles looked down at the pack. "What's that hissing noise?"

Pongo recognised his carbon dioxide cylinder. His dinghy leapt out of its pack, and Achilles disappeared under a sheet of yellow rubber.

Pongo sat up to see the lyrist looking back at him. She threw her head back and laughed as musically as she played the lyre. Then Pongo couldn't hear her anymore because the whole glade quaked with laughter.

Patroclus's hands shook as he hauled the dinghy off Achilles, but even Achilles was laughing. "Thank Zeus Hector didn't have one of those!"

He wheeled on Pongo and hauled him into an embrace that nearly put him back on the ground. "Some ambrosia for Elysium's newest guest!"

The lyrist put her lyre aside and produced a clay urn from somewhere. She strolled toward him in a way that made Ingrid Bergman look as graceful as a cadet's first salute. She stopped in front of Pongo. He forced himself to look up to her face. She nodded as though to say that he could go on looking if he wanted to. It occurred to Pongo that staring at the breasts of someone you hadn't been introduced to might constitute a gaffe. "My name's Pongo. How do you do?"

The lyrist held the urn to his lips. He almost took it before he remembered that the first drink always seemed harmless, but invariably put him on the path that ended in a blazing headache and a bill for broken furniture. "Oh no, not for me thank..."

She pressed the urn between his lips, and a liquid that surpassed sweetness bathed his tongue. He decided that his new friends probably didn't pay subscriptions to the Temperance Society, and swallowed. The lyrist lowered the urn. Pongo found that she'd become even more desirable.

She kissed his lips. "My name is Pulchrissimé. I do very well, thank you."

A cheer engulfed them. Pulchrissimé placed her hands on his shoulders and pushed him to the ground. She straddled his midriff and caressed his face.

Pongo remembered Old Cribb catching some of the boys with a magazine full of grainy pictures of undressed women. Cold showers for the lot of them, followed by six of the best and one for luck.

He looked around to see the heroes of a thousand years of battles exchanging grins and laughs. "Um, Pulchrissimé, this is all rather sudden..."

A finger over his lips silenced him. She kissed him again, and he decided that he'd spend the rest of eternity under a cold shower for one more kiss.

"Here he is!"

Pongo's lips froze on Pulchrissimé's.

"Ah, jolly good," replied another voice in English. Pongo didn't recognise the voice, but his spine prickled at the schoolmasterly inflection.

Pongo looked up. A tall man wearing a toga spoke to Pulchrissimé in the booming Latin of the first voice. "Get off him woman, he's a monotheist. These fools," he gestured at a small man sporting a tweed jacket and a pointed beard, "sent him here by mistake."

Pulchrissimé jumped off Pongo as though he was a wasp nest. "A monotheist! But I kissed him!"

She hawked and spat.

The warriors' grins dropped away. The Roman fingered the pommel of his sword.

The tweed jacketed man held up his hands. "I'm terribly sorry my dear. We get so many these days that we're bound to lose track of a few. We do our best, you know."

"Well do better." The toga pointed at Pulchrissimé. "And you had better take a bath immediately."

The bearded man pulled Pongo to his feet. "Oh dear, poor Hades gets so upset about these things," he said in English, apparently oblivious to the angry murmur swelling around them. "But really, we haven't lost anyone down here since the Black Death. You *are* Pilot Officer WR Ponsonby, five-oh-nine-two-one-oh?"

Pongo tried to assume the pose that seemed to work for the judges, but couldn't stop himself hanging his head as he had on the day he had to explain how astonished he was that his initials had carved themselves into a school desk. "Yes."

"Well that's a relief. I'd have some explaining to do if I came back with the wrong man. I'm Mephistopheles, by the way," he pumped Pongo's limp hand. "Aha, I see you've heard of me. I expect you're surprised to see me doing this job, but we're all rather rushed these days and we do our bit where we can. There is a war on, you know."

Pongo felt sick. Years of church instruction and he'd crashed on his first solo, but this was far worse than bending a Tiger Moth. Half an hour away from teachers and superior officers and he'd been fighting, drinking and fornicating. Now the demon who tempted Faust had turned up to take him to task for it. An eternity of cold showers was the best he could expect.

Mephistopheles rattled on. "Just a quick shout on the *wireless*, I think you chaps call it, and it's chocks away."

Mephistopheles took Pongo's arm and turned him around to face another pane of dark glass that had appeared from nowhere, this time without the decoration of an archway. Pongo found himself frog marched through it before he could say a word.

"Here we are, home at last and sorry about the detour," said Mephistopheles. "How d'you like it? Um, I don't mean to presume, but you'd find it easier to express an informed opinion if you opened your eyes."

Pongo took a tentative breath, and the pleasantly warm air persuaded him to open an eye. He expected to receive a red-hot needle in it, but all he saw was blue sky over white clouds.

Clouds. Sky. Nothing under his feet. His hand leapt for where his ripcord should be, but got a handful of silk robe. He didn't seem to be falling toward the clouds, so he looked down and saw why. He was standing on them. He took an experimental step and found himself walking across the cloud, though he could feel nothing beneath his bare feet.

"Ponsonby Minor? *C'est pas possible!*"

Pongo looked up and rubbed his eyes. It made no difference. The woman looking at him still had a faint nimbus of light over her brown hair.

She spoke in rapid French, and smiled at his blank expression. "Ah, but you never did pay attention to our beautiful language," she said in English. "But how did you come to be here? I don't remember seeing you in the chapel."

"I'm sorry? Have we met?"

Pongo scrutinised the woman's face. Her features were unremarkable, but they had a sort of purity, as though every blemish had been cleansed away. Pongo was sure he would have remembered such a face if he'd seen it before.

The woman opened her hands. "But surely you remember my voice, even if you don't recognise my face, *mon jeune brave.*"

Pongo sat down with a force that would have bruised his tailbone if there had been anything solid enough to bruise it. "Madame Brennier?"

"*Oui, c'est moi. J'ai...*oh, you never did pay attention in my lessons, did you? Even after I separated you from the Harris boy. I look thirty years younger than you remember of course. I was in church so much *more* when I was young, but what can you have to confess when you are nearly sixty and live in *England*?" she smiled. "But what are you doing here? I thought you were C of E?"

"Well, I..."

"C of E? Don't be ridiculous!"

Mephistopheles's voice cut off Pongo's reply.

"He converted last year, didn't you old boy?" Mephistopheles clapped Pongo's back. "Sorry to break up the reunion, but I need to borrow the man of the hour. Some forms to fill in before you get too settled. Frightful bore and all that, but needs must."

Madame Brennier genuflected and Mephistopheles pulled Pongo to his feet for the second time in ten minutes. He leaned toward him confidentially. "You didn't say anything about not being Catholic, did you?"

"I didn't really get a chance to say anything."

"Good, good, they've thought they've had the place to themselves for the last thousand years. Wouldn't do to disillusion them. Now, as for you. Frankly, it's a bit embarrassing to have misplaced you twice. Of course, we're all at sixes and sevens with the war, but you *have* been rather unlucky."

Mephistopheles's eyebrows pressed together, making him look more like a schoolmaster than ever. "What I mean is, the *headmaster* would like to see you in person. Hear *your side*, so to speak."

"The headmaster? You mean..."

"Yes."

Pongo stammered as his meagre social graces screamed inadequacy at him. "But I haven't a thing to wear!"

"You're fine as you are. Just call him sir and don't slouch."

Mephistopheles spun Pongo around into a pane of dark glass that had appeared behind them. Pongo didn't know what to expect on the other side, but found that he and Mephistopheles were simply floating in, well, nothing. It was neither cold nor warm. He could feel nothing supporting him, but he had no sensation of falling.

"Here we are," said Mephistopheles.

"But there's nothing here."

"There will be. Sorry must dash. Someone's sent a whole U-boat crew to the Zoroastrians. Ta-ta."

Pongo looked around to see that Mephistopheles had already vanished, but that order was appearing in the nothing. It was wrapping and folding itself into a dark face with a black beard and a turban.

Nothing reverberated to the clearing of an enormous throat and the words, "*Salaam aleikhum.*"

Pongo forced himself to speak. "How do you do?"

The dark eyes widened. "Are you of the faithful? You are very strangely dressed."

"People keep telling me that. Sir."

Pongo heard another voice, although he couldn't make out the words. The face rolled its eyes. "Oh, not again."

The skin lightened and became a little ruddy, while the dark beard faded to grey. The turban sank into a crop of grey hair. The new face had an air of experience and wisdom that did remind Pongo of his headmaster, though his headmaster had never started an interview by changing colour.

"I do apologise," said the voice in an accent that matched the new face. "One meets so many people these days that One is forever making these *faux pas*. I do my best, but no one's infallible."

"Not at all. Don't mention it, sir."

"Now what are we to do with you? You've seen far more of our premises than you're supposed to, but it was hardly your fault. To misplace you once may be regarded as misfortune. To misplace you twice seems like carelessness. I say, didn't somebody say something like that before?"

"Oscar Wilde wasn't it, sir?"

"Oh yes. Well at least you didn't see where we put *him*. Now then, do you have any preferences yourself?"

"Well sir, I must admit that I'm rather confused. I mean, how do things work here?"

"Ah now, that would be a bit complicated. I really haven't got time to explain a system that's taken seven hundred millennia to put together."

The indistinct voice floated through nothing again.

"Well tell them to wait," snapped the face. "Honestly, it's been like this ever since you people got it into your heads that you wanted to talk to me directly. Never a moment's peace. Why you can't make do with the demi-gods and avatars like you used to is beyond me. What else are they for?"

"Wouldn't that be idolatry, sir?"

"Call it what you like, it makes my day easier. When people first got the idea that they were too good for demi-gods, I sent them mad to try to put them off the idea. Gracious me, look what I did to Job! Much good it did."

A sigh ruffled Pongo's hair.

"I'm even more confused now," said Pongo.

The voice took on a hint of compassion. "Yes, of course you are. I'd forgotten that you English assume I was born in Berkshire and went to school at Eton. I should have seen this coming a couple of hundred years ago. It was a mistake to let the industrial revolution start in a country that thinks Yorkshire pudding is the height of good cuisine and that fornication is a sin."

"Sir?"

"Well, Yorkshire pudding's hardly the best the world has to offer, is it? We've got a program to get you English to take yourselves less seriously, but it won't really get going for another twenty years or so. If only I'd thought of John Lennon at the same time I thought of Queen Victoria."

"John who?"

The distant voice spoke again.

"I'm being as quick as I can! If you hadn't lost him, this conversation wouldn't be necessary!"

The voice resumed its conversational tone. "Apparently there's a queue building up, so we'd better make haste. The point is, where would you like to go?"

"I don't know sir. I'm just so confused. All my life, I've believed that you, well, that you looked like this all the time."

"Quite so. If certain creations had been doing their jobs, you would still believe it and much embarrassment would have been spared. However, I think the choice really ought to be yours, under the irregular circumstances."

This was worse than waking up to the ferryman. Pongo had never felt less able to make a decision in his life, or since. An idea struck him. "Can you tell me where Harry Harris is, sir? He bought it last week."

The face raised its voice. "Harry Harris? You hear that?"

The other voice replied, and the face grimaced. "Oh my word, they've done it again!"

"Sir?"

"I'm afraid your friend was mislaid as well. He was sent to the Hindus."

"The Hindus? "

"Yes, he seems to have got himself reincarnated."

"Sir?"

"Yes, he died in a fire didn't he? It seems they decided he deserves to be kept well away from the stuff this time round."

"Where is he?"

"They sent him back as a deep sea squid. About as far from fire as you can get, I suppose."

"A squid? Harry's turned into a squid?"

"Yes. He won't be too bright of course, but no one who went to your school would notice the difference."

Pongo liked swimming. "Can squid get confused and miserable over theology?"

"Not at all. They don't have expensive enough educations."

"Then I'd like to join him, if I may."

The face relaxed into a smile. "Good. That's settled then. Have a good time."

Pongo opened his mouth to say thank you, but a splash of salt water stilled the words, and he found himself unable to think about anything beyond getting out of his egg case and snatching a copepod in his gangling young tentacles.

Seeking Kailash

Ghandruk placed each foot as carefully as a snow leopard stalking its prey. The ice covering the bare rock only needed one false step to pull his feet from under him, sending him off the cliff beside the trail. Yet every time he placed a foot and straightened a leg, the crest of the pass came a little closer. By concentrating on placing his feet and straightening his legs, he could forget the pressing weight of the sahib who lay across his shoulders and the ache in his neck from the basket strapped round his forehead.

He was near the crest now, and he allowed himself to look up to see the white tip rising beyond it. He smiled but looked back to his feet; he had no wish to give his life to the ice, or the life of the man whose salt he had sworn by.

Then Ghandruk was on the crest of the pass, and there was nothing between him and the white mass that challenged the blue infinity of the sky. His feet fixed themselves to the ground as his eyes drank in the jagged silver flanks of Annapurna, the *himal* that had watched over his childhood. He had not seen her since he had turned his back on her, with a thousand questions on his tongue and the joy of devotion in his heart.

Now he was returning to her from the other side, as a retainer of the *Angreji*, his questions unanswered.

She chastised him for having been away. She welcomed him back. She wished him success, but refused to promise it. She nudged his eyes up to the lammergeier circling above to remind him that her slightest whim could kill him.

He smiled back and told her that his life was hers to take, but she could not keep him from the Himalaya when he was reborn.

"Do you see her, sahib? Do you see Annapurna?" he said in Hindi, which the sahib spoke fluently. He bowed slightly to Annapurna, to apologise for using the foreign tongue within her hearing.

Ghandruk felt the sahib move. His breath sighed past Ghandruk's ear as he struggled to speak.

"She's beautiful," said the sahib.

Ghandruk was pleased that the sahib used the word 'she'. Most sahibs called mountains `it', as though they were mere lumps of rock and ice. He lowered his gaze to see the trail opening out before him, leading down the side of the cliff and plunging into the deep green forest. Just above the edge of the forest, Ghandruk made out the red and white flicker of prayer flags flying from a *stupa*, and he suppressed a quiver of excitement.

"There is Radha's *stupa*," said Ghandruk. "We shall be there in time to eat our rice."

He felt every muscle in the sahib's body tense.

"You're sure? You're sure we're really here?"

His wheezing voice belied the excitement of his words.

"I'm sure."

A movement on the trail caught Ghandruk's eye.

"Sahib, someone is coming toward us. We should get out of the way."

Ghandruk placed the sahib on the side of the trail away from the cliff, and placed the basket beside him. He crouched beside the sahib and contemplated his bloodless face with concern.

"How are you, sahib?"

The sahib smiled weakly.

"As though I spent last night drinking that *raksi* of yours."

Ghandruk chuckled. He had seen many sahibs failed by their bodies in the Himalaya, but most blamed their porters and ordered them to camp in stupid places. He had never met any with the courage to joke about their weakness.

"How can you laugh up here? I can't even breathe."

"You have to be born to it. You sahibs are born to the sea, not the Himalaya."

"I'm no good at sea either. I was sick all the way to India. But if we really are at Radha's *stupa*, she'll have me fit by tomorrow."

Ghandruk heard all his hopes in the name of Radha.

"If what we heard is true."

"Don't say that, Ghandruk, we haven't travelled for three months to find out it's not true. She cured the Rajah of Kanpur's impotence didn't she? She must be worth the trip if she could do anything for that old drunkard."

He broke off as three men appeared around the curve in the cliff and fell to their knees. They lay down with their arms stretched in front of them. They got up and walked three steps, then knelt and lay down again.

"Ghandruk, who are they?"

"Pilgrims, sahib."

Ghandruk lifted the rugs out of his basket, and found one of the small sacks of rice beneath them. He stood against the side of the path and waited for the pilgrims.

"Help me stand, Ghandruk," said the sahib.

Ghandruk hid his surprise; he had known no other *Angreji* who would try to stand for Hindu pilgrims.

"They will not wish you to suffer for them," he said.

The sahib turned back to watch the pilgrims.

Ghandruk contemplated the pilgrims' unkempt beards and chafed knees with envy, for they showed the same joy of pilgrimage that had carried him out of sight of Annapurna. He hoped it stayed with these men for longer than it had stayed with him.

He held out the rice to the nearest man. The fingers that brushed his were as coarse and chipped as rotten wood, and the man's smile of thanks drew a trickle of blood from a sore on his lip as he passed. Ghandruk sighed at the retreating back that carried what he once had.

But now he had taken *Angreji* salt, so he could indulge his regret no longer. He placed a foot, straightened his leg, and was immediately back into his rhythm.

"We are favoured, sahib." he said.

"What was that, Ghandruk Gurung?" asked the sahib.

Ghandruk appreciated the sahib's attempt to use his Gurung name, although Ghandruk was actually the name of his village. He had abandoned his Gurung name when he had turned away from his pilgrimage.

"We are favoured," he repeated. "Lord Vishnu's pilgrims accepted our gift. Perhaps that means he will give us what we seek."

"I hope so," said the sahib with all his former strength in his voice.

Ghandruk could now make out the grey lump of Radha's *stupa* beneath the flags. He could no longer concentrate his whole mind on the action of walking. A sense of unease was creeping up his back, and he found himself wanting to turn around and return to the village where he had left the rest of the bearers, although he knew he would be caught on the pass when night fell. Annapurna loomed sardonically, reminding him no life lasted for long. She only made him realise that it was not death that he feared. He had agreed to be the sahib's sirdar because he was as curious as the sahib to find out whether the stories about Radha were true, so he invited Annapurna to send what she would and concentrated on placing his feet and straightening his legs.

"Why do they make it so hard? The pilgrims?" The sahib's voice broke into his thoughts.

Ghandruk wanted to tell him of the thrill of discovering that pain crippling to a man of the world was no more than a mosquito bite to a man who had given himself to Lord Vishnu, but he knew the sahib would not understand. For the *Angreji*, pain was an enemy to be driven away lest it blight the only life they believed they had. They did not understand that pain was inevitable, that it was fear of pain that must be mastered rather than pain itself.

"Why do you?" Ghandruk asked him. "Why don't you play polo and drink whisky with the other sahibs? Why come here where the air's so thin you can't even walk?"

Ghandruk felt the sahib's weight shift.

"Why?" the sahib wheezed. "I joined the East India Company because my father..." He paused, his breath grating painfully. "My father wanted me to spend my life curing clerks of the gout in Edinburgh - in *Belayat*." Another pause for breath. "Then I found that the Company wanted me to spend it curing soldiers of the clap in Lucknow."

Ghandruk found himself remembering his own father telling him he would live his life in Lama Prakash's monastery. Ghandruk had looked forward to joining his brothers on their salt caravans for as long as he could walk, but his father just smiled with a father's certainty and said he would understand when he was a man.

Perhaps the sahib was on his own pilgrimage. It had not occurred to him that the sahibs knew anything of pilgrimages before.

"So you begged the company to let you leave your whisky and

your polo to look for an old woman in the Himalaya because of some *bazaar* gossip, and to ask why Hindu pilgrims make their lives difficult?"

"I came for medicine."

"Of course." Ghandruk heard Lama Prakash's voice in his own throat, giving the reply that Lama Prakash always gave when Ghandruk told him less than the whole truth.

Ghandruk looked up at Annapurna, and hoped she approved of the new warmth he felt for the sahib.

~~~~~~

As they neared the tangled scrub of the highest part of the rhododendron forest, Ghandruk saw the *stupa* was barely more than a pile of broken rocks. The prayer flags that he had seen from the top of the pass hung from a single frayed rope.

He felt a little disappointed. If the stories about this place were true, it should have a richer *stupa*. Then he discerned something that quickened his pace until his fingers hovered over the exquisitely etched figures on the stones.

"Ghandruk, would you put me down?"

Ghandruk realised he had forgotten the sahib in his excitement, and set him down next to him. The sahib swayed for a moment, then placed an arm around Ghandruk's shoulders. He exclaimed something in *Angreji*, and his hoarseness owed as much to reverence as exhaustion. "The *stupa* of Radha?"

"It is."

"It must be," he reached out a finger but, like Ghandruk, stopped short of touching the stones. "The richest temples in India have nothing more beautiful."

Ghandruk turned his head from side to side in agreement, and thought how much work would be needed to repair the damage of the scouring ice that would cover them every night.

"It is the *Bhagavada Purana*," he said. "See, here is Lord Krishna with his flute, leading the women from their homes. Here they are in the forest. And here, he is hiding from them with Radha - his special love."

"Who is Lord Krishna? He is beautiful, almost like a girl himself."

"Lord Vishnu came to our world as Krishna. He became a great warrior, but in his youth he was not always serious..."

The sahib yelped with astonishment and his hands jerked back from one particular image. Ghandruk was startled until he remembered that the *Angreji* god did not couple with mortal women, which was strange as he did not think the *Angreji* worshipped any goddesses either. No wonder the *Angreji* god gave them such cause for fear.

"*Namaste* friends!"

Ghandruk turned at the shout to see a man and a woman pushing their way out of the scrub. He pressed his hands together and made the best bow he could with the sahib leaning on him.

"*Namaste* elder brother. *Namaste* elder sister."

The man's youthful stride belied the years chiselled into his face as he advanced on Ghandruk and the sahib. The woman followed more slowly.

"Are you here to see Radha-mother, younger brother?" the man asked in Pun, although there could be no other reason for Ghandruk and the sahib to be there.

Ghandruk was relieved to hear a language he understood. The sahib, who spoke none of the Himalayan languages, smiled politely.

"We are, elder brother," said Ghandruk. "You and elder sister?"

"We are. My name is Purna. My wife's name is Ganga."

The look in Purna's eyes begged Ghandruk not to ask why he was there, yet his voice rolled on as though he were powerless to stop it.

"Our son is sick. Very sick. Fever. He will die soon."

Purna stopped and drew a long breath, as though relieved to have finally spoken his fears. He continued, "He did no evil in his life, so I'm sure he will be reborn well. But my wife..."

He waved a helpless arm at Ganga, who had stopped some distance away and was keeping her hand in front of her face.

"What to do?" sighed Purna. "But Radha-mother will help us."

The sahib shifted against Ghandruk.

"Radha? Did he mention Radha?"

"He did, sahib, and we are favoured indeed." Ghandruk threw a glance at Purna to see that he was not following the Hindi. "They have come to Radha because their son is dying of fever. I think we can see her do some of her magic."

"They've come here to save their son? Then the stories about her were true?"

Ghandruk was about to answer when he saw a flash of colour in the scrub. Then sunlight burst on long black hair and a crimson *lunghi*.

Purna and Ganga pressed their hands together. The depth of their bows identified the newcomer as Radha, because she was years younger than them. She returned their bows with little more than a nod. She turned to look at Ghandruk and the sahib. Ghandruk knew he should make his own bow.

He could not.

He could not move a single muscle because one look at that impossibly smooth, unweathered face had told him that all his years of wandering had only been steps on his journey to this place. This woman.

"Ghandruk, who's that?" asked the sahib. "Is it..."

His voice trailed away as though he lacked the strength to pronounce her name.

Ghandruk could no more answer him than he could take his eyes off the woman striding toward him, whose very presence held his mind immobile. The sahib's weight left Ghandruk's shoulders as he determined to stand by himself. The movement knocked Ghandruk's mind into action. He was being offensive. He pressed his hands and bowed deeply, and was relieved to see the sahib following his lead.

When he rose, he saw her eyes were not on him but on the sahib. The creases in her brow were not from the anger that he feared, but from amazement.

The sahib stepped forward. "Radha?"

Ghandruk felt his aching shoulders tense in irritation at finding himself behind the sahib. He wanted to speak to her first, and was surprised to find himself wishing that the sahib's legs had not found their strength.

Radha's eyes were frozen to the sahib's face as she replied. "I am Radha. Who are you?"

Her Gurung made the sahib throw a helpless look to Ghandruk, who seized the opportunity to step forward.

"My name is Ghandruk," he said. "My companion's name is Balfour. He is *Angreji.*"

Ghandruk felt he had won a small victory when Radha's startled gaze jerked toward him.

"A sahib?" she said. "He is a real sahib?"

"A real sahib."

Radha stared at the sahib, and Ghandruk found his fingers

tightening into fists. He was horrified that he had introduced the sahib as his companion instead of his master. It was the first time he had been untrue to a man whose salt he had taken. His feelings had not betrayed him as much since he was a child, receiving his first lessons from Lama Prakash.

Radha snapped her head around at the sound of Purna shuffling his feet. The look of wonderment dropped from her face like a Shiva's Night mask. Her chin lifted and her mouth tightened. She was Radha-mother again, the end of so many journeys made by so many people who remembered to bow deeply.

"Follow me," she said, and strode back toward the forest. She did not look back to see if her visitors were following her. This, thought Ghandruk, was a woman used to being followed.

Ghandruk looked back at the *stupa*, then up to Annapurna. Prakash thought he was sending me to Lord Vishnu, he told her silently, have you brought me here to fall in love with His lover?

He looked around to see the sahib, who was following Radha unsteadily. He wondered how the warmth he had felt had been joined by a resentment that he did not understand.

What would Prakash say?

He would say that if you did not feel some warmth for the sahib as a man, he would be no more than a duty and so you could not resent him as a man.

Why did he feel no more settled now that he knew that?

Prakash would smile his benign smile and tell him it was because he had answered the wrong question.

Ghandruk hurried after the sahib, through the green and red rhododendrons. The branches were so tangled that they ensnared every movement, and the sahib's clenched jaw revealed the effort that it cost him to fight his way through them. Normally, Ghandruk would have cut a path with his *kukri*, but he did not want to use it on Radha's forest.

The sahib said something so weakly that Ghandruk did not hear the words. "Sahib?"

"I said is she really Radha? She's barely more than a girl."

"She is Radha. It seems the *bazaar* gossips did not know everything about her."

The scrub was so thick that Ghandruk did not know they were close to Radha's hut until it was five paces in front of him. He was relieved to see that it was an ordinary hut made of mud on a wicker framework; after the etchings on the *stupa*, he had half expected to find some celestial palace. Unusually, the door was on the uphill side of the hut. When Ghandruk reached it, he understood why. A section of the rhododendron had been cut back so that Radha could look up at Annapurna, as Ghandruk found himself doing now. He pressed his hands together in entreaty, and followed the sahib into Radha's home.

He paused in the doorway, bent double, for he saw that this was no ordinary hut. The orange light of the fire in the centre flickered off rows of pots lining the walls. A few were made of crude Himalayan clay, but many more were made of pewter or copper, which meant they had come from India. He even saw a few with the delicate blue designs that he had seen once or twice in the hands of the *Angreji*, who brought them from somewhere called *China*. Radha's name must draw visitors from a very long way away.

He felt, rather than saw, a sharp glance from Radha. He was keeping the door open when the heat of the fire could be warming the hut. He closed the door and sat beside the sahib, who was slumped against a corner-post. The brush of the sahib's arm against his own stirred his concern even as his eyes sought Radha. Purna crouched before her with his head bowed while Radha listened to him, her arms folded like a rani hearing a suitor. Ganga crouched behind Purna, hiding her face with her shawl.

Purna finished with a final nod, and gave her a bag from under his shawl. He opened the bag to show her two plucked chickens, and placed it before her. Radha stood without speaking. Unlike Ghandruk, she could stand upright in the hut but outside, he had not noticed her small stature for her regal demeanour. She selected a few pots and placed them on the floor, then sat next to them.

She rolled back her sleeves, and Ghandruk caught his breath at the golden skin of her forearms. Four pairs of eyes followed her hands as they dipped into the pots with the deftness of kingfishers into a stream. Ghandruk did not doubt for a moment that the quantities she dropped into a tin mortar were exactly right. She reached for a pestle and filled the hut with its rhythmic thump, the heartbeat of hope brought to life.

A painful cough turned Ghandruk's head to the sahib. The smoke that filled the hut would not help his laboured breathing. Sometimes Ghandruk wished that the huts of the Himalaya were built with chimneys like those of India, though the cold of the night would be far worse than the smoke.

"You feel worse?" Ghandruk asked the sahib.

"I feel more alive than I have since I arrived in India," said the sahib in a voice that did sound firmer. "What do you think she's making?"

"I don't know," said Ghandruk. "I've seen a lot of healers, but fever is death to a child."

"No wonder they're talking about her in Lucknow."

Ghandruk was about to answer him when he saw Radha's head turn toward them. He hoped he had not offended her by speaking unbidden, but the beat of the pestle did not change and her expression was serene. She looked like a lady fit for a god, with the firelight dancing across her wide Tibetan cheeks and glinting in her hair. The realization that she was looking at the sahib was almost more than Ghandruk could bear.

"Perhaps she can even make you walk again, sahib," he heard himself say. He was startled at the steel in his voice as he reminded the sahib of his weakness, but the sahib did not seem to notice.

"Yes I hope so," said the sahib. "But what else can she do? What else can she give the world?"

Ghandruk wondered what she would give to him.

"If I had this sort of medicine in Lucknow! What I could do!"

Angreji always talked like novice monks seeing their first tree when they found something new, and Ghandruk no longer had the patience to listen. He wanted to make the sahib reveal the true subject of *Angreji* reverence. "You could become a rich man."

"Perhaps. But have you seen Calcutta? Or London? So many sick and here we've found the cure."

Ghandruk's head sank forward in shame. Perhaps the sahib deserved Radha's attention more than he did.

"Sahib, you are a good man."

"I'm a doctor."

Radha gave some of her concoction to Purna and Ganga, who put it in their mouths. She went back to her pots and added more herbs to the mortar. By the time the beating resumed, Ganga's head had risen out of her shawl and she was shuffling toward Purna, who put his arm round her shoulders. Radha offered a smile to the sahib, and Ghandruk closed his eyes so that he would not see.

~~~~~~~

Purna and Ganga left with a bundle of herbs. One look at the sahib told Ghandruk that they were not leaving with them. He hoped Radha would let them sleep in her hut. He had woken with his rugs stiff with ice many times but whatever his confused feelings for the sahib, he was still afraid of the effect that such a night might have on him.

"How will those herbs help the boy?" asked the sahib, as soon as Purna and Ganga were out of hearing.

Ghandruk translated and Radha's eyebrows arched in confusion.

"I gave them to the parents, not the boy."

Ghandruk told the sahib, who had the face of a blind man groping for a gold nugget, terrified of not finding the wealth that lay within a hand's breadth.

"What will they do with the herbs?" he asked.

"They will mix them with their food. They will keep the sadness at bay until it begins to leave them," she said.

"But the boy is dying of fever, not sadness."

Radha looked at the sahib.

"I thought the *Angreji* knew everything. Why can he not understand this?"

"Please forgive us," said Ghandruk. "In India, we heard that you could cure diseases that *Angreji* medicine is helpless against."

"Oh, the men of India are fools. They come here asking for the silliest things. Last year, some men came and asked me to make their Rajah a whole man again. No one can do that."

"But everyone in Lucknow says you succeeded. They say he was a new man after his caravan came back from you."

The sahib fidgeted. While Ghandruk had Radha's attention, the sahib could go on fidgeting.

"He may have been a new man, but he wasn't a whole one," said Radha. "I cured his spirit, not his body."

Ghandruk heard Annapurna chuckle. The sahib heard nothing.

"And the herbs for the boy's parents?"

"For their spirits."

Her patient smile reminded Ghandruk of Lama Prakash when he was slow to understand him.

"What's she saying, Ghandruk?" the sahib broke in.

"She's saying that the herbs won't cure the boy. They will stop his parents grieving for him."

The sahib's face froze like a mouse before a cobra as his gold nugget revealed itself as a lump of coal.

"But the Rajah of Kanpur?"

Ghandruk told him about the Rajah's manhood. The sahib's voice quivered as he asked, "and me? Can give me my strength back?"

Ghandruk translated and Radha looked at the sahib with the same expression she had worn while gauging her herbs. She started toward the sahib with a sudden decision that told Ghandruk that she was thinking about more than just healing him. She took his face in her hands. Her thumb slid slowly across his cheek. Ghandruk would have given the strength of his own legs to change places with the sahib. The sahib met her eyes and smiled uncertainly.

"Do all *Angreji* have blue eyes?" asked Radha without looking away.

"Some have brown eyes, like us. But I saw one whose eyes were green."

"Green? You're joking with me, Ghandruk-younger-brother."

The 'younger-brother' stabbed Ghandruk. He was years older

than her, but he would always be younger-brother. All men were to Radha.

"I've seen many things that made me think my eyes were joking with me."

Ghandruk despised his boast even as he spoke it, but something inside him could not let her caress the sahib with a lover's intimacy. Radha did not even glance toward him.

"And the *Angreji* conquered them all," said Radha. "Radha-grandmother told me they conquered all the world beyond the Himalaya."

"India is not all the world."

"She said they defeated the Gurkha with machines that made the gods themselves tremble. And the Gurkha had conquered the whole Himalaya."

"Their machines are called *cannon*, and there's nothing magical about them. The *Angreji* beat the Gurkha, but they couldn't conquer them because they are too weak for the Himalaya."

"Balfour isn't too weak for the Himalaya. Is he one of the strongest of the sahibs?"

Radha was looking at the sahib as though he was Lord Krishna himself, and hearing Radha speak his name without adding 'younger-brother' lashed Ghandruk like a whip. If Ghandruk told her how he had carried the sahib for half the day, she would see that the sahib was not a god but the lesser of the two men before her.

His mouth was open to speak when Prakash's voice asked him, "why do you want to do that?"

Ghandruk looked at the sahib and saw the man who had been willing to destroy his body to find cures for others. The man whom Ghandruk had sworn to help and protect. The man whose dignity he was about to take away to make a woman turn her head.

He could only tell the truth. "He's one of the strongest."

The smile on Radha's lips filled Ghandruk with fear that his courage would not survive the next question. He had to speak before she could. "Who is Radha-grandmother?" he asked.

"She recognised me."

"I'm sorry?"

"You know that the *Bhagavada Purana* tells that Lord Krishna left Radha when they were both young? Well, it doesn't tell how he taught her the secrets of Radha - how to kill sadness - and caused her - me - to always be reborn in a village near this place. Because of Krishna's love for me, I am reborn before I die, so that I can remind myself of the secrets. Radha-grandmother recognised herself in me, and now she is dead and I am whole again."

Lord Vishnu, thought Ghandruk, you have lost none of Krishna's mischief.

Radha tore herself away from the sahib, and gathered leaves from some of her pots.

"I'll grind these and Balfour must take them with his food."

"I'll make dinner," said Ghandruk. "We have rice."

Rice was rare in the Himalaya. Radha smiled a little girl's smile.

~~~~~~

Ghandruk was about to put Radha's herbs in the sahib's rice, but he paused to smell them. He backed away from the smoke and sniffed again. He remembered a leering apothecary he had met in Bhaktapur, two years ago.

The sahib was sketching some leaves that Radha was showing

him. She was watching with a devotion that would make Lord Krishna tear his hair with jealousy.

Ghandruk dropped the herbs in the fire.

~~~~~~~

"We should be happy," said Radha, after they had eaten. She produced a pipe with a long stem and a large bowl, etched with dancing figures.

"What does she mean?" asked the sahib, when Ghandruk translated.

A day before, Ghandruk would have warned him, but he just said, "you will see."

So when Radha lit the pipe and passed it to the sahib, he inhaled as deeply as though it was one of the foul smelling *Angreji* cigars. Ghandruk loathed his disappointment when the sahib stayed sitting up and put the pipe down very deliberately. Then he bolted for the door.

Radha looked stricken. Ghandruk took a rug and motioned her to stay where she was. The sahib was on his knees outside the door, sobbing air into his lungs. Ghandruk was surprised that he had not vomited.

The sahib said something in *Angreji*. Ghandruk did not think he needed to understand the words.

"It's called *bhang*," he said.

"No, no, Ghandruk, I said isn't she lovely?" said the sahib in Hindi

"Sahib?"

"Radha. Lovely."

Ghandruk's shoulders sagged against the hut at the words he

dreaded.

"I think I'll marry her! That's what I'll do. She's lovely and brilliant and knows how to cure all the sickness in the world. I'll marry her!"

"Sahib, she knows no more about how to cure sick people than any village healer in the Himalaya. She just knows a little more about *bhang*."

The sahib did not seem to have heard.

"Do you think she'll marry a man who can't walk? No, that's no bar, I'll never seem old if I can't walk to start with."

"I think you should sit down, sahib," said Ghandruk, setting down the rug.

The sahib sat on the rug and took deep draughts of air. Annapurna gleamed like a piece of the moon fallen to Earth.

"What am I saying?" said the sahib at last. "I can't marry her."

Ghandruk remembered that *Angreji* did not marry ordinary people. He had always been amused by the *Angreji* belief that any kindness they received just confirmed their natural superiority. Now he wanted to take his *kukri* and cut off a sahib's head for it. His teeth ground with anger as Balfour dismissed Radha, the lover of Lord Krishna whom parents left dying children to visit, as easily as an untouchable.

"What would she want with a man who can't stand up by himself?" said the sahib.

Ghandruk bowed his head in shame.

"You know Ghandruk, I should worry about what the Company will think, but I just don't care. All their accountants and lawyers, telling a man how to live, who he can love. Right now, the whole herd of them could be on the moon. I've often wished they were."

They sat in silence until the cold drove them back into the hut.

They smoked the *bhang*, but the sahib soon fell asleep and Ghandruk covered him with his rugs. He hoped that he would have Radha's attention at last, but Radha only wanted to know about the *Angreji*. Her admiration stung his eyes more and more with every draught of the pipe.

"How did you meet Balfour?" she asked.

"The sahibs often ask for me when they want to go into the Himalaya. There aren't many men who speak Hindi that can bring them here."

"Yet you do?"

"Like you, I had heard many stories of the sahibs. I wanted to know if they were true, so I went to India."

"Are they?"

"Some of them."

"What kind of answer is that?"

Her sharp look reminded Ghandruk that she was used to being answered directly, but he saw the chance to talk about something other than *Angreji* greatness. "I asked a man that once."

Radha glared through the smoke with the royal rage of a thousand rebirths. Then she giggled. "I suppose you're going to tell me what he said?"

"He said I should make a pilgrimage to Kailash, and all my questions would be answered."

"What were the answers?"

"I haven't got there to ask them yet."

She smiled as though she was playing a game with a child.

"Why not?"

Ghandruk took a long draught from the pipe.

"I met another pilgrim, and we started talking of how Lord Ganesh lost his human head. My friend said it was because Shani burned it off in a moment of anger."

"That's foolish. Everyone knows that Lord Shiva cut it off because he thought he was Lady Parvati's lover."

"I thought that."

"You gave up your pilgrimage because of this fool?"

"I went to find answers to my questions. Then I found I didn't know what questions to ask."

Radha's indulgent look made him wish they were still talking about the sahib.

~~~~~~

"Some of these herbs are extraordinary," said the sahib. "I've never seen anything like them before."

The sahib was much stronger this morning. He thought it was because of Radha's herbs. Ghandruk did not know how to tell him that the Himalaya could give a man his strength back as quickly as they took it if they were so disposed.

"We'll be ready to leave soon, sahib."

"Not yet. Radha's gathering a few more leaves for me. I can't wait to try some of these out."

"The sick will forget their sickness, sahib."

"No, not that stuff. It's all very well for the Rajah of Kanpur but I'm talking about real medicines."

Ghandruk sighed. No *Angreji* had ever sought the medicines of the Himalaya before, so he could not know how much more easily he could have found Radha's few genuine cures.

Ghandruk turned back to his basket and groped beneath his rugs. His hand closed on coarse cloth.

"I'll help Radha," he said.

He headed uphill, away from Radha, until he was above the forest and stood before the *stupa*. He opened his hand and shook out the prayer flag he had made when he turned away from Kailash, toward India and the sahibs, vowing to release the prayer when Lord Vishnu answered his questions. He tied the flag to the line, and watched it twitch in the light breeze that would carry the prayer to Lord Vishnu. Ghandruk knelt and bowed to Annapurna. He looked up as a shadow swept over him from behind. The lammergeier told him nothing.

He found Radha bending over a small plant. The worst passes and ridges had never filled him with such fear.

"Radha," he croaked.

"Yes Ghandruk-younger-brother," she said, sharply enough to remind him that he had omitted the word 'mother'.

"May I ask you?"

"What?"

"Radha, are you a nun?"

It sounded like a child's question. Ghandruk's face burned at his clumsiness.

Radha smiled her understanding and he breathed again.

"Ghandruk, I was afraid you were not going to ask!"

"You were?"

Had Annapurna heard him?

"No, I am not a nun. And there is no one to prevent me from leaving this place."

Pure joy swept through Ghandruk. He wanted to clutch her to him where they stood.

"Please tell Balfour I will be overjoyed to go with him."

"The sahib?"

She turned toward her hut, pushing her way through the tangled branches.

"I will be ready to leave very soon."

Ghandruk dashed after her and caught her by the arm. She glared at his hand as though it was filthy. He let go and looked at his feet so that she could not see his pain on his face.

"You have more to say?"

"I didn't mean - I don't know if he wants you to go."

"Oh Ghandruk-younger-brother, I know you want to marry me but surely you know I could not? You're a strong man and a good man, but so many strong, good men have asked me. But Balfour . . ."

"Radha, I mean it. He hasn't asked me to..."

"But he will," she said confidently. "I'm sure he will."

"Don't be. I've taken great care that he hasn't been taking the aphrodisiac you said would restore his strength."

Ghandruk looked up. The stricken face and wringing hands before him did not belong to Radha the great healer, but to Radha who was barely a woman and mother to everyone. Radha who was beloved of a god, and whom he had robbed of her chance to be anything but utterly alone on Earth.

"We shall see the sahib. But if he asks you to go with him, it is because he wants to and not because of your *bhang*."

~~~~~~

The sahib's fingers drifted across Radha's back as he followed her out of her hut. All three of them had made their choices. He felt stronger than he could ever remember. He stood up and returned their smiles.

"I hope you will be happy," he said in Hindi, then in Gurung.

They thanked him.

"Radha will take you back to the bearers," Ghandruk said to the sahib. "They will take you both back to Lucknow."

"You're not coming with us?" The sahib was startled.

"I have more travels in the Himalaya, sahib."

The sahib was about to argue, but Ghandruk caught Radha's eye. She pressed the sahib's arm. The sahib pressed his hands together and bowed as deeply as he had bowed to Radha the day before. Ghandruk returned the bow equally.

Ghandruk watched them leave and wondered which would be the first to curse him for bringing them together, when they struggled with each other's' languages and each realised they had chosen a mere mortal. He would make a prayer flag for them when he reached Kailash, to ask Lord Vishnu to smooth the path they had chosen. He would make another for Lama Prakash, and his answers that had taken him twelve years to understand.

A plume of snow trailed approvingly from Annapurna's peak.

Ghandruk turned his back on the morning sun. He walked three steps, dropped to his knees and lay flat. He got up. He walked three steps. He dropped to his knees.

Foreclosure

"Plenty of warm bodies at home. The debtor and the donor should be in there, with any luck."

Colin looked up from the infra-red image on his laptop and grinned at Greg. The roll of the River Thames was making him queasy. If the Haywards were home, he wouldn't have to sit in the boat and wait for them.

He guided the quadricopter camera drone back to the boat. When he stood to stow it, Ellen nudged the throttle and sent him staggering against the donor cage in the stern.

"Careful there," said Ellen.

Colin turned his face away from her to hide his scowl. If he challenged her, she'd say she thought he could manage the motion of a boat. Her words would be deferential, but her tone would convey how little she cared if he believed her.

Junior loan facilitators like Colin didn't get to choose their own security personnel.

They were heading for a red brick building that had been a Bankside squat since the rising estuary swallowed every ground floor in London. Colin sat down before Ellen nudged the boat alongside the building's floating jetty. If he hadn't, she'd have hit it a lot harder.

"Guess I'd better stay with the boat," said Greg as he tied up.

Ellen cut the engine. "Fair enough. We won't need both of us up there."

Colin looked up at the building. He couldn't tell how many people lived there, but the cluster of canoes and rowing boats tied to the jetty suggested most of them were in.

"Are you sure?" he asked. "There could be trouble..."

His voice tailed off. Ellen was looking at him as though he was explaining the tooth fairy.

"I expect I'll manage, Mr. Hooper. I think we should be more worried about whether the boat will be here when we get back, or whether the local anarchists will have found a way to entertain themselves with it."

"There's narchs round here?"

"Possibly."

Something in her tone let Colin know his question amused her, though he couldn't have said exactly what it was. He stepped on to the jetty and looked back at the clasped hands logo of the Bank of Friends on the donor cage. Among the weed-coated walls of buildings that had become islands, the motorboat's unchipped paint stood out. If there was a place where people had reasons to join the anarchists, he had to admit he was floating in the middle of it. A boat belonging to a bank would draw them like magpies to silver.

"Ready?" asked Ellen.

Of course he was ready. Did she think his shoelaces needed tying? He brandished his briefcase and hoped his smile didn't look as idiotic as it felt.

Ellen turned to the building's fire escape, which was now the main staircase. Why couldn't Ellen have stayed with the boat, leaving him with the more personable Greg? The steps put his eyes level with Ellen's backside as it undulated under her trouser suit. He found it hard not to look, even though he was convinced she knew it.

They entered the building on the fifth floor, beside the lift shaft. The lift hadn't run in decades, so all the shaft did was funnel the brackish smell of the estuary into the corridor. If he'd been with Greg instead of Ellen, Colin would have mentioned these flats had once been worth a couple of million pounds each, back when that was real money. As he wasn't, he said nothing and followed Ellen to the door marked '52'.

The man who answered his knock bore the sunken-eyed look of someone introduced to poverty late in life.

"Mr. Hayward?" asked Colin.

The man nodded. He didn't look as though he had much fight in him, which was a relief. Colin already had the uncomfortable feeling a biomedical repossession put in the pit of his stomach. It only made it worse when they made a fuss about it.

"I'm Colin Hooper from the Bank of Friends. This is my associate, Ellen Reid. We're here to help you with the repayments on your loan."

"Help me?"

"Yes, of course." The hardest part was getting through the door. Not that it would stand up to the gadgets hidden under Ellen's jacket, but he'd resorted to assisted entry a couple of times this year. It would look bad on his next appraisal if it became a habit.

"Our policy is to provide our valued customers with every assistance in meeting their commitments."

The trick was to make the smile friendly without overdoing it.

"If we could just come in for a few minutes, Mr. Hayward, I'm sure we can settle everything to your satisfaction."

Banksiders didn't get called 'Mr.' very often. A little deference was often a good investment.

"It's Doctor Hayward, actually," said Hayward.

"Ah. I beg your pardon, sir."

Hayward stepped back. Colin strode in before Hayward changed his mind. He found himself in what had once been half of a large lounge. Someone had put a chipboard partition across the floorboards, splitting one penthouse into two squats. Colin hadn't been able to see that with the infra-red camera, but a hasty calibration with the plans he'd memorized confirmed he'd seen two people on this side of the partition.

The original owners must have taken everything when they left for a drier part of the country because the only furniture was a pine bench that Hayward probably liberated from a park. Hayward had placed it at the window, angled so he could gaze at the dome of St Paul's. The cathedral loomed over the drowned city from the top of Peter's Hill, the only ground in central London that stayed dry at high spring tide. "Please, have a seat," said Hayward. "I'll just call my accountant in and we can get started."

Colin looked at Ellen. Banksiders squatting in unfurnished flats didn't have accountants. If Hayward left the room, they would never see him again. Ellen sidled toward the door. She was a head shorter than Hayward, but he'd have more luck trying to go through the wall.

Hayward rapped on the partition.

"Coming," called a woman's voice from the other side.

Hayward smiled amiably. Colin allowed himself to relax and sit down. She hadn't sounded like a gang of narchs. Hayward's 'accountant' was probably just a helpful neighbor, but he wouldn't be calling her an accountant if he didn't have something to negotiate with. Perhaps it wouldn't come to repossession after all.

Ellen stepped aside to admit a woman whose salt and pepper dreadlocks placed her a world away from the Bank's dark suited accountants. She was the shortest person in the room, but her straight back and level gaze betrayed none of Hayward's air of being ground down.

"This is Ulrika Philby."

The empty room made Hayward's voice sound flat.

Colin stood up to shake her hand. She gave his fingers a quick squeeze without looking at his face.

"You said your name's Colin Hooper? H-O-O-P-E-R?" asked

Philby.

Colin suppressed a frown. What did the spelling of his name have to do with anything?

"Yes," he said.

"As you can see," said Philby, "my client's resources are limited."

In spite of her Bankside looks, Philby spoke with the accent Colin had spent years trying to cultivate.

"I appreciate that, and there's some scope for flexibility," he said. "However, I have to point out that Mr. Hayward has been in default for over a year now."

"My client no longer owns the house he took out the loan for. He sold up and moved here, paying most of the money he received to you."

"I know he did. Unfortunately, it covered less than half the value of the loan."

Colin shuffled the papers in the briefcase. He hoped they'd take the hint that he could back up what he was saying and wouldn't make him waste time leading them through the documents. You didn't get into management by letting clients talk you round in circles. You made sure you knew the facts.

"Well of course," said Philby. "Property prices in London have been in freefall since the Thames topped the Flood Barrier. That was entirely predictable when you granted the loan."

Colin wanted to roll his eyes at the word 'you'. The loan had been granted twenty years ago, when he was a toddler. He knew clients saw him as an extension of the bank, but he went out of his way to be courteous. It wouldn't hurt them to do the same once in a while.

"The terms of the loan make no provision for changes in property prices."

Didn't people ever read the terms and conditions?

"Besides," he said, "the loan was granted on the assumption that Mr. Hayward would remain in full employment. He's been out of work for eleven years now."

"*Doctor* Hayward lost his job through no fault of his own. He developed cancer and Caxton Limited replaced him when the laws mandating sick leave were rescinded."

Colin arranged his features into the appropriate expression of sympathy while Philby blithered on about Hayward's recovery and his wife's unexpected death. They didn't seem to realize a sob story only made it obvious they had nothing to offer. Hayward had met with a run of bad luck, but it wasn't Colin's job to worry about that.

He'd taken out a mortgage, not insurance against bad fortune.

Colin waited for Philby to pause.

"I'm happy to hear Doctor Hayward's cancer was successfully treated," he said. "Now, if we can come back to the matter of the loan. The Bank's made every effort to be lenient since Doctor Hayward lost his position at Caxton."

"I'm sure you have," said Philby. "Are you aware of what Ken did for Caxton?"

"He was their director of research and development."

A hint of exasperation dislodged Colin's carefully nurtured accent. He couldn't help glancing at Ellen, just as her lips twitched into the inevitable smirk. Easy for her to mock. Security didn't have to worry about how they sounded, but the days when talent found its own level were long gone. Colin's grandfather had never lost his Dagenham glottal stop, but it hadn't stopped him retiring as a company director. These days, if you talked Estuary, you stayed Estuary.

Hayward spoke before Colin could get all his consonants in place to bring the conversation back on track. He cursed Ellen for putting him off his stride.

"Your suit came from a tridee printer?" asked Hayward, as though the Bank paid the people sent on house calls enough to buy cotton clothes.

"Well, yes. From a Caxton store as it happens."

"I designed the system that scanned and tailored you."

Finally, perhaps they were getting somewhere.

"So you still receive royalties?" asked Colin.

"Oh no, Caxton retained all intellectual property."

Colin sighed through his nose, hoping they wouldn't notice.

"I just thought you might be interested," said Hayward.

"Fascinated. Perhaps we could return to the point. There's a biomedical clause in your loan agreement. The purpose of my visit is to inform you that unless we can arrive at an arrangement for

resuming payment, we'll have to act on it."

Colin kept his voice level, as though he was continuing an ordinary conversation. The right tone of voice could go a long way to keeping clients calm when the biomedical clause came up. He flicked his eyes to Ellen, who had a hand under her jacket, caressing one of the persuasion tools on her belt.

Hayward and Philby exchanged a grim look, but neither ran for the door or tried to strangle Colin.

"Let me be clear," said Hayward. "You're going to take one of my kidneys to settle the loan?"

"I'm afraid it's gone beyond a kidney," said Colin. "For one thing, even a complete set of organs wouldn't cover the loan, although the Bank's willing to write it off when we receive them. For another, you've had cancer, so your organs aren't eligible for donation."

For once, Philby had nothing to say. She confined herself to raising an eyebrow.

"The biomedical clause includes a next-of-kin sub-clause," said Colin. "Your next-of-kin is your son. He turned sixteen last month, so he's eligible. He's at home now, I believe?"

Best to say he knew the boy was in before they had a chance to deny it.

Hayward nodded. "In his room."

"Good. If you'd be kind enough to call him, we can settle the loan now. I'm sure you're keen to be free of it as soon as possible." Colin smiled his friendliest smile. He didn't look at Ellen.

"Before I do," said Hayward, "I'd like to be absolutely clear about this. You're going to take my eldest son to pieces to cover the loan."

Colin restrained himself from frowning. According to the paperwork, Hayward only had one son.

"I assure you the process is entirely painless. It's all done under anesthetic."

"But he won't wake up. He'll be dead."

"That's right. Naturally, the Bank will return any non-valuable remains to you."

"How thoughtful of you." Hayward pinched the bridge of his nose. "I have a few questions."

There was something strange about Philby. A friendly neighbor would be dismayed if she failed to fend off a repossession. Philby glared at Hayward as though he'd said something wrong. Colin didn't know what to make of it, but he'd put up with a few questions to keep Hayward compliant.

"Of course," he said.

"I'd like to know how you feel about a job that involves taking a teenager to be carved up."

So much of customer relations came down to choosing the right smile. Colin assumed the most professional smile in his repertoire. He couldn't understand why so many of them asked that question. Did they think he'd have some sort of existential crisis and walk out on a job he'd been damn lucky to land in the first place? Or that he'd reveal himself as some sort of emotionless automaton after he'd put so much effort into making it easy on them?

"I'm just a functionary." He gave his standard answer. "You signed the loan agreement, and my job is to represent the Bank's position."

The first time he'd been asked, he'd explained he needed the job because he'd met the woman he loved and he wanted to raise children with her in a decent home. He'd wanted the client to understand he had feelings and aspirations of his own, that he didn't do the job for the fun of it. It hadn't gone down as he'd hoped. Since then, he'd never told a client anything personal. Better to keep a safe distance.

It seemed to be working. Philby's face was a study in dislike and Hayward didn't look any happier, but neither reached for his throat.

"Mr. Hooper, you're a young man," said Hayward. "Twentythree? Twenty-four?"

Colin tipped his head in a minimal nod. He was twenty-three, but that was more personal information than he cared to share.

"About the age I was when I signed that contract," said Hayward. "I didn't have kids then and I thought I had a job for life, so it seemed safe to mortgage my future. I was wrong, but it taught me that if you make a decision when you're young, you have the rest of your life to regret it."

Was Hayward trying to talk him out of doing his job by playing the 'I'm older and wiser than you' card? Sometimes it was hard to keep a straight face with these people. Colin lifted his eyebrows, letting Hayward know that if he had a point, he hadn't made it.

"I made a mistake." Hayward didn't change his theme. "A big mistake. All I'm asking you is to let me pay for it. Take me with you."

"Ken!" Philby gripped Hayward's arm.

"No, Ulrika," said Hayward. "I mean it. I'm willing to meet my obligations."

"He won't let you, Ken," she said.

At least Philby grasped the situation.

"I'm afraid she's right," said Colin. "The recipients expect reliable organs and you simply can't provide those."

Hayward sighed. "Well, it's your decision. Your regret."

Philby squeezed his arm. The look she gave Hayward struck Colin as more triumphant than sympathetic.

"I'll get his birth certificate," she said.

That was odd. Why would Philby have Hayward's son's birth certificate? Not that it mattered. He could summon a copy on his laptop if there was any dispute. He handed Hayward the release forms.

"If you'll just sign here, sir? These will end your relationship with the Bank of Friends. I'm sure that will be a relief to you."

Colin expected Hayward to spend the next half hour scrutinizing the forms for a loophole, but he'd signed them before Philby returned with the birth certificate.

"And now, if you could just call your son?"

Things could still go bad, but a shot or two from Ellen's taser would settle things. There wouldn't even be any property damage to explain.

Hayward and Philby hadn't moved. They were both looking straight at him. The corners of Hayward's mouth betrayed regret, though not as much as Colin expected.

"But you're already here," said Philby.

"I'm sorry?"

"The biomedical clause states Ken's next-of-kin can be called to fulfil it in his place," she said. "Ken doesn't have a will so the next-ofkin is automatically his oldest child. You."

Colin chuckled. That was why they'd been taking it so well. They'd had this trick up their sleeves, for all the good it would do them. He took the birth certificate, catching sight of Ellen as he did so.

She winked. Did every little effort to put him off balance amuse her?

"I'm sorry, this isn't even a good fake."

As he said it, Colin realized it wasn't true. He couldn't see anything to criticize, even though the certificate must have been printed since he'd entered the room. They couldn't have known in advance who the bank would send.

He remembered Hayward was an expert at tridee printing. The raised printing under his fingertips felt definitive. Something about seeing his own and his mother's names printed alongside the name of Kenneth Hayward, named as his father, sent cold footsteps scuttling up his spine.

Banksiders could vanish by moving from squat to squat, seen only by people who were struck blind, deaf, and dumb by a question from a loan facilitator. Sometimes it took Colin months to track down a client. Hayward hadn't moved. He'd laid a trap, and only a fool would let bank security into his squat unless he was confident of the trap. Whatever

Hayward was, Colin was sure he was nobody's fool.

He didn't want to laugh at these people anymore.

"Look, I know who my father was," said Colin. "He lived in Essex his whole life and never learned one end of a tridee printer from another. A forged certificate doesn't change the public records. I'm not your son, so can we move on?"

Philby touched Hayward's elbow.

"I'm afraid you are my son." Hayward stared over Colin's shoulder, trying to look fascinated by something out of the window.

He was a poor liar and knew it.

"No, I ain't!" Colin took a breath. "I have my birth certificate at home. Your next-of-kin is in that room there."

Colin waved at the closed door of the Hayward boy's room.

"Your birth certificate is in your hand," said Philby.

"You printed it while we were talking." He pointed at Hayward. "Forgery would be easy for you. That's why she got me to spell my

name. So your friends in there would know they got it right."

He jerked a thumb at the partition, wondering how many people were listening from the other side.

"Please, go on," said Philby. "This is better than a novel. Presumably the sole point of our conversation in here was to give them time to print it?"

"Yes!"

Philby met his eyes with the indulgent look of an adult being lied to by a five-year-old. She was as bad as Ellen.

"Well, perhaps your associate would like to look at the certificate," said Philby.

The last thing Colin wanted was to involve Ellen's warped sense of humor, but he couldn't stop her sauntering over. It was unprofessional to give a direct order in front of clients so he let her take the certificate. The corners of her mouth twitched as though she'd read a joke so bad it couldn't help but entertain.

"Looks like the real thing," she said.

Colin glared, hoping she'd understand it as an order to stop fooling around.

"Perhaps you'd like to check your bank's records," said Philby.

Ellen joined Hayward and Philby in looking at him.

Philby's expression hit him like a punch in the stomach. She was certain of what he would find. Somehow he couldn't stop his hands from opening the laptop and his fingers from tapping keys. When he'd checked Hayward's records two hours ago, the name in the nextof-kin field had been 'Daniel Hayward'. Now it was 'Colin Hooper'.

He didn't have a smile to cover the situation.

Philby took the laptop from his hands. "There we are."

She passed it to Ellen and took the forms Hayward had signed.

"And all the paperwork seems to be in order," she said.

She turned to Ellen. "I think it's your job from here."

"Yes. I see it is."

Why did he have to be working with Ellen when someone tried this? She seemed to think the whole thing was a piece of theatre for her benefit.

Colin turned to Philby. "You're a narch. You must have someone inside the Bank to pull this off."

"I'm sure I've no idea what you're talking about," said Philby. "But unless your systems are very unsecure indeed, I'd need more than one person on the inside to fake something like this. Even if I had them, your bank would never admit their people were so unreliable.

Just imagine what it would do to customer confidence." "I

assure you our security is extremely tight," said Ellen.

"Thank you," said Philby. "That is reassuring."

"Ellen..."

She'd overstepped the mark this time. She didn't have to like him to back him up. She just had to do her job. Now he couldn't move forward without admitting a breach in the Bank's security. All she'd had to do was keep her mouth shut until someone needed tasering.

Then he looked at her face and saw she had no intention of letting him move on. Her job was to protect the Bank of Friends, and a bank was nothing if its customers lost confidence in it. Backing him up had become more difficult, and less amusing, than accepting the evidence Philby and Hayward had manufactured. Any of the security personnel would make the same call, though Greg probably wouldn't be struggling to suppress a smirk.

Fear churned like strong coffee on an empty stomach. Once in the donor cage, there was no way out before he got to the John Radcliffe Hospital's operating theatre where donors would say anything, so everything was ignored.

He made himself look straight into Ellen's smirk. He had one chance to talk her out of this.

"My wife's pregnant," he said. "She's due in a couple of months. Please let me see my child."

The silence grew heavier as seconds ticked past. He'd never understood the depth of Ellen's contempt for him until that moment.

She had even less regard for Colin than she did for a client.

"We've heard that one before, haven't we?" said Ellen.

"I imagine it's often true," said Philby.

"I asked you not to do this," said Hayward. "I was serious when I said I'd go in your place, and you'd regret it if you refused me. You made your choice readily enough when you didn't realize you were making it for yourself."

Colin sprinted for the door. He didn't expect to make it, but anything was better than meekly walking into the donor cage. He managed three strides before taser pain seared his back.

Things got rather indistinct. He was vaguely aware of being dragged out of the door and manhandled down the fire escape. The first thing he saw clearly was a patch of light, sliding across dents left by feet and fists on metallic walls. It took him a moment to recognize the light was coming through the grilled window in the donor cage and that it was moving as the boat rolled. He leapt to his feet, cracked his head on the ceiling and landed on his backside.

Ellen's eyes appeared at the grille. The tiny window was too small to see any more of her face.

"Not to worry," she said. "I've heard you tell donors it's entirely painless at least a dozen times. I'm sure you said it to my husband, the day I didn't get home in time."

Summer Holidays

Barry ran up the steps into the old portacabin and yanked the door shut behind him. As the door thudded into the frame, its last hinge gave way, crashing it to the concrete below.

"Now look what you've done." Barry had left his mum crying over a cigarette in their flat but he'd brought her voice with him. "Your favourite place to hide and you've gone and broken it."

He didn't want to hear how he'd end up like his father, wherever he was now, so he screamed. He clenched his fists and screamed and screamed through his knotted throat until he had to lean on the broken-legged table to get his breath back.

All because she'd found his fags, and she said he was too young to smoke. Barry had tried to say he was thirteen. He'd tried to shout it at her in the voice grown-ups used when they didn't want to be argued with, but his stammer pushed his tongue against the roof of his mouth and shattered the words into grunts and clicks. Mum hadn't waited for him but decided they needed to have a serious talk, as usual, and somehow ended up talking about his father and started sniffing, as usual. Her shaking hands had fumbled for her fags, only this time they were Barry's fags, "and now you've started me smoking again when I've gone all day..."

Barry's scream filled the portacabin's wooden walls until he was sobbing for breath. He cuffed the tears off his cheeks and found himself looking at the charcoal drawing on the cupboard above him. It was a harrier jet, like the ones that sometimes flew over the derelict holiday camp the portacabin had been abandoned in. Like the ones he wanted to fly one day.

One day. But now he was too young. Too young to smoke.

The jet looked like something a kid would draw. No kid would know where to put the serial number, or where the refuelling probe was, but jets were what kids drew. Jets were what kids wanted to fly. Barry wasn't a kid. He was thirteen. Yet almost every flat surface in the cabin was covered with charcoal jets.

He flung open a cupboard door and grabbed the box of charcoals he'd blagged from an art lesson. The sticks scattered across the faded linoleum floor. He got hold of one and slashed it across the harrier. It hurt to destroy his drawing but he slashed harder and harder and his grunts became words.

"Not! Too! *Young!*"

The charcoal snapped.

"Not too young."

His voice was more level now.

He turned away and found himself facing a patch of blank wall at the end of the cabin. It was so clean he didn't understand why he hadn't drawn on it before. He picked up a new stick of charcoal. He would fill this space with something no kid would draw. Something Dad would draw if he was still around. Dad had left nine years and three months ago. Barry knew exactly. His mum said he'd just walked out and never come back like the total waster he was, but Barry knew she'd driven him away with her serious talks. One of Barry's earliest memories was her snivelling, just before Dad walked out the door for the last time.

What would Dad draw?

He let the charcoal lead his hand up to the wall. It moved as though it knew where it wanted to go and Barry's hand was just there to hold it up. Its determination startled him and he jerked it away. He'd drawn a small circle inside a large one. What was that supposed to be? It looked like a polo mint, or one of the empty rawl-plugs in the walls. A kid might think it looked like an RAF roundel but Barry wasn't a kid so it looked like...

Barry moved his hand deliberately this time, putting an oval around the circles to make them the iris and pupil of an eye. He added lashes and the tear gland. It was definitely an eye, looking over Barry's shoulder.

An eye needed a face and a face has two eyes, but he found his hand working on the mouth. He drew half of the upper lip and was surprised to find it was a woman's mouth. It wasn't like his mum's hard line but a swan's wing like the ones Barry saw on the posters outside the cinema his mum never gave him the money to go to. It was a lip that should be the blood red of the poster's lips. It would be if Barry ever managed to nick a set of paints.

While he was thinking about it, his hand had finished half the lower lip and curved down to the chin. Again, not like Barry's mum. His mum's face was all straight lines. His hand was using the cheekbone to pull the outline into another smooth curve while he pondered.

Barry didn't have a watch, so he didn't know how long his hand followed the charcoal while he thought about what it was doing. He did know that when he stepped back, he understood for the first time why men called women beautiful. He stood and drank in the elegance of the black curves on the dirty white wall that formed half of a face.

Why only half a face?

Not a problem. He reached out to draw the second eye but his hand paused just before the charcoal touched the wall. He just couldn't see how that eye should be. The charcoal slid down the side of the neck. That wasn't what he'd meant to do. He placed the charcoal where the line of the upper lip ended and was about to draw the other half of the mouth.

He dropped the charcoal and jerked his hand away. He stifled a yelp, because kids don't yelp, and because the eye couldn't really have moved to look at him. Of course not. It was where he'd drawn it.

Or was it? Barry couldn't remember exactly where it had been. But he knew his charcoal half-face couldn't move and the half-lips couldn't be stretching into a smile, revealing perfect teeth he hadn't even drawn, so he was through the doorway and running across the cracked concrete before he realised he was frightened.

He felt the sun laughing at him, like Dad would if he saw him running away like a scared child. Barry made himself slow down and lean against the wall of the burned-out ballroom. He took deep breaths and thought of the boy and girl from the year above him at school, who'd come in here last week. Barry had crept round to where there had once been a wall, and was now only thick vines. He'd watched them fumbling around with their jeans around their ankles, bathed in green light. It was better than thinking about the eye that couldn't have moved and the mouth that couldn't have smiled.

He wandered around the ballroom toward the beach, which happened to be away from the portacabin. A movement in the corner of his eye stopped him dead. He stepped back behind the wall. He replayed what he'd seen to himself: a girl, about sixteen years old, wearing a black T-shirt, a short tie-dyed skirt and a red rucksack, heading toward the chalets by the beach. He was proud of himself. A kid would have stood there gawking until she saw him. Not Barry, who could tell everything he needed to know with one glance and get out of sight. Dad would have been proud.

Barry edged his head back round the wall and watched her stroll up to the open doorway of the first chalet she came to. He imagined her dismay at the broken beer bottles and stale vomit from the teenagers' beach parties. She backed out and tried the next one but Barry knew they were all the same. That was why he liked the portacabin. It was far enough from the beach that the teenagers left it alone.

The girl looked around. Barry flattened himself against the wall. She must have come to the same conclusion as Barry because she made straight for the portacabin. Barry moved back around the ballroom so it was between him and her, but where he would see her when she came round it. He was playing his favourite game and he was good at it. He preferred stalking local teenagers who came here to drink beer until they spewed, or smoke their sweet-smelling fags until they lay on their backs giggling. Barry would laugh to himself and imagine how he'd wait till the next time they shoved him around or dissed Dad, then he'd say he'd tell their parents. But next time they called him 'B-B-Barry the b-b-bastard' he'd never say anything, because they'd give him a kicking.

He hadn't seen this girl before so she must be from the holiday site down the road. Sometimes the grockles wandered around the derelict site and said how bizarre it was in their funny accents but they never did anything interesting. This girl was interesting, even if she was a grockle.

The bits of her he could see from behind all seemed to be curves, which was good. Her hair fell in brown curls over her round shoulders. The bulge above her waist didn't belong on a film poster, but he was more interested in the larger bulges above and below it. They held his gaze as she paused at the portacabin's door, saw there was no broken glass, and climbed in.

She would see his pictures! All those pictures that looked like they were drawn by a kid. He ran to the end of the portacabin where he could put his eye to a crack between two wall panels.

The girl was looking straight at him.

He dodged away from the crack. How could she know he was

there? What would she do now?

Two footsteps thudded in the portacabin. Barry had to run but he couldn't resist one last look. The girl was at his end of the cabin, staring over his head. She hadn't seen him. She was looking at the half-face on the panel he was hiding behind. He heard himself breathing fast and noisily, so he made himself slow down before she heard him. He was pleased but he didn't know whether it was because the girl was looking at the picture, or because the picture would be looking at the girl.

She reached a hand toward the picture but stopped just short of touching it. She turned away suddenly, took off her rucksack and shook out a black polyester swimming costume. This grockle was getting more and more interesting.

She put her head out of the door and looked around, but she couldn't see Barry from there. She took hold of the bottom of her T-shirt. She paused and looked at the panel. She turned her back on it and pulled her T-shirt over her head. Barry was disappointed that her bra was like his mum's, all off-white elastic and nothing like the ones in shop windows. Then it didn't matter because her hands reached around her back and unhooked it. Barry saw red dents pressed into her white skin. He felt more of himself pressing against the panel than there had been before.

She stepped out of her sandals and bent over to slip down her skirt and knickers, thrusting her bum toward Barry. It was the best thing Barry had ever watched, but *please, please make her turn round.*

She spun around so quickly that Barry thought he'd made a noise, but she was looking at the picture again. She stared at it while her hand drifted in front of something that Barry didn't know the name for. He decided he preferred looking at her than at any of the women in the magazines left behind at the teenagers' parties. The girls in the magazines, with shins that would snap if you kicked them and breasts like balloons, were probably the way girls were supposed to be but this girl wasn't crumpled by a dozen boys' stares and she didn't smell of stale beer.

The girl's shoulders twitched as though she were cold and she pulled her costume on, slipped on her sandals and strode toward the beach. Barry slid along the panel so he could watch the bits of her that bumped up and down. He was about to follow her when he remembered she had left her clothes and rucksack in the portacabin, so she would be coming back to take her clothes off again.

He dashed into the portacabin and looked up at the half-face on the wall. The eyebrow slid upward, raising a crease on the forehead. The face seemed to be waiting for something.

"Thank you for showing me." The words came out in the deep voice he often tried but had never quite managed. There was no trace of a stutter. He felt six inches taller.

The half-mouth stretched into a smile and the eye pointed Barry toward what he had to do next. Barry lifted the bra with trembling fingers and put his face in the cup. He was disappointed that it smelled like the school cloakroom after football. A narrowed eye reminded him that he was acting like a kid, so he put the bra back exactly as he'd found it and went through the rucksack. Nothing but a towel in the main part, but he found a purse in the pocket in the lid. He opened it and released his breath slowly. "Wow!"

Three ten-pound notes and a lot of change. His mum never let him have more than a couple of quid at a time. He thought of what he could buy with thirty quid but he knew where to nick fags and the girl might not take her clothes off again if she noticed something missing.

He closed the purse and put it back in the rucksack. He looked up to a sneering mouth, mocking him for his petty ambitions.

"Another look's all I'll get from her."

He jumped at the sound of his own voice.

"I can't make her give me any more."

The girl would be like every good thing. He'd steal a glimpse of her and try to make the joy of theft make up for never having more than a glimpse. Like watching his classmates getting together to drink beer and knowing they would never let him be together with them. Unless...

"Can you make her do things?"

Barry found himself picking up one of his scattered charcoals and letting it lead him back to the half-face. It needed to be stronger to help him. To be stronger it needed to be whole.

"She'll notice you've changed," he said.

But the picture didn't reply. It waited, motionless. The charcoal found the line of the neck where it curved into a shoulder. Barry didn't even try to draw the other side of the face. The mouth smiled its approval as his hand framed the fingers. He let the charcoal lead his hand at a speed he could never manage by himself. If it wasn't strong enough to make the girl do what Barry wanted, he'd have to do some of the making himself and he probably wasn't up to it.

"I *am*." But the whine belonged to a kid.

He dropped his voice. "I fucking am."

That sounded better. That's what Dad would say. But Barry wasn't Dad and he wanted to finish the picture quickly and get out of the portacabin. Then he could leave it to work on the girl until she took her costume off and was ready for him.

The charcoal was running down from the armpit and began the newly familiar outward bulge, to make room for what half a tongue was sliding between parted half-lips in anticipation of being given.

The charcoal snapped.

Barry picked up the longest end and put it to the panel. It didn't move. The eye widened to goad him. He put the charcoal where he should start the semi-circle of the curves that would reach forward from the torso. Nothing happened. He put it where the pinnacle of that curve should be. Nothing.

Barry tried to coax his hand to follow the shapes he knew should be there but he couldn't make himself see where the charcoal should go. It scratched a broken line across the flaking paint and Barry pulled it back quickly before he ruined what he had already drawn.

The picture wasn't smiling now. The eyebrow had flattened into a straight line that joined the dangerous vertical lines on the forehead. It looked like Mum's face when she found his fags. The half-face wanted a whole half-body, otherwise it wouldn't be strong enough to help Barry. Barry wouldn't be able to help himself. The girl would walk out of the portacabin leaving Barry with nothing but the memory of what could have been his.

A clatter of sandals announced that he'd run out of time. Barry decided whether the picture could help or not, the grockle wouldn't just walk away from him like everyone else did. He turned over the table with the broken leg, braced a foot against it, and wrenched out one of the good legs. The rusty screw at the top was bent sideways so the point stuck through the side of it.

Good.

He peeped through the empty window frame. He'd taken too long because the girl was already past the ballroom and heading straight for him. The picture shook with silent laughter at his dithering but he could only cower by the window and tremble at the meeting he'd lost his chance to dominate.

The girl ran her fingers through her wet hair where it tangled forward from her shoulder. Her black costume glinted in the sunlight as the curves underneath bobbed in time with her walk. The sight pushed its way through Barry's terror and down his spine into his balls. The portacabin rocked and she stood in the gash of sunlight at the doorway.

Her hand leapt up to cover her cry of surprise. She stepped out of the sunlight toward Barry.

"I'm sorry," she said with a nervous smile. "You startled me."

Her voice was very posh, like someone on the telly on Sunday evening, but why was she apologizing to him?

He glanced back at the picture, which was rolling its eye at his stupidity. Of course, she was a grockle so she didn't know to swear and laugh at Barry like the local girls did, and she didn't know he'd been watching her. He made his legs stop shaking so he could stand on them.

"My name's Fay," she said.

Barry knew he had to tell her his name, and it was silly to be scared when he was taller than her.

He took a deep breath. "Ber-rr-rr."

His stammer was back. He tried again.

"Berr-arry."

"Barry?" she asked.

Barry nodded, not wanting to risk speaking if he didn't have to. His eyes flicked from Fay to his pictures, back to Fay, not settling on anything.

Fay waved at the panel behind him.

"Did you draw that?"

Barry nodded again.

"It's very good."

Barry grinned. If she liked the picture, it must be working on her.

"It's very...lifelike." She shivered, although it was a warm afternoon.

Barry decided to take a chance. "Thank you."

He got it out without stuttering. He found the confidence to let his gaze settle on Fay's costume. Small curves mounted on larger ones. He wouldn't be able to speak again for a while.

"Do you mind me using your cabin to change?" said Fay

The picture was definitely helping him. She was already talking about taking her costume off. His part would come soon, if he could only work out what to do. He remembered the teenagers in the ballroom. It hadn't looked as easy as it did on telly.

"I'm sorry if you do," said Fay.

Barry realised she was waiting for him to reply so he shook his head so fast he made himself dizzy. He made a couple of grunts that sounded enough like 'no' that she got the message.

"Well in that case," she said slowly, as though she meant more than she said, "perhaps I could change back?"

She stepped to one side. Barry would have thought she was making room for him to leave if it wasn't for the picture. He stepped toward Fay, eyes fixed to the curves pulling him toward her. His hands leapt forward, just as they had to draw the picture. Barry's every sense was concentrated in his palms as the cold wet cloth pressed against them.

Something smashed into his mouth from in front, and something else from behind, and his back was sliding down the wall panel.

Fay's mouth gaped and her clenched fist sagged to her side as Barry rocked back and forth. Grunting, mewling noises forced their way up from his chest as he waited for her to start kicking him.

"I'm sorry", said Fay. "You frightened me. You shouldn't...oh look, you're bleeding."

She pulled out her towel and advanced on Barry.

"Here, let me see. I'm sorry."

Barry almost wished she would kick him now. If she was angry, it would show that she was at least a little scared. She was treating him like a child she'd hurt accidentally. He hid his face behind his arm and the noises got louder. Fay backed away.

"Perhaps I'd better go. But I'm sorry, okay Barry? I'm sorry."

Barry kept his face behind his arm. He heard her gathering her clothes and rucksack, then the rattle of sandals as she faded back into the sun. He huddled under the picture while his lip leaked blood into his mouth, to remind him he was still a kid. He turned himself around to look up at the picture. It looked back, unmoving. Exactly as he'd drawn it.

Barry noticed a spot of blood over the last line he'd left broken. His blood. It was in the right place and of the right colour for the part that he hadn't been able to draw. Part of him had become part of the picture. The picture that had made Fay take her clothes off for Barry, then made Barry get hurt by Fay. That tiny part of him now had more power than the whole of the rest of him. What was left was nothing, but the drop showed him how strong he could be.

He picked up the table leg he'd broken off and dragged his left wrist across the point of the screw. He dipped a finger in the gash but there wasn't enough blood to do much with. The charcoal eye shifted slightly as it looked down at him. He placed the screw above his wrist, pushed it in and dragged it down toward his hand. He hardly noticed the pain as the red paint he hadn't been able to steal spilled on to the floor. Now he had something much better than charcoal. He dipped his right fingers into the flow and set to work. Breast, belly, hip, leg all flowed out of him. He didn't stop until all five toes were perfect. There was a lot of blood on the floor by now but he'd managed to keep it from splashing on the wall and spoiling the picture. Half a face of charcoal tilted forward to examine its half-body of blood. It nodded its approval and Barry knew he'd passed its test, and what it wanted him to do next.

He dragged the screw down his right forearm and his left hand set off to fill in the other half of the face. He was tired by the time he finished but he would have to finish the body to share its full strength. His legs folded when he got to the waist. He could reach it from the floor so it didn't slow him down.

Soon he was able to lie on his back and look up at the best picture he'd ever drawn. His masterpiece. It stared over him, eyes fixed on the doorway for the next person to come through it. It had already lost interest in what was left of Barry. Barry's eyes closed and his arms and legs were too heavy to ever move again, but he smiled because when he woke he would be able to watch and act with real strength. He would do what he liked.

He wished he'd hidden some fags in here.

Steel in the Morning

A knock on the door. Le Méridien rose from his chair and picked up the lantern from the floorboards. He turned it in a slow arc so the figures on the diagrams of fencing actions seemed to move with the shadows it cast. He buckled on his smallsword and paused by the door, breathing the aura of sweat that never quite left the air.

Le Méridien opened the door to Sarratt, whose smile looked forced even in the flicker of the lantern.

"A fine morning for it," said Sarratt.

Le Méridien followed him down the stairs to the street. Sarratt knew better than to intrude on his mood.

Sarratt had a hackney carriage waiting. Le Méridien's breath misted in the light of the driver's own lantern.

"'Morning sirs!" The driver made to open the door, but Sarratt deftly placed himself between the driver's ebullience and Le Méridien. Le Méridien climbed in and arranged his cloak around himself.

"Hyde Park it is then," said the driver, "and seeing how it's such a fine morning, I think we'll make it a crown."

"That wasn't what we agreed." Sarratt's voice was as frosty as the April morning.

"That it weren't," said the driver, "but I didn't know why we was going there when we agreed it."

"You've no idea why we're going there, and it would be none of your business if you did," said Sarratt.

"Beggin' your pardon sir, but when a gentleman asks me to take 'im and 'is sword to Hyde Park this early in the morning, I don't have to ask for why. Also beggin' your pardon sir, I might agree that it's none of my business but his honour the justice o' the peace might not agree with me. So it's a crown."

Sarratt glanced at Le Méridien.

"Very well. A crown." His voice came from between clenched teeth.

"Thank you kindly, sir." The driver shook his reins. The dull ring of horseshoes on cobblestones greeted the grey dawn that trudged between the rooftops.

Le Méridien allowed his eyes to close and his mind to wander. Fencing actions clamoured for his attention, but he knew he must not heed them now. He must not allow the feel of a blade snared into *counterquarte* to occupy his mind lest it was still in possession when his life depended on his wrist turning into *septime*. Time enough to consider the moment when an opponent's parry would signal the second part of his *une-deux* when there was no danger of his anticipating it before it happened. He clasped his hands gently so his right hand would not stray to the hilt of his sword. How could a man who had gambled his life on the events of the next two hours think of anything but his gamble?

Le Méridien allowed himself to think of where the gamble began. He was handing a towel to a pupil sweating from his third lesson. "You've a good wind, Ensign Downe, but you mustn't let your body escape your mind."

Downe answered with a puzzled look that made him look much younger than his seventeen years.

"A fencer needs a quick body and you have that. But he also needs a strong mind, otherwise he becomes a brawler with a sword. I can train your body, but only you can keep it under your mind's mastery."

Downe bit his lip and nodded up at Le Méridien, whose six feet placed him a head higher. Le Méridien sighed. Downe learned the actions quickly enough, but something prevented him from putting them together correctly.

"I'll make a pact with you," said Le Méridien, "I'll answer your question if you answer mine."

"My question?"

"The question you ask every time you flick your eyes at me. Like that." Downe looked away. "My father was Le Vicomte d'Arles. He took my mother as his mistress while on his plantations in Martinique, and took her back to France when she fell *enceinte*. I was born on their last day at sea, hence my name. My mother was born a slave, but the Jacobins raised her to the aristocracy when they guillotined her. I escaped to your own fair land, where I found that life on a country estate had taught me only one way of earning my bread."

He tapped the button of a practice foil.

Downe's eyes were as wide as cannon muzzles. "You've hardly any accent," he said at last.

"Thank you. Now you must answer my question. Why do you wish to learn to fence?"

Downe's eyes wandered round the room, and Le Méridien saw a dozen lies rise to his lips and pass them by. They both knew he would tell the truth.

"I must kill my brother-in-law." He spat the word 'brother'.

"Why? Has he cheated you at bridge or merely spoken slightingly of your regiment?"

Downe's mouth hardened into a line that was beyond humour. "He seduced my sister."

Le Méridien almost asked whether she enjoyed it. Downe's hands bunched into quivering fists and Le Méridien held his peace.

"He slipped laudanum into her wine. She was only sixteen. She didn't know what was happening to her. My uncle found them..." Downe's voice tailed off, but left no doubt as to what he found them doing. "My mother paid him my father's legacy and ruined our family to make him marry her. I'll never forget Caroline's face the last time I saw her. She made one mistake and now her life is sold for our family's *reputation*."

"So now he must die?"

"Then Caroline can return to my mother with the legacy and her reputation. But I don't think I could kill him for those reasons alone. I must kill him for seducing her."

"And you'll all be a happy family again?"

A ghost of fear paled Downe's cheeks. "My regiment takes ship for Moore's army in the Peninsula in six weeks. I don't know when we'll come back."

Le Méridien paused for a moment to rue his question. He'd seen Downe as just another guinea-a-week pupil for the last time.

"Monsieur Le Méridien," said Downe, "I think this might be a fool's question, but is there - can you teach me - the perfect thrust?"

"Yes. Perhaps not today, but yes I think I can teach it to you."

Downe looked surprised. "Captain Fisher - the best fencer in my regiment - says it doesn't exist."

"It exists. A perfectly executed lunge with the correct disengagement at the ideal distance is impossible to parry."

Downe looked disappointed. "I've heard rumours of other actions. Secret actions."

Le Méridien smiled. "You've been listening to rumours of *bottes secrètes*? Secret thrusts?"

Downe didn't meet Le Méridien's gaze. "They say my brother-in-law knows one."

"He's been out before then?"

"Several times. He's always killed his man."

Le Méridien raised his eyes to the ceiling. "I've met many swordsmen who strike with a favourite move that's difficult to parry if you're not anticipating it, but they all *can* be parried. The thrust that I shall teach you is known to every man who ever took lessons in fencing, and if any could execute it in more than one attempt of a hundred, fencing would be a dead art. Now to business. Is your brother-in-law right handed or left?"

"Right"

"How tall is he?"

Le Méridien saw steel in Downe's eyes as he spoke of his brother-in-law, and began to believe that it might be possible to keep him alive.

~~~~~~~

A keen wind blew across London Bridge. Sarratt nudged Le Méridien and offered his hip flask. Le Méridien shook his head, as Sarratt must have known he would. Le Méridien felt a twinge of sympathy for Sarratt, who would prefer a late night discussion on the latest Proceedings of the Royal Society to helping Le Méridien risk his life early in the morning.

The riding lights of barges moored near the bridge glowed like the eyes of beasts of prey, their bulk just visible in the twilight. The great dome of St. Paul's Cathedral loomed ahead, promising the judgment the morning would bring. Le Méridien closed his eyes again, and saw Downe's customary pensive look.

"Will you act for me?"

Le Méridien raised his eyebrows. "There must be officers in your regiment who know the conventions as well as I?"

Who wouldn't be mulattos, but there was no reason to labour the obvious.

Downe picked up a foil and practiced a few parries without looking at Le Méridien. His silence told the story of a friendless boy who could not tell his brother officers of his family's shame.

"I'd be honoured." Le Méridien was surprised to find he meant it. "Smallswords, I presume."

"He always fights with smallswords."

Downe's hand shot out to lead his body in a lightning lunge, bending the foil against the exact centre of a target.

"Downe, you may not thank me for saying this, but I must say it."

"Yes?"

Le Méridien inhaled slowly. "The ball of a pistol usually misses, however deadly the aim. The edge of a sabre cuts to the bone, but rarely deeper. The point of a smallsword needs only to enter a finger's length into a man's body, and if he doesn't bleed to death in an hour, he'll die of putrefaction in a week. Sometimes - often - the best choice is forgiveness."

Downe hit the target again and followed with a perfect recovery to the *en garde* position. "I must kill him."

"Then you had better tell me his name."

"William Olde."

~~~~~~

Sarratt glared at the carriage driver and handed him a crown.

"I won't go far," said the driver, "It's only sixpence to go back."

"Damn your insolence," muttered Sarratt.

Le Méridien's feet were already crunching the morning frost as he strode into the park.

"Good luck, mate." The driver's voice sounded subdued as it floated after him.

Le Méridien raised a hand in thanks, but did not turn back.

He strode the mile or so to the meeting place, feeling the exercise pump his blood around his limbs and drive out the cold and stiffness of the carriage. He'd need that blood flowing fast before long.

He wasn't surprised to find they were the first at the meeting place. Le Méridien felt a coldness that did not come from the air as he recalled that his challenger liked to appear late, to give his opponent time to nurture his fear. Today, Le Méridien vowed, he had mistaken his man. All he would nurture would be that coldness, and to do that he must not think of the last time he had waited for the same man in the same place. To do that would be to risk rage, which was as dangerous as fear. Yet he could not keep his eyes from straying to the grass where he fancied he could see the indentation of a body, and the memory of a bloodstain that would be revealed when the frost thawed.

He could almost see the footprints on the patch of ground where he had given Downe his last minute practice. Practice would not help Le Méridien now, but Downe was of a different temperament and it had kept him from dwelling on what was to come. There had been a mist that morning, and the four figures were only fifty paces away by the time they took shape. A man as tall as Le Méridien led with a much smaller woman on his arm. Her features were hidden by the hood of her cloak. Two fat men waddled behind. One carried a surgeon's bag and Le Méridien guessed the other was Olde's second. Le Méridien looked back to the tall man, who must be Olde. He was about forty, with the florid complexion and bulging midriff of a man who lived well, but there was a strength and quickness in his stride that belied his inelegant figure. He would be puffing like a grampus by the end of one of Le Méridien's lessons, but Le Méridien guessed his wind would last for the few minutes the encounter would probably take.

The woman stopped dead, dragging on Olde's arm. He jerked her forward. "Come along, Caroline," he said as though to a disobedient dog.

Her hood slipped back from her head and Le Méridien saw she was barely more than a girl with the same wide eyes as Downe, on whom her shocked gaze rested as she stumbled after Olde.

Le Méridien turned to Downe and his heart sank. Downe's eyes and mouth gaped in an exact reflection of the girl's.

"Caroline," breathed Downe, then he called her name aloud. Olde's second glared at the breach of protocol.

Le Méridien knew the reins that he had taught Downe's mind to control his body with were tenuous at best, and he could see the girl's presence sawing through them. He guessed that Olde had told his wife she was coming to watch him fight, but not that he was fighting her brother. She looked as astonished as Downe.

Le Méridien stepped in front of Downe, blocking his view of Olde's party, and seized his shoulders. "Look at me Downe. *Look at me.* Now listen to me. Are you listening?"

Downe swallowed and nodded.

"Don't look at her. She isn't here. The only people here are you and him. Do you understand?"

Downe nodded again.

"You can fight for her, but don't look at her because she isn't here. Just you and him, and he's a dead man who still thinks he's alive.

Isn't he?"

"He's a dead man."

"Good man. Now turn to face the tree behind you, and take your cloak off while I meet his second."

Downe's jaw tightened and he didn't look so young any more. "He's a dead man."

Le Méridien searched his mind for a way to postpone the meeting, but there was none. He could no more stop it than he could stop a falling stone pushed off a cliff, and the stone had been pushed before he even met Downe. It was too late now because he was face to face with Olde's second. Le Méridien imagined the man's doubled chin flapping with laughter when Olde explained his plan to unman Downe with the presence of his sister. He had to offer the man his hand.

"My name's Le Méridien. Your servant, sir."

The other man guffawed and pressed Le Méridien's hand as briefly as protocol allowed. "Servant? Look more like a slave to me. My name's Theobald Inkham. Are you really the best the pup could do?"

Le Méridien raised his chin. He looked down his nose at the cat's cradle of veins tangling across Inkham's face.

"I acknowledge I'm a nigger, but I am at least a sober one."

Inkham snorted and his nose grew even redder. "I'll be sober when you're still a nigger."

"I'll wager you won't be sober for as long as I remain a nigger."

Inkham's jaw quivered, sending a wave of tremors across his chins. "Damn your eyes! Tell the pup we're ready as soon as he's got his nerve up. You can tell them to begin. See if I care!"

He turned and clumped back to Olde, who stood with a hand resting on the hilt of his sheathed sword. His posture was a study in nonchalance. Le Méridien doubted anyone without his fencing master's eye would see the tension in his shoulders.

He got Olde and Downe *en garde* as soon as he could. He did not want to allow Downe any time to think, though he could see how taut his muscles were. It was a far cry from the fluidity that allowed the explosive movements he'd mastered over the last month, but there was no help for it now.

"*Allez!*"

Le Méridien could see Olde's sneer was studied, but it probably looked confident enough to intimidate Downe. Olde tapped Downe's blade with his own a couple of times. Downe's sword jerked into an unnecessary parry. Le Méridien winced. He saw exactly what was going to happen, how Downe would try to follow his teaching and get it disastrously wrong.

It happened. Downe stepped forward into the perfect distance for the perfect thrust, and lunged. His point dropped to deceive Olde's parry and flicked up to drive into the torso. But Olde hadn't parried. Downe had anticipated a move that Olde hadn't made. His blade rang on Olde's and scraped harmlessly past his body. Olde riposted. Downe somehow managed to parry it as he stumbled back.

Olde stepped back to avoid a wild and mistimed thrust. They came back *en garde* and Le Méridien let out his breath. It was a miracle Downe had survived that riposte.

Downe's lips were drawn back to reveal the bared teeth of a cornered animal that might run away or fight desperately, but couldn't think so couldn't fence. A grim purpose that Le Méridien did not doubt was entirely authentic had replaced Olde's sneer as he advanced and beat Downe's blade. Downe parried wildly. Olde stepped back. Downe followed and Olde was flying back from him, but for all the apparent panic in his attempts to catch Downe's blade, Le Méridien saw Olde's feet fall exactly where they should fall. He saw Olde's back leg stretch behind him, take his weight, then snap straight like a spring. He closed his eyes so he didn't see Olde's perfect thrust impale Downe. A falsetto scream bored into Le Méridien's skull and tore his eyes open.

Downe's contorted body lay before Olde, who threw his head back, stretched his arms out to his sides and bared his teeth at the sky. Air rushed out of his lungs in a hissing roar of exultation. He took one more look at Downe, and turned on his heel.

"Inkham. My cloak if you please."

Inkham scurried forward, his congratulations stumbling over each other. Le Méridien realised Inkham was here as much to do Olde's boasting for him in the drinking clubs of the gentry as to hold his cloak.

Caroline Olde's dull eyes moved from her brother to her husband. Her jaw hung as though she was unsure of what she had just witnessed.

"Caroline," barked Olde. "Stop dreaming. Time to go."

He pushed his arm through hers and towed her after him. She turned back once more, and Le Méridien saw comprehension beginning to dawn. It was the face of a girl who had thought she had already lost everything, and just discovered that she had been wrong.

Le Méridien forced himself to look at Downe. Blood poured from a slash that ran six inches to the left from just below his sternum. Olde must have sliced his blade across after he drove it home. No wonder he always killed his man. The surgeon lifted Downe's head and tried to force a bottle between his lips, but Downe's mouth was clamped shut so tightly that he had bitten through his bottom lip. He was determined not to scream again.

The surgeon shrugged and took a pull from the bottle himself. "I loathe these encounters," he said to Le Méridien, "but it was a decent enough thrust in all fairness."

Le Méridien shook his head. "A man takes a bribe to make a girl his slave, kills her brother for loving her, and the only one who sees wrong in it is the dingy Christian."

It took Downe an hour to bleed to death. It took Le Méridien less than five minutes to decide another man must die.

~~~~~~~

There was no mist this morning; just the usual haze of smog, so Le Méridien saw the three men coming some way off. He shook off the memories, annoyed with himself for succumbing to them when he needed a clear head.

Olde strode in front, unencumbered by his wife today. Inkham and the same surgeon scuttled behind him. Le Méridien forced himself to stand calmly. He would have preferred to sit, but the grass was wet from the recently melted frost. Le Méridien was a fencing master, but it had been years since he had last fought in earnest. Olde was a skilled swordsman who had earned his lethal reputation. Le Méridien closed his eyes and pushed the thought from his mind.

It had taken some finesse to bring Olde here. A direct insult from a mulatto would just invite him to break down the door with a riding crop in one hand and a pistol in the other, even if he had tacitly accepted Le Méridien as an equal by not objecting to his seconding Downe. Instead, Le Méridien had sent a letter to Inkham on the previous Saturday afternoon, asking if he was aware of Olde's conduct towards the Downe family. As Le Méridien had foreseen, Inkham thought it was a huge joke and spent the evening in his club blurting the contents of the letter to anyone who would listen. By Sunday morning it was the talk of the

Fancy and Olde's reputation depended on sending a formal challenge.

Le Méridien opened his eyes as Olde strode to the same spot he had occupied when Le Méridien had last seen him. Le Méridien turned towards him but kept his eyes unfocused, allowing his mind to remain clear. Olde looked everywhere but at Le Méridien, but Le Méridien caught the occasional raking glance that Olde did not want him to see. Le Méridien smiled inwardly. A swordsman sees a man best when he does not look directly at him.

The time for smiling was past. Sarratt was going to meet Inkham, and Le Méridien allowed himself a single sharp look at Olde. This man would die. No, not this man for it's no easy thing to cut into a breathing, sweating man's body. This beast who had taken a defenceless girl. This thing.

Sarratt was coming back. His angry flush told Le Méridien that Inkham had not improved his manners. Le Méridien knew what the arrangements would be so he allowed Sarratt's explanation to wash over him while he took off his cloak. He unbuttoned his shirt to the chest to show he was wearing no amour, and felt the cold caress of the morning on his bare skin.

He drew his sword from his scabbard and raised it before him. He tilted it so the reflections of the wan sun chased each other up the Solingen steel to the point. Their smooth progress told him his hand was steady. His gaze lingered for a moment on the point, so sharp he could plunge it through an inch of cured leather with a good lunge. He took a deep breath, drawing sharp air into his nostrils and savouring the cleanliness of it. So different to the stink of too many people in one place that he could never escape in the city.

Le Méridien realised Sarratt had unbuckled his scabbard. He walked towards Olde, who was walking towards him. For a moment,

Olde could have been his reflection in a looking glass as both men converged on the same point. Le Méridien felt the slight impact of his feet on the ground with a keenness that he welcomed as an old friend.

Sarratt stood between them, slightly to the side. "*En garde.*"

Le Méridien's muscles slid his limbs into the stance as easily as putting on a well-fitting jacket. Sarratt passed his own sword between their points to show they were separated. Le Méridien looked at Olde's face for the first time. He wore the same sneer that he had worn against Downe. The sneer of an aggressive man with no fear of his opponent. A man who expected to attack, who would not retreat unless he found himself desperate.

"*Allez!*"

Olde advanced. Le Méridien let him, keeping his grip slack so he did not react when Olde tapped his blade. Olde tried a more aggressive attack, though without closing the distance. Again Le Méridien did not react, watching what Olde did without revealing anything of himself.

Olde attacked again, trying to take Le Méridien's blade aside. Le Méridien stepped back. Olde stepped forward in a way that announced he was ready to raise the tempo. Le Méridien stayed on the defensive, parrying and retreating. Olde's aggressive look may have been studied but it wasn't a sham, and there was a chance he would get carried away and over-commit himself.

The firm ring of a perfectly placed parry. Le Méridien's right hand shot out in an almost involuntary riposte. Olde sprang back and parried weakly. Le Méridien seized the initiative and advanced and suddenly Olde was flying backwards, his blade frantically seeking Le Méridien's.

It was the moment Le Méridien had been waiting for and he followed, waiting for the slight stiffening of Olde's posture *there* that warned him to stop his weight on the front leg *there* so he was in the right place to parry the thrust that killed Downe. He bound Olde's blade out of the way with a sweep of the wrist. Hurled himself into his own lunge. Olde's left arm shot in front of Le Méridien's point. Le Méridien swept his point up so it didn't touch Olde. He stepped back.

Olde was frozen, his blade out to one side, seemingly unable to believe he was not cut. His face was crimson and streaked with sweat and confusion. He raised his eyes to Le Méridien's. Le Méridien raised an eyebrow and nodded as he would to a pupil acknowledging his own mistake. Olde's mouth tightened as he realised that Le Méridien had pulled back because he did not want the encounter to end with a wound. He wanted a death.

Olde came back *en garde* and advanced, but the resolve was gone from his step. The sneer was trying to return to his face, but it was an insipid shadow of what it had been. The habit of aggression was still with him, and Le Méridien suppressed a surge of triumph as he saw Olde following him, unwittingly allowing him to set the distance.

Le Méridien continued his slow retreat. Back foot, front foot, back foot, front foot, back foot just a tiny way back and Olde fell for it. He made a full step forward. Le Méridien lunged. The merest twitch of the beginning of Olde's panic-stricken parry as he saw Le Méridien closer than he expected. Le Méridien dipped his point under the parry, dropped his left hand to his thigh, drove the point into the open line. The grate of a rib. The grudging yield of flesh. Le Méridien's right hand flew across to cover Olde's blade with his own before he had even withdrawn the point. Olde tried to step forward, the vestige of his sneer still on his face. Blood foamed from his mouth and poured down his shirt. He sank to his knees, his elbows, his side.

Le Méridien's legs, so supple he had not even been aware of

them a moment ago, threatened to drop him to the ground. His fingers locked on the grip of his sword so hard his forearm ached, and he had to press the hilt against his hip to keep the blade from shaking. He felt a burning need to empty his bladder.

"Damn it all, Le Méridien, how do you manage to look so calm?"

Sarratt's face swam before him, looking every bit as strained as Le Méridien felt. Sarratt offered his hip flask and Le Méridien took a pull. He shuddered with pleasure as the rum burned down his gullet.

He took another breath of the wonderful, clean air and looked down at Olde convulsing in the arms of the surgeon. Le Méridien's eye fell on the slash below the sternum. Had he intended to kill Olde with the same wound that had killed Downe, or had he simply returned to a position of defence before he fully recovered from the lunge? He knew he would believe both possibilities when he was in different moods, but now with the act fresh in his mind, no answer came to him.

Le Méridien took another mouthful of rum and handed the flask back to Sarratt. He smiled. "Thank you, my dear Sarratt. Now shall we to breakfast?"

Sarratt's grin broke through his furrows of worry. "Excellent idea. Before the justice asks if he may join us."

"Or if we may join him. I don't doubt that he's a man of parts, but I have a widow to return to her mother and I fear his company may be a hindrance."

Newgate Jig

Le Méridien's Hackney carriage shuddered to a halt on Gracechurch Street. Through the side windows, he saw people looking toward a commotion ahead so he stepped out to see for himself. A draper's wagon had broken a wheel while turning across the street and blocked one of London's main thoroughfares.

The driver of Le Méridien's Hackney was one of half a dozen people gathered to shout advice and imprecations at the hapless draper's assistant examining the wheel. The Hackney driver hurried over when he saw Le Méridien.

"Not to worry sir, we'll 'ave it shifted in two shakes. You just wait here." He glanced around the gathering onlookers. "And look to yer pockets, if you follows my meaning sir. I'll just give him a hand and we'll be on our way."

The Hackney driver turned back to the draper's assistant, who was still peering at the broken wheel.

"It's broken, you great ninny! We can all see that so get it off the bleedin' road before you swing at Newgate for blocking the King's highways!"

Le Méridien smiled but stayed beside the carriage door. He was returning from giving fencing lessons at a Bond Street club and his foils and plastrons would be a rich haul for a footpad. He glared at a pair of urchins sidling toward him, but their looks of slack-jawed astonishment showed more interest in the novelty of a black man wearing a burberry jacket and waistcoat than any larcenous intent.

He noticed a couple of other boys quartering the crowd. One slipped toward a well-dressed tradesman enjoying the altercation. The tradesman's fist shot backward and sent the boy sprawling. The other boy joined the crowd's bellow of laughter.

Le Méridien's eye was drawn to a man whose broken nose and uneven teeth made him look more like a pugilist than the gentleman he was dressed as. The few boxers who had become wealthy were well known but Le Méridien did not recognise this man. Le Méridien turned his face to the stricken wagon but kept his eyes trained on the man, who was edging toward a young woman. He walked with a feline grace that belied his broad frame and confirmed Le Méridien's first impression that he was a fighter of some sort. He would make an excellent swordsman, but the scars on his face told of fists and knives rather than the gentile blood-letting of the duelling ground.

The fighter glanced around, checking that everyone's attention was occupied. A deft hand slid toward the girl and withdrew. The girl did not start as she would have done if the hand had insulted her, and the hand left open and empty. The man disappeared around the corner of Fenchurch Street as quickly as a pickpocket anticipating a hue and cry. Whatever the man had done, the girl had not noticed.

Le Méridien turned back to scrutinise the girl, who was perhaps fifteen or sixteen. Her jacket and shift could have been worn by a Duke's wife or an actress's maid, but a lady of wealth would not be walking alone and there was something about the stoop of her shoulders that spoke of someone more accustomed to receiving orders than giving them. He shook his head. No small incident in London ever failed to draw a crowd, and no crowd of Londoners could gather without spawning intrigues worthy of the Prince Regent's court.

He was about to forget the matter when the fighter strode out of Fenchurch Street. He pointed at the girl without breaking stride

"There she is," he shouted. "Hold the thief!"

The girl's head turned to him with the rest of the crowd.

"Hold the thief!" shouted the fighter again.

Le Méridien saw the look of perplexity on her face when she saw the fighter was pointing at her. She did not even try to run. Someone seized her arm, almost jerking her off her feet. Someone else grabbed her hair, which spilled from under her bonnet in a brown cascade. Her wail of pain was drowned by shouts of triumph.

Now, Le Méridien told himself, was the moment to allow sense to triumph over curiosity and stay by the carriage door until he could go back to his *salle* in Southwark. He sighed a lament for his feeble sense and pushed into the crowd, which was ebbing from the wagon and flowing toward the fresh drama.

"My name is Jonathon Norbury." The fighter's tone was conversational but he spoke loudly enough to carry over the chatter of the crowd. "Warranted thief taker of the city."

That got everybody's attention. Thief takers were unpopular but they could be counted on to add drama to any situation. Norbury drew a fistful of silver spoons from a pocket inside the girl's jacket. Le Méridien, standing at the side, saw the shock on her face that would be hidden from the men holding her from behind.

Norbury offered the crowd a broken-toothed grin.

"Don't think a kitchen maid can afford the likes of these but I think your master might recognise them, eh?"

The girl shook her head but Norbury spoke over her. "Thank you for your help, sirs." He dug in his pocket and handed coins to the men who held the girl. "Now if you'll hand her to me..."

Willing hands pushed the girl to Norbury. More than one hand squeezed her bottom before surrendering her to a short fate that could only end with a shorter rope.

Le Méridien spoke over the buzz of conversation. "A moment, Mr Norbury. Was it not you whom I saw lingering by this young woman before you dashed into Fenchurch Street, only to return a few moments later?"

Norbury's grip on the girl's arm made her wince, and he did not slacken it as he turned to Le Méridien. Norbury did not speak immediately and people began to back away from the ground between them as though to clear a line of fire between two duellists. Norbury slowly raised his eyebrows. The unspoken meaning was as clear as if he had shouted it. *Who put a big black bugger in those fancy clothes and taught him to speak like the quality?* Le Méridien heard a couple of sniggers as others noted the mockery. He knew that Norbury was drawing out the moment to make sure no one else would say they had seen him.

When Norbury spoke, it was with a courtesy that could only exaggerate the ridiculous figure he was making of Le Méridien.

"Begging your pardon sir, but you must be mistaking me for some other gentleman. If, that is, I may have the honour of naming myself a gent before so fine a gentleman as your good self."

Laughter bubbled around him. Le Méridien saw how Norbury's coins and wit had drawn the crowd to his side, thief taker or no. It would take more than simple truth from Le Méridien's thick lips to change their minds.

Le Méridien bowed his head. "No doubt you are right, sir. May I offer you the use of my Hackney to take her to Newgate? I presume that is where you are going?"

Norbury's expression did not change, but Le Méridien saw discomfort in the shift of his weight from one foot to the other. Norbury could have no desire to share a Hackney with Le Méridien's suspicions, but to refuse would be to risk someone asking why and raising London's traditional distrust of thief-takers.

Norbury nodded. "Thank you kindly. I'd be glad to accept your offer."

The row over the draper's wagon raged on as Le Méridien's Hackney turned around, toward Newgate. Le Méridien opened the door and Norbury half lifted and half threw the girl before him. Norbury sat beside her and Le Méridien opposite. The girl cast her eyes to the floor and made no sound beyond an occasional sniff that betrayed barely suppressed hysteria. Norbury fixed his eyes on Le Méridien's and backhanded the girl across the face.

"Enough of your noise, girl. You'll disturb this kind gentleman who saved us a walk."

As a fencing master, Le Méridien taught his pupils to read what an opponent's body unwittingly betrayed, and how to choose what they communicated themselves. He was engaged in such a contest now, so he stifled the cry of protest that Norbury's violence dared him to utter and kept his face impassive. He opened his handkerchief and mopped the blood from the girl's lip.

"What is your name, my dear?"

He sensed Norbury shift, confused by his failure to monopolise Le Méridien's attention. The girl shrank away from the handkerchief so Le Méridien placed it in her hand and raised it to her mouth. "Your name?"

"Carrie Barlow."

"Tell me Carrie, why is this man so interested in you?"

Le Méridien saw Norbury's knuckles whiten as his hand tightened on her arm. Carrie gasped with pain but did not speak.

"Stuck her fingers in her master's cutlery draw, didn't you girl?"

Said Norbury.

Le Méridien looked for defiance or denial in Carrie's face as she raised her head, but saw only bewilderment.

Norbury's fingers shifted on her arm and dug between bone and bicep. Carrie's back arched. "Yes! Yes I did!"

Le Méridien did not believe it for a moment.

~~~~~~

Le Méridien stood in the public gallery of the Newgate magistrate's court when an usher manhandled Carrie Barlow into the dock. Some impulse made him look at his watch to time the proceedings. It took Mr Justice Chatterton forty seconds to read the charge and persuade Carrie to plead loudly enough for the court recorder to hear the words 'not guilty'. It took two and a half minutes to hear Norbury's evidence. It took twenty seconds to pronounce a sentence of death by hanging. Three and a half minutes in all.

Le Méridien left the gallery, strode to Newgate Street and stood for a moment before the place where the gallows stood every Monday morning. He looked at the gates of Newgate prison, imagining the wheeled scaffold stored behind them, awaiting its next tribute of life. He sighed a last lament for sense and rapped on the keeper's door. A hatch opened and an unshaven face appeared. The keeper's eye travelled from Le Méridien's dark face to his apparel and his jaw sagged with the effort of deciding which to adjust his manner for.

Le Méridien spoke first. "Good morning to you."

"Morning."

"I wish to visit an acquaintance in the women's quadrangle." Le Méridien held up a shilling.

"Not allowed."

Le Méridien held up a crown.

"Billy!" The keeper opened the door and took the coin as Le Méridien came in.

Clumping footsteps announced the appearance of a young man who looked too thin for such a heavy step. "What is it, Tom?"

"Take this, this *gentleman*, to the women," said Tom the keeper, "and mind they don't clout his purse while he's in there."

"Who are you visiting?" asked Billy the turnkey.

"Her name is Carrie Barlow. She was sentenced not half an hour ago."

"Sentenced for what?" asked Tom.

"Theft."

"She'll hang then?" Asked Tom.

"In three days."

"Not allowed," said Billy.

Le Méridien gave him a crown. Billy pocketed it and led Le Méridien down a tight corridor and unlocked the door at the end. They emerged into the daylight. A couple of women looked up from the water pump in the middle of the open quadrangle.

"Bleedin' hell Billy, what's this? The black baron of Newgate?" The shrill voice echoed around the quadrangle and women appeared in the empty doorways to stare at the newcomer.

"Oi Billy, leave him in here will you? We'll look after his grace!" A woman in one door yanked down her blouse to expose underfed breasts. Laughter cackled from the room behind her.

A voice from the other side of the quadrangle took up the challenge. "Nah, bring him here and he'll thank you. Long as you don't mind carrying him home, that is!"

More women joined the fun and Le Méridien was caught in a hailstorm of laughter and obscenities. Billy touched Le Méridien's elbow.

"Beg pardon, sir. They're for Botany Bay in a couple of weeks and serve 'em right. We're for this ward here if she's a thief."

A woman with grey-streaked brown hair stood in the doorway with her back to them, wagging her bottom. Billy slapped her and she stepped aside. "Ooh Billy, I wish it weren't just your hand you could do that with!"

Cheers drowned her voice as their ward won the contest for Le Méridien. The stink of the room burned into his nostrils. It took a moment to gather himself enough to see Carrie sitting against the wall with her knees against her chin. For a moment, he thought she was unaware but her face turned to him as he stepped toward her.

Something brushed his side and he saw Billy grasping the wrist of a woman who had tried to pick his pocket. Billy punched her and she landed on her back.

She flung open her arms. "Come to me, Billy love, come down here!"

Le Méridien closed his eyes and tried to clear his head. "Billy, could you give us a few moments alone? We have some matters to discuss and, excellent as the company is, we would prefer confidence."

Billy opened his mouth to speak. Le Méridien patted his purse. "I know. Not allowed."

Billy's lip twitched in something like a smile and he raised his voice. "All right, you ain't in Drury Lane no more! The gent says out, Billy says out, so out you goes!"

Billy swore and cuffed and the women shrieked and laughed, but they filed out. Le Méridien squatted in front of Carrie. He spoke her name. She looked up, but there was no comprehension in her unfocused eyes.

"Carrie, do you remember me? I brought you here after Norbury slipped the spoons into your jacket. I'd like to talk to you."

"They'll hang me," she said. "I'll dance the Newgate jig. For a bunch of spoons I never took."

"That's what I'd like to talk about."

Carrie's face showed no sign of understanding. "Didn't do nothing and they'll hang me."

Her jaw quivered. Le Méridien watched as facts she must have been hiding from her consciousness burst forth in one howling sob after another. He took her hands in his and she fell forward into his arms, clinging as though he was a stout tree in a storm. He held her tight and tried to restrain his impatience. He would learn nothing until the storm passed, but Billy's forbearance would not be infinite. He waited for the worst convulsions to pass.

"Carrie," he said, "Carrie you must listen."

She showed no sign of having heard him. He prized her arms from around his neck and seized her face in both his hands. She tried to shake him off but he held her with a grip that must have hurt.

"Carrie, will you listen?"

He felt her try to nod in his grip and released her.

"I didn't steal them spoons," she said at last.

"I know. I saw Norbury put them in your jacket, though I didn't know what he was doing at the time."

Her eyes focused on him and for the first time, he saw something other than despair in her face. "You did?"

"I did. But as you see, I don't have the sort of face that commands the respect of magistrates."

"Cos you're a coon?"

"If you want to put it that way. The point is that perhaps if I know why he did it, I can find a way to prove it. But first you must tell me why, if you know."

Her eyes dropped. "You a devil?"

"I'm sorry?"

"I heard the devil's black and you got a funny name. Now here you come offering temptation cos if you can show I didn't steal the spoons, I won't hang. But the devil always wants his due. I heard that too."

"My name is French, not diabolical." Le Méridien allowed irritation to creep into his tone. "My father was an *aristo*, my mother was his slave and the only devils I know are the Jacobins who guillotined them. Now are you going to tell me whatever it is that you're ashamed of, or would you prefer to hang?"

Her head jerked back as though he had slapped her, but he saw her register the sense in his demand.

"He must of put the spoons there because my master paid him to."

"And who is your master?"

"His name's Theobald Gudgeon. You heard of him?"

"I've been spared the pleasure. Would you like to explain the charade with the spoons? Most employers simply dismiss their maids when they tire of them."

"Oh he's tired of me, that's for sure." She dropped her voice to a mumble that Le Méridien could hardly hear. "Not just as his kitchen maid."

Le Méridien's lips formed a silent 'oh' but he did not speak.

Words poured out of her in a torrent. "I needed the extra money. My sister got the consumption, me dad's dead of it two years back, me mum's on the gin and we've had no wages for six months. He weren't so bad. Then he said he were getting married and I shouldn't come back. I told him I'd starve without the wages I were waiting for and I'd had to borrow money, which weren't nothing but the truth, and I told him about me mum and me dad and me sister. He says he weren't giving me no more money and I said he would if he knew what was good for him and he didn't say nothing then and I kept coming to work like nothing was different. I thought I'd keep the job till he paid up and we'd say no more about it, but he must of sent that man instead."

It was all spoken in one breath and she stopped talking when she ran out of wind. Le Méridien was gratified to see defiance in her glower. She would need all the courage she could muster in the next two days.

She dropped her gaze. "You're still here."

"I am."

"You still going to help me now you know I'm a whore?"

"I am."

"How?"

"I don't know yet."

They regarded each other for a silent moment.

"Tell me," said Le Méridien, "why did you tell me your father is dead?"

"Sounds better than run off with another woman, don't it?"

~~~~~

Sarratt sipped his coffee and regarded Le Méridien with a raised eyebrow.

"My dear Le Méridien, we've been here ten minutes and you haven't asked me about the latest Royal Society meeting once. I can only surmise that you are in thrall to your Quixotic muse again."

Le Méridien had to smile. Sarratt's fascination with natural history was usually a welcome diversion from the drudgery of raising the rent for his *salle*, but today he could not deny that his mind was elsewhere.

"You have me," he said, and told the story of Carrie Barlow's impending execution.

Sarratt frowned when he finished. "You say her employer is Theobald Gudgeon? There's a name I've heard."

Le Méridien's interest stirred. "You've met him?"

"No, he's very much one of the Fancy so our paths haven't crossed."

"The Fancy. He's something of a rake, then?"

"No more than is usual in the Fancy, which would make seducing his maid more or less compulsory. But it's rumoured that his real vice is gambling."

Le Méridien nodded. One of his pupils was an heir to an earldom who had gambled so heavily on how far an acquaintance could throw a stone that he could no longer afford lessons in Harry Angelo's fashionable *salle* and had to depend on Le Méridien to keep him in preparation for the duels that the Fancy was so fond of.

"As his gambling is a subject for rumour, I presume it is usually unsuccessful?"

"Disastrous by all accounts. He's said to be a good enough player who never knows when to stop. The man's ruined himself and nearly taken his family with him. His father, by some sleight of hand we can only guess at, has arranged a good marriage for him but only on condition that he swears off gambling and shuns the Fancy."

Le Méridien was conscious of well-fitting cogs beginning to

turn.

"And presumably off kitchen maids?"

"I imagine that went without saying. His unfortunate bride-to-be is Miss Henrietta Burnfield."

"Related to the Burnfield wool merchants?"

"Old man Burnfield's only surviving child. Henrietta's a widow with two daughters and she's already thirty-five, so Burnfield must be in a hurry to marry her off while there's still a chance of a son and heir. Though the more I hear about Gudgeon, the more desperate I think Burnfield must be."

"Probably not desperate enough to weather the scandal Carrie Barlow would stir up."

"So Gudgeon seems to think. He would probably buy her off if he could afford it, but you say he isn't even paying his servants' wages and paying her after the marriage might involve explanations he'd rather avoid."

Le Méridien nodded. "While he could come up with all sorts of reasons for needing to pay Norbury. All the same, he could face some very uncomfortable explanations if he doesn't have the money when Norbury wants it."

The two men shared a smile, but Le Méridien's mind was already forging ahead. He reached for his coffee and became aware of the resignation in Sarratt's smile.

Sarratt spoke first. "Before you ask me what you are going to ask me, may I ask what this girl means to you?"

Le Méridien's cup froze in mid-air. He could not help but laugh at himself. He was so used to depending on his inscrutability that he forgot how long Sarratt had known him.

"Shall we say that she is a fellow traveller who has fallen and requires assistance?"

"And you to her?"

"She asked me if I was a devil."

"Then you may depend on me."

"I intend to. You have the sort of face that will be believed when you give your word of honour that Carrie Barlow is innocent."

There was a hint of concern in Sarratt's reply. "My word of honour is not something I give lightly."

"That is why it will be necessary for Gudgeon to confess to you before you give it."

"Ah. A plan with the virtue of simplicity. There is but one complication."

~~~~~~

"We are not assaulting the Bastille," said Le Méridien.

Sarratt snapped the pistol's lock to check the flint.

"Humour me, Le Méridien. I don't intend to shoot my way into a Berkeley Square house but I will find it easier to look Mr Gudgeon in the eye with these in the gig. It will offset the knowledge that he's already tried to kill to hide what we threaten to bring to light."

"To kill certainly," said Le Méridien. "To spill blood on his own carpets I doubt."

Sarratt loaded the second pistol and returned it to its box under the seat. Le Méridien held himself motionless and watched furrows of tension ease from Sarratt's brow while Sarratt's mouth assumed the firm line of purpose. Sarratt had been one of Le Méridien's best pupils before he discovered that defeating fear before a duel was far easier than defeating remorse afterward.

Sarratt's gig bumped to a halt outside Gudgeon's house and Le Méridien stepped down. The afternoon's still air left a shroud of coal smoke over the city and brought twilight at three o'clock. Sarratt told his driver to wait and rapped on Gudgeon's door. The valet who opened it was identifiable as such only by his manner, for his jacket, breeches and cravat would have passed inspection by Beau Brummell.

Sarratt gave him a card. The valet gave it a glance and tipped his head back to a patrician angle. "May I enquire Mr Sarratt's business?"

"Quite so. Please be so good as to inform Mr Gudgeon that Mr Sarratt does indeed have business." Sarratt's voice was low and level. Only a man who knew him as well as Le Méridien could hear the tension in it.

The valet managed to convey insolence without actually glowering as he showed them into the parlour and left them to find Gudgeon. A hint of perfume tickled Le Méridien's nose. He shared a look with Sarratt. Gudgeon's finances may have been in a perilous state but he was determined to maintain the façade of opulence.

The valet returned. "Mr Gudgeon will see you now, Mr Sarratt. Perhaps your footman would care to wait in the kitchen."

Le Méridien turned his whole body toward the valet but kept his face blank, letting the valet torture himself by guessing what he was currently suffering in Le Méridien's imagination.

Sarratt waited until the valet began to visibly shrink before he spoke. "Mr Le Méridien is my particular friend and is as anxious as I am to see Mr Gudgeon. Now if you please."

The valet practically scurried ahead of them to the drawing room door. "Mr Sarratt and Mr, er, Lemennon."

Le Méridien strode in first and stretched out a hand. "Le Méridien. Your servant sir. Delighted to meet you."

In the two steps from the door to Gudgeon's hand, Le Méridien recognised a considerably less formidable opponent than Norbury. Gudgeon's slight stoop made him look as though he was in his mid-forties, but the debauched red of his cheeks spoke of a man younger by several years who was aged by ill-usage. Gudgeon's feet shuffled with surprise at seeing a six foot black man in his drawing room. Gudgeon took Le Méridien's hand before knowledge could restrain habit. His mouth curled slightly as he realised that he had just accepted a black tradesman as his guest.

Le Méridien stepped aside and allowed Sarratt his turn with Gudgeon's hand.

"Please take a seat, Mr Sarratt." Gudgeon pointedly ignored Le Méridien. "Tell me of your business."

Sarratt exuded affability as he sank into an armchair. "Carrie Barlow."

There was no change in Gudgeon's demeanour. "I'm sorry?"

"Carrie Barlow. Your kitchen maid who will be executed at Newgate the day after tomorrow."

"Ah. Yes. Carrie Barlow. Now I remember."

"I imagine you do," said Sarratt. "I doubt you hang a kitchen maid every day."

Le Méridien would have kept silent and let Gudgeon realise for himself how foolish his denial had sounded, but Sarratt had succeeded in unbalancing Gudgeon. The turmoil behind Gudgeon's smile was as plain as if he had been thrashing on the floor.

"No, no of course not." Gudgeon managed a chuckle. "But look, I can't leave my guests dry. Brandy? Good, good. One moment, one moment."

Gudgeon left the room for a little longer than seemed necessary to tell the valet to bring brandy, but then he could have called the valet into the room and given the order in front of Le Méridien and Sarratt. Gudgeon returned with his shoulders relaxed and his stoop gone. His cheeks were a little redder, showing he had anticipated the arrival of the brandy by a glass or two. Gudgeon sat opposite Sarratt and darted a glance at Le Méridien, who had placed himself at a right angle to the two of them.

"Mr Sarratt," said Gudgeon, "You were speaking of Carrie Barlow."

"Actually Mr Gudgeon, I came to discuss a hundred guineas. I merely mentioned the Barlow girl by means of illustration."

Gudgeon confined his reaction to a single raised eyebrow. He had assumed his card-table manner. "Blackmail is it?"

"Good heavens no. What possible grounds for blackmail could there be?"

Another glance at Le Méridien showed that Gudgeon was as unsettled by Le Méridien's silent presence as by Sarratt's changes of direction.

"What indeed?" asked Gudgeon.

"Of course, some might consider your liaison that you ended by having Jonathon Norbury send the girl to the gallows."

Gudgeon said nothing. Le Méridien's stomach muscles tightened. The critical moment was approaching and Gudgeon's thoughts were hidden behind his face.

"You're not going to waste our time by denying it are you?" Asked Sarratt. "I had understood that you are a man amenable to business."

Gudgeon smiled the thin smile of a gambler trying to hide the crippling damage that the last hand had cost him. "If you know this much about my affairs, you know I do not have a hundred guineas. I may raise a little perhaps, but a hundred is entirely beyond my means."

Le Méridien relaxed.

"Then we may indeed discuss business," said Sarratt.

"Business be damned. You people came here to blackmail me so let's call the devil by his name."

Gudgeon threw another glance toward Le Méridien.

Or did he? Le Méridien summoned the map of the room he had committed to mind before he sat down. The door was behind him and immediately to his right. Had that been the real focus of Gudgeon's nervous glances? Had he half heard a rustle of cloth or the brush of a boot on a carpet? Had the brandy been the only thing that Gudgeon had ordered from the valet, or had there been a summons as well? He found himself as convinced of a presence outside that door as if he had heard a knock.

Sarratt was reacting to the suggestion of blackmail with theatrical mortification. "Dear me, a horrible accusation. I don't ask a penny for myself but I'm sure you would not deny Carrie Barlow a pension after the ill treatment that she has suffered. Ill treatment that will end directly when you tell the Justice that the spoons weren't yours, or whatever you choose to tell him before I speak to him myself..."

Le Méridien cut him off. "Please come in, Mr Norbury."

Silence fell. The door opened and Norbury's lithe step carried him to the middle of the room. There was something feral about his stance. He brought the violence of the rookeries into a house of embroidered tablecloths and chairs covered in faux-chinoiserie. Sarratt, Gudgeon and Le Méridien stood.

"Course he ain't here to blackmail you."

Norbury's words were to Gudgeon but he did not move his gaze from Le Méridien. Although Le Méridien had not spoken since he sat down, Norbury showed no doubt as to who his principle adversary was.

"Mr Le Méridien ain't the blackmailing sort. Leastways, that's what them what know him say, and one or two who only heard of him. I been asking. The sort to take the part of a poor girl sent to hang by the likes of you and me, but not the sort to blackmail you over it."

Le Méridien saw both the respect to himself and the implied insult to Gudgeon in Norbury's refusal to acknowledge anyone else in the room. He also recognised a man who was likely to show respect for a worthy opponent by waiting for him to turn his back before he struck.

"So now Mr Le Méridien's mate here can go tell the magistrate that he put it all before you and you didn't deny it. And because he's white and he'll give his word of honour with a straight face and a clear conscience, the magistrate will believe him. You bloody, bloody fool."

Le Méridien nodded. "Actually, Mr Gudgeon will be as delighted to tell the magistrate himself as he will be to pay Miss Barlow a pension of a hundred guineas. He is very keen to spare the Burnfield family the embarrassment of reading about Carrie Barlow in *Town and Country* before his marriage."

Le Méridien's hands were by his sides, but Sarratt caught the wave of his finger and made for the door.

Norbury nodded, some of the tension easing as he saw a way to keep the money promised to him. "He's very keen indeed."

"Then you gentlemen must have things to discuss. Good day to you." Le Méridien strode round Norbury without touching him. He followed Sarratt out of the house and into the hazy gloom of the street.

Sarratt opened the gig door. "Home Johnson, quick as you please."

Johnson the driver looked dubious. "She might manage a trot, sir."

"Well be a good fellow and make it a *brisk* trot."

Le Méridien climbed in beside Sarratt. Sarratt let out his breath. "Damn it, I was enjoying myself before that bruiser turned up. You certainly have some interesting friends, Le Méridien."

"I meet them in coffee houses."

Sarratt doffed the strain of the last half hour by laughing much harder than the joke warranted. He slumped back and the two men pulled on their cloaks against the cold of the approaching evening. A clatter of horseshoes on cobblestones preceded the blur of a galloping horse past Sarratt's window. Le Méridien saw several pedestrians scatter out of the way.

"A pity we can't just go to the magistrate now," said Sarratt. "I'd like to finish this wretched business."

"I too," said Le Méridien, "but Chatterton is not bound to believe us, while he can hardly fail to heed Gudgeon if he says there was no theft in the first place."

Sarratt nodded and they both lapsed into silence. The sound of galloping approached from ahead. There was a whinny of pain. The gig stopped dead and lurched backward.

"What the devil?" Sarratt reached for his door.

Le Méridien gripped his shoulder. "Gudgeon is a gambler who doesn't know when to stop and your word of honour could cost Norbury his thief-taker's warrant. Stay inside."

Le Méridien pulled a pistol from the box under the seat and cocked it as the gig lurched back again. He slid out of the cart and slipped the pistol under his cloak. Johnson was trying to calm the horse that was rearing between the gig's traces. Men and women were gathering, drawn by the disturbance, but there was still enough light for

Le Méridien to be sure he recognised none of them.

"What happened?" Le Méridien asked.

"Damned galloping blade on his fancy horse." said Johnson. "Begging your pardon sir, I mean some *gentleman* come galloping past and gave Strawberry here the end of his crop on her nose. She ain't used to it, are you my dear?"

Le Méridien was no longer listening. He worked his way around the bucking gig, scrutinising every figure his progress revealed.

A man much nearer than anyone else appeared around the gig's corner. Le Méridien just had time to note that he slouched and walked with a shuffling gait unsuited to approaching a panicking horse before the man straightened up and levelled a pistol at him. There was no triumph on Norbury's face, just the concentration of a craftsman at a challenging task.

Sarratt, thought Le Méridien. Sarratt was the reason he was still alive. It was Sarratt's word of honour that must be silenced, and Sarratt who was out of clear sight and could be pointing a pistol of his own at Norbury.

Le Méridien turned side on to Norbury like a duellist presenting the smallest possible profile to an opponent's fire. Norbury was a fighter but not a fencer so he did not see the significance of Le Méridien's feet shifting into the stance of *en garde*, nor the way he placed his weight over the front leg.

Both men stood still, waiting for Sarratt to perpetuate a situation he may not even have been aware of. Le Méridien focused every sense on Norbury until it was as though they were alone in the grey smog. The rocking gig and the people shying away from Norbury's pistol could have been on another continent.

A click from the gig's door announced that Sarratt coming out.

Norbury's pistol swung to the gig as though attached to his eyes. Le Méridien flicked his cloak aside from his own pistol. The half-inch eye of Norbury's pistol jerked back to Le Méridien. The flint snapped. Priming powder flared. Le Méridien did not try to point his pistol but threw his front leg straight and hurled himself forward in the *fléche*. Two pistols banged. A ball plucked at Le Méridien's cloak.

The *fléche* carried Le Méridien three steps before he arrested his momentum and swung back to Norbury. He just had time to see Norbury crumpling to the ground before vanishing behind the smoke of Le Méridien's own priming powder a moment before the kick of the discharge.

Le Méridien stepped through the smoke to see Norbury sprawled on the street. He looked round to see Sarratt half out of the gig, his pistol sinking to his side. Sarratt's pistol was still cocked.

"Hesitated," said Sarratt to nobody in particular. "I hesitated and then he dropped."

Le Méridien thought back. He was sure he had not been mistaken when he heard two reports, yet Sarratt had not fired. He looked at the gathering crowd and his eyes were immediately drawn to the one man who was moving away while everyone else had decided that the shooting was over and was coming closer. Le Méridien saw that the man was making his way toward a horse that was ambling away. He felt everything fall into place.

"Mr Gudgeon. A moment of your time." Le Méridien's voice cut through the growing buzz of conversation. The man walking away stopped in his tracks. "We'd like to thank you for shooting this…footpad…in the back."

The man abandoned the idea of escape and strode toward Le Méridien and Sarratt. Le Méridien nodded to himself when he saw it was indeed Gudgeon

"Thank God I was in time," said Gudgeon when he was close enough that only Le Méridien and Sarratt could hear him. "I tried to persuade him to accept your terms but he seized one of my horses and took off after you. I gave chase of course, but it was a damned near thing. A damned near thing indeed."

Le Méridien could detect nothing in Gudgeon's manner to show he was lying. If only the man had known when to cut his losses, he could have been a successful gambler but even now he could not resist trying his luck against the clear evidence of his actions.

"Then you had no reason to slip away," said Le Méridien, "and I only see one horse wandering off."

"I beg your..."

"I'm sure Norbury carried on abusing you after we left. That must have dented the pride of a man who feels free to dispose of anyone who doesn't wear silk whenever they become inconvenient to him." Le Méridien kept his voice as low as Gudgeon's.

"This is ridiculous..."

"You saw a way to solve all your problems at once. Norbury was ready to accept our terms so you must have offered him more money. Whatever you offered, you rode us down with Norbury on your own horse, probably because he couldn't ride. You dropped him ahead of us and turned back to whip Sarratt's horse and stop the gig. Norbury was waiting for Sarratt to step out so he could silence his word of honour. I doubt you cared about me, but Norbury would have shot me even if you didn't tell him to. He knew both of us couldn't outlive Sarratt for very long."

Gudgeon's mouth opened and closed in a face set in an expression of denial, but no words came out.

"But you had an idea you didn't share with Norbury. Perhaps he offended you or perhaps you woke up to the fact that you can't let a man like that into your life and expect him to quietly walk away when you finish with him. Either way, you stayed back so you could shoot him down as a footpad as soon as he shot Sarratt. You're not a bad shot, Gudgeon, but if you've ever fought a duel, you're still alive by sheer luck. You had him covered because you knew he'd shoot you if he even suspected what you had in mind. But you panicked when he fired and shot him before you made sure he'd hit anyone. You probably didn't even mean to shoot, did you?"

Le Méridien sniffed Gudgeon's breath. "I'll give you this. You're a much better dissembler after your fourth drink than when you're sober. If you had been as transparent as when I first met you, Norbury would have seen through you in a moment and you would be a very dead man by now."

Gudgeon looked as though he had contracted a sudden bout of ague. "This is…absurd. You're insane."

"Do you give me the lie?"

Gudgeon's protests died in his throat. Le Méridien watched the thoughts chase each other through Gudgeon's mind. Gudgeon had accepted Le Méridien as a guest so could not insist on a difference in class. Gudgeon's gaze dropped to Le Méridien's cooling pistol, then rose to regard the cool expression and consider the clear thinking in the aftermath of mortal danger. He glanced at Sarratt, who was within hearing of the deadly sleight on Le Méridien's honour that he was on the brink of making.

"No, no. Dark. Easy to make a mistake."

"Quite. The dark often affects my hearing as well. Now go and get your horse before the watchmen decide it's safe enough to come and find out who was shooting at whom. You'll need it for you visit to Mr Justice Chatterton tomorrow."

Gudgeon backed away, nodding like a clockwork bird.

"Mr Gudgeon," said Sarratt. "Carrie Barlow's pension now stands at two hundred guineas."

~~~~~~

Le Méridien was putting away foils and plastrons after a class when he heard the knock. He went down the stairs that connected his *salle* to the street and opened the door. The girl outside gave him a hesitant smile and it took him a minute to recognise her as Carrie Barlow. The healthy flush to her complexion that had been bleached out by fear and dismay whenever he had seen her before.

"Come in, Miss Barlow."

Her face showed a moment's confusion at being addressed as 'Miss', but she stepped in and allowed him to take her cloak as she climbed the stairs.

"Please have a seat, Miss Barlow. Would you care for some brandy?"

"Brandy? Not 'alf!" She grinned like a child offered a special treat. "I mean, I'd love some, sir."

She looked around the *salle*. "This is where you work? I thought Mr Sarratt said you live here."

"I have a small room at the back." He handed her a glass of brandy.

"Oh, I thought you was a gent. I mean a gentleman."

Le Méridien pulled a chair opposite her. "I'm afraid I have no debts to anyone. A most unfashionable condition among the gentry."

"Oh." She sipped the brandy and squinted at the glass. "Funny taste. Well, so much the better. I haven't done very well with gents."

"How is Mr Gudgeon?"

"Married, and looking ten years older." She grinned again. "Looks like he had a right scare. Perhaps it was Mrs Gudgeon. I do hope so."

"I hope the poor woman can give him a scare as well. I'd have tried to confound his marriage plans, but I had to offer him a way out to be sure he would see you released.

"He's a gent. He'll always get what he wants in the end. It's the rest of us who have to make do."

"Very true. But I trust he gave you a generous pension."

"I'll say. He sent for me and gave me two hundred guineas. I couldn't believe it. I mean, why'd he come over so generous all of a sudden?"

"Why indeed?"

"Perhaps it were that Mr Norbury. Heard he got shot trying to rob some gent. Typical bloody thief-taker." Her hands shot to her mouth. "Oh I'm sorry, I'm sorry."

Le Méridien inclined his head. "As you said, I am no gentleman."

"No, s'pose not. Anyways…" She tilted her head on one side and gave him a different sort of smile. "I came here to thank you for…well, for everything you done to keep me from the Newgate jig."

She stood up and slipped her shift down to her elbows. She was fashionably naked underneath. Le Méridien stood and pulled it back up.

Carrie's smile faded into open-mouthed confusion.

"If you please." Le Méridien could think of nothing better to say.

"Why not?"

"It is not why I did what I did."

"It weren't? But it's like I said in Newgate. You must want something, don't you? I asked a few people and they put me right, said you black fellows ain't devils but that you can't never get enough of white..."

"Nevertheless."

"Right. Well." Carrie drained the brandy in one swallow. "Reckon I prefer beer. You don't want no thanks then?"

"You have already thanked me."

"Right. I'm taking my sister to my Dad's cousins in Bristol. Going to buy a pub with Mr Gudgeon's money, so I don't think I'll see you again."

"Thank you for coming."

"You was right. You ain't no gent." Le Méridien thought she meant it as a compliment, but she was gone before he could be sure. He sighed and put the rest of the foils away.

Virulence

The street children came from nowhere, as much a part of Davao City as the aroma of chicken frying on sidewalk grills. They appeared between me and the Public Health Laboratory, pointing to their mouths and piping "Hey Joe, hey Joe". The security guard stepped forward to chase them off, but I threw a few coins after them.

"You shouldn't do that, sir," he said in his precise English. "Now they will wait for you to come back and annoy you again."

I wondered how he kept his white uniform looking freshly laundered all day in the glaring heat of the Philippines. I could feel sweat running down my face, and my shirt felt like a dishrag where it clung to my back.

I mumbled something about supposing so and retreated into the air-conditioned cool of the lab.

"Hi Tony," said Karla. "The director was in earlier. He's sure we're looking at dengue fever."

Her voice was a monotone, and I noticed that she didn't say what she thought herself.

I sighed. Somebody had used the word 'dengue' in front of a health minister who probably didn't know a virus from a bacterium, so the recent outbreak on Mindanao was henceforth caused by dengue. Dengue was untreatable, which saved anybody in the Public Health Department from answering awkward questions about who was going to pay for treating the victims. Karla's job was dependent on the good will of the director, whose job was dependent on the good will of the minister, so she wasn't going to be the first to say what no one wanted to hear. I couldn't blame her. She had two children and an unemployed husband to support.

I nodded at the paper strips wallowing in the antibody solution. "Well, we'll find out in twenty minutes. I'll just check my e-mail while we wait."

She brightened when I didn't pursue the subject.

"Is that the third or fourth time today?"

"I'm waiting for something important."

I felt a smile warming my lips when I saw Sahar's daily message in the inbox. As usual, the connection was agonisingly slow, so I sat back and remembered the evening before I left Glasgow for the Philippines. We'd shared a pleasant meal with pleasant conversation, but the smile was in memory of the goodbye hug that lingered on and on, and the promise in her rolling Glasgow vowels.

"Come back soon, Tone, and don't you forget me, now."

I won't, Sahar, I won't.

Hi Tone,

Guess what, you're hearing from Dr. Sahar at last! Just finished defending my thesis and I'm shaking too much to type properly but hey, it's over! Only funny question was about the wider significance of those rats that got parochial. Waffled my way through it, now I hear the call of the pub.

Know when you're coming back yet or have you fallen for some nubile Filipina? Don't you dare!

Sahar

Always that hint of promise. We'd been getting closer for months, but her studies had been her priority recently. Still, now that her thesis was out of the way…

My attention drifted back to the beginning of the message. What was the wider significance of a rat turning parochial in response to a disease? As far as I could remember, her rats had become parochial, or very aggressive towards unfamiliar individuals, when they were exposed to influenza. I'd been preoccupied with grant applications at the time and we'd never discussed it in depth.

"Time to develop the test, Tony," called Karla.

I forgot about parochial rats and went back to the paper strips in the lab. Karla laid them in the developing solution one by one. If black dots appeared, I would owe Karla lunch.

"It will take ten minutes or so," she said.

"If it happens."

"God will tell us."

She touched the crucifix around her neck. God kept us waiting.

"Here," she said eventually, "and here. You're buying lunch, Tony.

"That's two out of two hundred. Give it a few more minutes."

We waited. Dots appeared on another strip.

"I don't understand," she said. "Why only three?"

A weight descended on my shoulders.

"Because," I said, "while we've been spending the last damn month trying to track an outbreak of dengue fever, people have been going down with something completely different."

She frowned at the 'damn', but if I'd said what I really felt about the customs officer who'd impounded the test kit, she would have taken sanctuary in a convent.

Now the disease had spread half way across Mindanao and thanks to an over-zealous bureaucrat, we had only just got around to establishing that we didn't know what was causing it.

"But that's impossible," said Karla. "There must be something wrong with the test."

"We'll run the test again, but I bet you lunch for a week that we get the same result. Whatever this disease is, it's spreading much too fast for dengue. And we're not seeing any haemorrhaging, which we'd expect, but a lot of pneumonia which we wouldn't."

"What is it then?"

"I don't know," I said, hiding my suspicions. "But let's run the test again."

I won a week's lunches. Unfortunately, I was too busy to eat them.

~~~~~

A percussion of coughing accompanied the hum of the ceiling fans that struggled to stir the thick air of the hospital. I picked my way between rows of bleary eyes that demanded to know why I could hide behind a face-mask while they had to breathe the air that was killing them. They could demand all they liked, but I wasn't breathing this air until I knew what was in it and neither was Karla. Not that I blamed them for being bitter as they shivered and sweated in each other's stench.

"This is Mr. Juliani," said the tired nurse, and hurried away.

Karla called our thanks after her, and we knelt beside the man on the floor. Sample 5E3 glared at us through fever-bright eyes.

"Good morning, sir" I said. "I'm Tony Reade from the Glasgow University Department of Virology. I'm here to study what we thought was a new form of the Dengue fever virus."

The curve of Mr Juliani's mouth told me he didn't know what I was talking about and didn't care. I was more used to dealing with the parts of people that fitted in Sarstedt tubes than the people themselves. "They told me you're getting better."

Actually, nobody had told me anything. The hospital's administrators had long since lost track of their patients. It had taken us half an hour to find out where they'd put him. Sometimes it's easier to be cheerful than truthful.

Mr. Juliani held my gaze, but said nothing. A muscle pulsed in his jaw. I edged back, then caught myself. It was crazy to be afraid of an invalid.

Karla asked him if he spoke English. His eyes flicked to her crucifix and he nodded reluctantly.

"You're getting better?" asked Karla.

"With God's help," he said, sharing his belief with her as a charm against the stranger.

"Can you tell us something, Mr. Juliani?" I asked.

He refused to look at me. His lips moved in what might have been a curse or a prayer.

"May I ask you a question, Mr. Juliani?" said Karla.

He nodded.

"Have you had dengue fever before?"

"Yes, when I visited Manila four years ago."

"Thank you, Mr. Juliani. I hope that God will make you well soon."

"Thank you," he said. "Go with God."

"Thank you," I mumbled.

He didn't reply.

We picked our way over or around the prostrate bodies to the exit. I looked up at the tortured Messiah over the door. He's never far away in the Philippines.

"Lot of help you are." I said it under my breath so Karla wouldn't hear.

We took off our masks as soon as we were outside and I breathed in a deep draught of the humid air. After the hospital, it was almost bracing.

"So all of our positive blood tests were only positive because they've had dengue before," said Karla. "You were right."

Being right gave me no satisfaction. Something to do with Sahar was nagging at the back of my mind, but I couldn't pin it down.

"What was all that with Juliani?" I asked as we got into the department car. Karla's government salary wasn't enough for her own.

"What?"

"Did he have something against me?"

"You thought so?" said Karla. "I didn't notice."

"Perhaps I imagined it."

I took a deep breath to say what I didn't want to say, and what Karla wouldn't want to hear.

"Look Karla, I think we should test those samples for influenza."

I expected her to argue, because influenza wouldn't be any better for her career than it was for Mr. Juliani. She didn't answer until she stopped at a red light.

"Yeah, I guess we should."

I looked away and tried to tell myself I hadn't underestimated her too badly.

~~~~~~

The effort of keeping my eyes focused ground a dull knot of pain between them. I was gazing at, rather than reading, the reports on what had been dubbed 'Maranao influenza', since we had traced the outbreak to the Maranao communities in Cotabato. Karla had wept for them. "They have so little down there, and the government won't lift a finger to help them because they're Muslim."

Influenza, I thought. Sahar. Parochialism. There was a connection in there somewhere. Sahar's rats were parochial. She'd told me about them over a flavourless canteen lunch, back in Glasgow.

"I see Kilmarnock lost again," I'd said.

"Shut up and eat."

Sahar's grandparents may have been practicing Muslims, but she was the second generation born in Glasgow and her only religion was football.

"Aren't you used to it yet?"

"Shut up and eat."

"Okay then, I'll change the subject. How're the studies coming along?"

"Aye, some good results on the rats with influenza."

Our conversations in this canteen would make any eavesdropper stop eating for a week, but I just said, "tell all."

"Well, it seems crazy but when they get a dose of flu, they turn, well, parochial."

"Parochial?"

"They get very aggressive toward rats they haven't seen before, but not toward their own social group. So much that some of the randiest males I've got chase off strange females in heat if they don't know them. I've never seen the like of it before."

"Any idea why?"

"I think it's some sort of behavioural mechanism to keep them away from anyone carrying the disease. I mean, if there's a bug about, you want to keep strangers that might have it away from your wee 'uns."

"Isn't it a little late by the time you've already caught the virus?"

"No, you see it in individuals that have never shown clinical signs. It's the presence of the virus that does it, you don't have to get the disease. Though they're more likely to get parochial if they have the flu and recover. The more virulent the virus, the more parochial they get."

I sawed at something the canteen called chicken but looked like a cremated sparrow. "It sounds kind of like an immune response."

"How d'you mean?"

"You react to a virus - or any other bug - by producing antibodies and white blood cells to fight it, right?"

"Aye," Sahar nodded.

"And you produce them when you're exposed to the bug, whether or not it actually makes you ill."

"Oh *right*."

Sahar dropped her knife and fork and sat back to think. I stared at her unfocused eyes. She really was beautiful.

"You mean that the same immune response might actually be changing their behaviour?"

She was grinning with the joy of elegant explanation. I was grinning because she was sharing her joy with me.

"So you stay away from anyone who might give you the bug in case your antibodies aren't quite up to the job," she finished the story.

"A sort of behavioural immunity," I said.

"Scary thought, isn't it?"

I laughed. It was funny then. Now I wished I'd concentrated more on what Sahar was saying and less on Sahar herself.

A long sigh from Karla hauled me back into the present. I

realised that she'd just hung up the phone, and that she hadn't enjoyed the conversation. Her feet dragged as she walked back into the lab. Three weeks of bad news had taken its toll on both of us.

"What now?" I asked.

"The bad news is that they've been reporting outbreaks in Cebu and Palawan in the past week. They want us to confirm. The worse news is that the government won't even think about restricting travel, so we're going to have it everywhere in a few weeks."

"But it could kill thousands!" I stifled a blasphemy. "Don't they understand what we're dealing with?"

"They're politicians, Tony. If they pretend there isn't really a problem down here, they've got time to find someone else to blame before it gets to Manila. They'll manage to ignore it until then."

"But it'll be too late by then! It'll be all over the Philippines and probably the Asian mainland as well!"

I realised I was marching up and down, waving my arms around like the archetypal mad scientist. I sat down and reminded myself that Karla was putting her job on the line by even making these phone calls. The word 'pandemic' drifted through my mind, but I didn't want to say it. We'd both hear enough of it before long.

Karla sat down and looked at me closely.

"Are you okay, Tony?"

"Nothing a good night's sleep wouldn't cure."

"Just tell me where to find one," she said. "I'll get back on the phone. Perhaps I'll find someone with half a brain in the government."

"Good luck," I said without conviction.

I tried to concentrate on the reports, but I found myself staring out of the window at the empty street, which had been packed with vendor's stalls only last week. I knew the conclusion I'd draw from the reports before I even opened them: Maranao flu had swept through the whole of Mindanao. I felt too miserable to calculate the number of deaths. The reports would be out of date by now anyway.

Oh God why can't I be back in Glasgow? With Sahar?

Sahar. Parochialism.

Karla came back.

"Can't get through," she said. "Half the telephone operators are sick and the rest are at home because they don't want to catch it. I need coffee before I try again. You?"

I rubbed my temples and scribbled a note that the telephone system had joined the general collapse of Mindanao's infrastructure. The epidemiologists back in Glasgow would want to know that.

"Yes thanks. Karla, wasn't there a pandemic in nineteen eighteen?"

She stiffened at the taboo word.

"Yes, why?"

Because that meant that the rank and file of the SS, and Stalin's bluecaps, had been exposed to a virulent influenza as children.

"Thinking aloud," I said. "What about the others since then?"

"Fifty-seven and sixty-eight. They both hit China hardest."

"Fifty-seven? Just before the Cultural Revolution?"

"Well, that started in sixty-six."

So Mao's Red Guards had been exposed to a pandemic strain as well, then another one at just the right time to make sure that the savagery lasted its eight bloody years.

I was shivering. I moved out of the draft of the air-conditioning unit but I was just as cold. It was the same lack of sleep that was making me dream up connections between the villains of the last century and Sahar's rats.

"And now there's a whole generation that's never been exposed to a really nasty influenza?"

"I guess. Are you sure you're okay?"

Her brow wrinkled with concern. Perhaps she was right to be concerned. Perhaps this was what a nervous breakdown felt like. "I'm fine. Really."

"Well, here's your coffee. I'll try the phone again."

I thought back to the hospital, and Juliani's barely restrained hatred. What would he have done to me if he'd had the strength to stand? Did that look in his eyes belong under a blue-banded cap as he battered somebody's door down in the middle of the night?

My teeth rattled on the cup. Karla's voice from the next room was a long way away, echoing around my head, reverberating with my own thoughts.

~~~~~~~

Karla found me face down in a pool of coffee. I can't remember much about the next few weeks and I wish I'd forgotten the rest. Unlike most of the victims, I was insured. I got one of the last private hospital rooms in Mindanao, so I had a better chance than most when the pneumonia set in.

Eventually, I began to recognise the difference between night and day, and the looming white figures that stabbed needles into me were nurses instead of the demons of my fevered nightmares. I still shrank away from them, feigning sleep to avoid talking to them. I couldn't forget that the barbecue smell that overwhelmed their cheap air fresheners was their friends, their family, burning in the pyre outside the public wing of the hospital. I couldn't forget that they had to feed me and clean me like a newborn baby because my country was wealthier than theirs. I wanted to beg them for their forgiveness so much that I dreaded their presence.

One day I woke up to find Karla in the room. There were new crow's feet around her eyes and her hair fell in greasy strips. I must have looked worse, and it was as well that I was inured to my own smell. My sheets hadn't been washed since before the electricity had failed for the last time, and condemned the hospital to suffocate without ventilation or air conditioning.

"Hi, Tony," she said.

"Hi."

"Glad to see you're better."

"Am I?"

I twisted my head towards her, and noticed that she was wearing a black armband. Her family had been dying while money that she could only dream of had kept me alive to bemoan the heat and the smell. I felt she must despise me but she hid it well. I wanted to yell that it wasn't my fault, I came here to help so don't thank me by blaming me.

"Better than you were," she said. "I've been here a few times but you probably don't remember. Can you sit up?"

I pushed myself into a sitting position and drifted up off the bed while the room spun around me. I fell on my back and the room was still again.

"What's the latest news? I don't know anything since I passed out," I asked when I could.

"Not so good. It's reached the mainland, Tony. Singapore first, but it's already spread as far as Turkey. And the first outbreak in the States last week."

"Oh."

"Tony? Tony, are you okay?"

I was shaking, but not because of my illness. I found I was angry. The virus was marching across Asia, toward Britain. My Britain! What had these bloody Filipinos unleashed on us? On us? And all she can say is 'are you okay?' Damn her!

"I'm okay," I said, between clenched teeth.

Calm down. Nobody caused it and it's certainly not Karla's fault. Calm down. Must be the fever. And the guilt.

"I'm okay."

Karla opened her purse.

"I've got a message for you, from Glasgow. It came through the fax, just before the phone system went down. They must have thought the e-mail wasn't working when you didn't reply."

She handed me a sheet of fax paper. I noticed Sahar's signature, but instead of the inner smile I anticipated, all I felt was a void.

"Hi Tony," I read. "We've just heard about you. We're all really worried."

Poor you, having to sit safely in my country and worry.

The sarcasm passed through my mind so fast that it barely interrupted my reading.

"I assume you're still out of it," the message went on, "but I had to write, I'm frantic about you. I just heard my uncle and two cousins in Karachi died. We're all so scared it will happen here."

I stopped reading as a torrent of bile poured into the gap where my love for her had been. She had cousins in Karachi. She'd been born in Britain, but not to a British family. She was one of *them*. She was like the Cotabato Muslims that the outbreak had started with, and now she was in my country telling me how hard it was for her. I'd known her for years and I was so stupid I'd never even thought about what she was.

I made myself read on. I had to know the worst.

"I was so scared I'd lose you too. I'm going to give you the biggest hug of your life when I see you.

"Love, Sahar."

The biggest hug of my life. My skin crawled. And love? *Love*?

"Look Tony, can you travel?" Karla's voice snapped me back to the hospital. "There's a military plane taking British citizens with the virus home this afternoon. There's an embargo on commercial flights, so you may not get back for a while if you can't go now. Do you think you'll feel well enough?"

Home. Back to my own people. People I could trust. People who would need help to defend themselves against whatever *they* had brought down on us.

Can't let Karla see how much I want to go. Can't trust her.

"I could try."

~~~~~~~

Karla brought my belongings in the car. I shuddered at the thought of her packing my clothes; I'd wash them all twice before I wore them again.

I refused to let the nurses help me dress but I had to endure their support to get from my bed to the car. I'd thought the hospital was hot, but the sun beat its way through the haze of smoke and reduced me to a dead weight before I was ten paces from the door. I didn't see the street children until they were swarming around me like maggots at a corpse. I tried to kick away the tugging hands and dribbling noses, and above all the cacophony of "Hey Joe, hey Joe", but my feet were made of lead and I couldn't lift them off the ground.

I heard a man shouting, then a tattoo of explosions battered my ears. The children vanished and I looked around to see the hospital security guard pointing a smoking revolver into the air. His gritted teeth told me that it wouldn't be pointing that way next time.

"I'm sorry, Tony," said Karla as the nurses lowered me into the car. "There's a lot more of them than there were."

"Suffer the little children," I said vindictively.

Her eyes flashed as she crossed herself. I cursed myself for showing my real feelings. She took a deep breath, but her hand was shaking as it turned the key in the ignition.

"Suffer the little children," she said quietly.

I kept my mouth shut.

We rounded a corner and Karla slammed on the brake. A crowd of men was gathered around a row of shanties, shouting and throwing bricks and bottles. Two men dashed through a low door. They reappeared, dragging another man. One of the crowd ran forward and punched their captive in the face. As though at a signal, the rest surged at him. He disappeared behind a riot of kicking legs. Two hands holding a brick appeared above their heads and shot downward. The crowd roared.

A man ran into another shanty and a woman in a chador flew through the door and landed on her face. The crowd fell on her like rats at a feast. I heard her screams even over the baying mob.

"Only Muslims," said Karla as she backed out of the road. She sounded relieved.

I looked at her with disgust and thought that these people deserved all they got.

Scary thought, isn't it?

"What did you say, Karla?"

"I said it's okay, they're only Muslims."

Was this the same woman who had shed tears for Cotabato?

"Our people know it started with them," she said. "God sent the plague to *them* and they gave it to *us* because we let them live among us. We get angry when our family..."

She choked off a sob and concentrated on the road.

"Make the most of your time with your lady, Tony," she said eventually. "You may not have so long."

Rage flared behind my eyes at the thought of her reading the fax and I nearly barked at her when she called Sahar my 'lady', but the thought of Sahar lead to another thought and I knew what had happened to Karla.

She had been exposed to a virulent strain of influenza.

I found a part of my mind that sneered at my anger at a woman who had watched her country tear itself apart, who had watched her family die, then had fought her way past the revulsion she must feel for me to visit me in the hospital and drive me to the airport. I watched myself hating her for reading a fax and I shuddered because I knew what it took to drag someone out of their home and smash out their brains for their race or their religion or whatever it was that separated *them* from *us*.

Just like Sahar's rats. Sahar, I thought, and shuddered again as I imagined my hands around her throat and I heard my voice screaming, "This is for making me love you!"

I slammed a door in my mind and opened my eyes. Karla was calmly watching the road. I hadn't screamed aloud, then. I made myself look at Karla and see my friend, who had remembered me when her world was falling to pieces. I had to keep that door shut.

How could I do that when my feelings were part of an immune response? How could I keep myself from joining a mob like that any more than I could stop my bone marrow producing antibodies? Could I ever trust myself in the same room as Sahar? I realised I was huddled against the door, as far away from Karla as I could get. I wondered if I would find myself flying at her before the next five minutes had passed.

So why wasn't I afraid of Karla? She was having the same immune response as me, she must have the same aversion to me, but she was helping me when she could have abandoned me. I thought back to what I knew of the purges of Germany, China and the Soviet Union. I'd found out how millions had found it in themselves to kill millions, but when I looked at Karla, I also knew how so many had stood aside from the killing. Why Germans had hidden Jews in their cellars. Why Gulag guards had smuggled food to their prisoners. They had found the same door that Karla and I were struggling with. They had locked it and bolted it. If they could, so could I.

Davao airport was closed, but Karla drove straight through the open gates to the big jet. It looked like a gleaming silver and white arrow pointing my way out of the squalor of the last few weeks.

A burly man with a golden wing on his isolation suit helped me out of the car. My head spun as I stood up, and he had to almost carry me toward the plane. I was hazily aware of another suit waddling towards us, but I concentrated on placing one foot in front of another. Then the suit yelled, "Tone!"

We stopped. I stared stupidly at the dark-skinned woman behind the faceplate.

"I was so afraid you wouldn't make it," she said.

"Sahar? What are you doing here?"

"They asked someone from the department to come and collect some samples as soon as possible."

Talking very fast about something irrelevant was Sahar's way of hiding emotions she couldn't cope with.

"No one wanted to come because we'll have to go into isolation with you, so I volunteered because..."

Something slipped from behind the door to ask me how she dared to pity me while she hid from the place that had crippled me in that suit. Another part of me was revolted at myself.

She broke off and cried, "Oh Tony!"

She tore me away from the airman. The vision of my hands around her throat returned and I tried to shrink away, more because I was afraid of what I might find myself doing to her than because of the voice whispering that her touch was poisonous. I couldn't support myself and I fell forward on to her. I felt the firmness of her arms around me, and my face was aching with a wild grin. The murderer inside me was a petulant child that I could order back to its room and bolt the door.

I lifted my arms around Sahar's bulky suit and held on like a drowning man holds a life raft. I looked up and saw the airman's slack-jawed astonishment, and laughed aloud.

Then I looked around to the column of smoke rising over the roofs of Davao. I saw Karla watching Sahar and I from the world I was leaving behind. She wasn't about to escape from those burning shanties on a pair of silver wings, yet she'd begun to fight her murderer without even knowing what it was. All I'd thought about since I woke up was escape. Shame washed my idiotic grin from my face. I detached myself from Sahar and made myself walk back to Karla. I expected my legs to fold under me at every step, but it would be small enough punishment.

Karla watched me coming.

"Don't ask, Tony," she said. "Don't ask me to come with you because I can't. There's too much to be done here, for my people."

I stood on the concrete, feeling foolish. After all she'd done for me, and all I'd learned from her, she didn't want the only thing I had to offer in return.

"Go home, Tony," she said. "Get strong again. And when your people find out how to fight this thing, you make sure they remember us."

She held out her hand and I shook it. Could she really put so much faith in such a feeble clasp? But she'd done it, so she'd better not be disappointed if I'm ever going to look in a mirror again.

Sahar's arm slid around me.

"We have a lot of work to do", I said.

We shuffled toward the plane.

The Redeemed

"He showed us the way! By his agonies, he showed us the way to salvation! He taught us to turn from shallow comforts to earthly torment, and so to turn from eternal punishment!"

My father's blue eyes bulged. Spittle ran down his grey beard on to his goatskins. The people of the Sanctuary quivered, and not from the winter chill. They cried out to him, as they always did when the rage of the Lord was upon him.

"Help us, Redeemer!"

"Show us the way!"

"The way?" he bellowed. "The way, you poor sinners, is to abandon all hope of pleasure in this world! To throw yourself upon the ground before the Lord and to - to - to..."

I threw myself face down in the mud before his flock noticed him faltering. I looked for what he'd seen, but only saw a forest of legs. Then the forest fell as though to a scythe, to reveal a tall figure in a long, brown cloak whose back showed her contempt with every stride. Faces emerged to show their devotion by the filth that covered them, and with their devotion to my father came their hatred of my mother.

"See the poor, damned sinner," my father rallied. "See the degenerate! Come back, lost soul! Turn from the flames while you still can!"

She disdained even to turn her head as she faded into the drizzle. As he knew she would.

I hid my face in the mud so that no one would see that I was no longer listening to the Redeemer. My own anguish held me in a far stronger thrall.

My father taught us until we shivered in the mud, then he called me forward to receive his blessing first, mumbled in the language of the Lord that he alone could speak. I stood back and watched his smile grow every time one of his children bowed their heads and kissed his feet.

A man rushed into the back of the throng with a sack over his shoulder, and the Redeemer's blue eyes hardened dangerously. "Who disturbs a gathering of the Lord?"

The man pushed through the crowd to stand before my father, panting with exhaustion. For a moment, he seemed oblivious to whom he faced, then he laid the sack on the ground before him and threw himself beside it. A sob convulsed his shoulders. We backed away from him as though he had the plague. The Redeemer stepped off his stool and strode toward him. We stepped back, ending up in a ring around the Redeemer and the grovelling man. The Redeemer bent down and upended the sack.

I told myself that the thing that fell out of the sack wasn't the naked body of a dead boy, and that the brown crust that covered it wasn't dried blood from the cavity where his chest should be. Someone drew breath. The gasp whispered across the crowd and I knew I deceived myself.

A gaunt couple forced their way to the front and the woman gathered the dead boy into her arms. The man stood behind with his hands on her shoulders, his face blank.

"See the teeth marks in his neck," cried someone. "Wolves! Wolves!"

"Wolves don't do that," cried someone else. "It's a goblin!"

My father watched the shouting and wailing become more and more hysterical, then raised his arms. "You fools!"

Silence fell so suddenly that I might have gone deaf, if it hadn't been for the weeping of the boy's mother.

"What you see was not done by a wolf," said the Redeemer. "What wolf takes only the heart and liver and leaves the rest? Nor has it to do with a goblin. The goblin exist only in the minds of the unredeemed. You sin to even mention them!"

"Forgive me, Redeemer!" A man sank to his knees.

"No," cried my father. "What you see here is a punishment for evil in the minds of the people in this Sanctuary."

"What is it, Redeemer?"

"Tell us!"

"Very well," the Redeemer lowered his voice.

Nobody dared draw breath.

"Lycanthropy!" he thundered. "Men who become wolves by the power of the evil way. They take only the children. Those without sin."

His gaze touched mine, so I threw myself back down. I looked up to see the Redeemer surrounded by prone bodies. He took the dead child from the mother, who didn't resist but reached toward the boy with open hands. The Redeemer lifted the child over his head. "What you see is a test! Evil exists to test the Redeemed, and we will not fail the test, my children!"

"No Redeemer", cried somebody.

"Tell us what to do!"

"We must hunt down the lycanthrope! We must find it, whoever it may be!" He glared around us. Did the lycanthrope lie in this circle. The man lying beside me? The woman whose hand brushed my foot?

"The next person who sees any sign of the lycanthrope must touch nothing. Leave it, and come to my hut. We shall keep our axes and staffs ready for that day, because it will not be long in coming. Evil does not rest, and the lycanthrope will feed again."

~~~~~~

I felt the burning eyes of the Redeemer on me all the way up the wind-battered hillside, even though I knew he hadn't stirred from his hearth in the Sanctuary that these hills enclosed. I didn't know whether I was more afraid of what he would do if he saw me going to my mother's hut, or the lycanthrope that I saw in the jagged shapes of the rocks looming out of the drizzle. The hut was little more than a crevice with a wall of slate in front of it, and the meagre fire was only ever lit for my occasional visits. I draped my wet jerkin by it, and huddled close to it myself to dry the rest of my clothes.

I hadn't called Llinos 'mother' since I was a child, but the brush of her fingers warmed me with a mother's love as she handed me a flagon of hot water. The harsh taste washed my mouth but the warmth freed my mind from my body's discomfort. I remembered the question that I carried with me. I didn't know when the question first came to me, or how long I'd carried it in silence. Now a lycanthrope lurked the Sanctuary, and I couldn't face it without knowing the answer.

Llinos watched me with an intensity that etched itself into the lines of her face, as gnarled by the weather as the hillside she lived on. If she spoke, I would never find the courage to ask my question.

"Llinos," I said, "why do you hound my father? Why do you appear in the middle of his teachings just to walk away?"

Her mouth tightened. "Because I hate him."

I shifted uncomfortably.

"I'm sorry Gwyn, but it's the truth. He's false and he knows it."

I should cry 'blasphemy', but I just stared at the fire, knowing that my question had led me to the choice I dreaded.

"Look Gwyn, I know he tells you it's a sin to doubt him, but every word he says is a lie. Why else does he falter when I look him in the eye?"

"You'll only turn people against you."

I choked off the last syllable. I had betrayed the Redeemer by speaking anything but condemnation. Yet how could I condemn the only person who had ever smiled for me? She smiled now. "As if there's anyone in the Sanctuary that doesn't already hate me. He's seen to that."

"There's me."

She took my hand.

"Yes there's you. And I'm afraid for you. I'm afraid of what he'll make of you. I wish you'd leave him."

"Where would I go?"

She watched me for a moment, as if afraid to say what was in her mind. "Leave the Sanctuary. We'll both go. There's more beyond these hills than that man's Lord."

Thinking about leaving the Sanctuary was like thinking about jumping off a cliff to see if I could fly.

Llinos must have seen my fear, because she went on, "I've lived beyond these crags. It's not paradise, but you don't have to make your own tortures out there."

"Why did you come back?"

She sighed. "Because I found I'd carried my torture with me. I remembered the son I left behind."

I remembered the day I was watching the sheep, and recognised the figure coming toward me as the mother that I thought I would never see again. My throat was so tight that I could hardly speak. "I can't go now."

"Gwyn, you always say that. There's always a reason why you can't go now. There always will be. Please, let's just leave."

Her voice almost set my head nodding in agreement. I had to stop her pleading.

"I mean it. There's real trouble,"

So I told her about the boy, and the lycanthrope in the Sanctuary. She passed her hands over her face and I thought I heard her mutter something like, "had to happen."

Then she looked straight at me, and showed me a determination that I hadn't thought possible. "You must do two things, Gwyn. Watch, and think about what you see."

I didn't understand. Not then.

~~~~~

The only fear that dogged me on the way back was of the Redeemer. The lycanthrope took only those without sin, and I was the guiltiest man in the Sanctuary because I had betrayed the Redeemer. I couldn't hide the sin from his Lord, and I wouldn't have been surprised to find my father waiting for me with his whole flock, to throw me to the flames that he so often spoke of.

The village was quiet, so he must have decided to face me with only his family watching. I stopped outside the door of our hut and fought back the urge to run as my fingers clenched into fists. There was no point in hiding from a man who heard the voice of the Lord. I could at least show him that I still knew my duty.

The Redeemer sat at the head of his table. His face could have been made of the scree that littered the Sanctuary. His head didn't move, but I saw his eyes following his disciple, Angharad, whose breath came in stifled gasps as she bent over the cooking pot. The Redeemer had been instructing her with his staff. Tears glinted in the firelight as her gaze held mine for a moment, and I thought I saw a plea in it, but perhaps it was just forbidden pity.

Gruffydd, my half-brother, tried to make himself inconspicuous in a corner, not succeeding because he was the largest man in the Sanctuary. He rocked back and forth in silence, as he always did after one of the Redeemer's rages. Nothing else had upset him since we found his mother's body beneath the crag from which she fell to her death. He'd hardly spoken in the three years since then, however often the Redeemer praised his many virtues.

I crouched against the wall in an equally futile attempt to avoid the Redeemer's gaze, but the grey head turned toward me and those blue eyes stabbed through my pretence to the guilt beneath.

"You see it, do you not?" He barked.

"See what, father?" I hated the quaver in my voice.

"What Angharad, the poor blind sinner, does not. Gruffydd sees it."

Gruffydd nodded in devotion rather than understanding. I was about to agree blindly when the Redeemer deigned to explain himself.

"Evil must be crushed whenever it threatens the Redeemed. Otherwise it leads honest souls into temptation, and to the flames."

"I see, father," I lied, though nothing I could say would save me.

"So when we encounter evil, we must do whatever - *whatever* - we must to destroy it."

"Of course, father."

"You see, my child," he said to Angharad, "as Gwyn sees. It was not pleasant for me to chastise you, but it was necessary to purge your evil. Neither is our next task pleasant, but so great an evil requires a great resolution. Gruffydd and Gwyn do not shrink from the task. Neither must you. Do you see?"

"Yes, Redeemer," she sniffed. "I see."

I loved him because he was talking about the lycanthrope, and not about me.

~~~~~

Rain turned to sleet, making our faces ache with cold, but it was the fear of what we would find that made me drag my feet and wish I could think of a reason to return to the village. Five paces in front of the rest of us, the Redeemer's straight back told me no excuse would allow anyone to turn from the trail of the lycanthrope's second victim.

The Redeemer stopped and we crowded around him. The trail ended at an outcrop of rock. The man who had rushed into our hut stepped forward, and his hand hovered over the rock as though afraid to touch it. "The body was here Redeemer, I swear it."

My father nodded slowly. "Surround the rock. Let us see what else has been here."

We were obeying even before he finished speaking, and found two more sets of tracks crushed into the frozen grass, one coming to the rock and one going away. They were the prints of a man, not a wolf, but the size of them brought back all my fear of the lycanthrope. The Redeemer set off along the trail without a word, but not even his stride matched the lycanthrope's. I tried to catch my companions' eyes to see if they shared my fear, but they were already pursuing the Redeemer. I hurried after them as though I hadn't betrayed our faith.

The sky darkened into night as we followed the trail. I began to share the excitement of the hunt. The lycanthrope couldn't be far from such a recent trail, and couldn't be strong enough to overcome all of us.

It was impossible to get truly lost in the Sanctuary because the village was always downward, but I didn't know exactly where we were. When a shape in the darkness solidified into Llinos's hut, the shock of it nailed my feet to the ground. A cry forced its way up my throat "Llinos!"

"Silence!" bellowed my father.

Llinos couldn't have heard us. Our loudest shouts wouldn't carry more than a dozen paces in the scouring wind.

"But Llinos!"

He struck a piercing agony into my cheek, and strode onward while I reeled away. The trail ended almost immediately under a rough heap of stones. We pulled them aside and found the frozen body of a child, the empty chest gaping like his mouth.

Some of our companions turned away and hid their faces in their hands. My father passed his hand over the boy's face and muttered in the Lord's language. He gathered the body in his arms and strode toward the hut. I followed him, and tried to prepare myself for the sight of some demonic creature feeding on my mother.

Instead, I could just make out a bundle on the floor, where Llinos stirred when the sleet followed the Redeemer through her door. I half crouched in the doorway behind him.

"You!" his voice filled the hut. "You of the dark ways!"

She rolled toward us with a groan, and froze when she saw him holding the dead child.

"You were my disciple." He spoke with the same harsh tone. "You had every hope of finding the true way. Yet you turned from me, and now you seek the *other* way."

I didn't understand what he meant. I just stood there, bent double and slack jawed. A growl from behind told me that the rest of the flock understood better than me.

Llinos threw back the blankets and pushed herself into a sitting position.

"Liar! You threw me out when you tired of me, and wanted my son for yourself..."

"Seize her!" He shouted her down as she struggled to stand on stiff legs. "Seize her before she changes form!"

My companions charged through the door, shoving me off my feet. They hurled her down beside me. She didn't cry out. She would show no weakness before the Redeemer. Or me.

"Bring her to the village," commanded the Redeemer. "For trial."

They half dragged and half carried Llinos into the tearing wind. Nobody looked at me.

~~~~~

The gale blew itself out that night, and the next morning brought one of the few still, clear days of that winter, as though the Redeemer's Lord had arranged it especially for the trial. The Redeemer stood on his preaching stool while two of his flock dragged Llinos behind us, so we had to turn our backs on the Redeemer to see her. She was bound hand and foot, and stood blinking in the frigid sunlight. She looked even frailer than she had in her hut.

She faced the Redeemer over our heads. I could smell the tension that surrounded me. Heads turned back and forth as Llinos and the Redeemer glared at each other, but nobody dared shuffle a foot.

"We of the Redeemed accuse you of practicing the dark way of lycanthropy." My father's voice rolled over us like a thunderclap. "This we know by the body of your victim found in your hut. We know that you turned from the true path some years ago, so this comes as little surprise. Nonetheless, you may speak for yourself."

Llinos's old spirit flickered across her face.

"You know that you didn't find the child in my hut but outside..."

"Note, my children," he barked, "that the atrocity is not denied."

"The child was outside because I'd never seen it before."

"The memory of what is done in the wolf form may not be kept by the human form."

"You invent this because you fear me!"

"It is wise to fear evil."

"You're afraid that because I don't fear you I'll show the lies you tell for what they are."

A murmur swept through the flock, like the gust of wind that precedes a storm. The Redeemer said nothing.

"If these people discover you lie, they'll stop fearing you. Then you'll be powerless!"

"See, my children, how the dark one desires power over mine."

Llinos's answer was lost in the yells of the Redeemed.

"Silence, children," shouted the Redeemer. "We will hear her. We will be just."

"I have one thing to say," she said. "This man rules you by fear, as he once ruled me. You'll never be free of him as long as . . ."

The children's' roar burst over her. She looked at her feet. She looked up and her eyes met mine. For a moment, our gaze held. My shoulders clenched at the feel of the Redeemer's eyes burning into my back. I looked away. He wasn't looking at me. When I looked back at my mother, she was looking down again.

"You try our patience," said the Redeemer. "can you prove your innocence or not?"

She looked straight at him. His head moved back a tiny distance, as close he'd ever come to flinching.

"Can you?"

She held his eyes with hers, not speaking.

"Very well. Burn her."

The Redeemer's flock roared.

I had looked away.

~~~~~

All I remember after that is staring at my goatskin boots rising and falling, carrying me away from that crowd. They probably cheered and capered and flames probably crackled, but the next thing I remember is the mud beneath my boots turning to stone. I looked up to see that they'd taken me back to the Redeemer's hut, where Angharad crouched by the ashes in the fireplace.

I had no real feelings for Angharad, although I still remembered her rescue by my father as a time of relief. Her predecessor had brought shame on our house by her sinful thoughts, and even more shame because she kept them so carefully hidden. The Redeemer himself only knew of them because the Lord sent her a daughter rather than a son, and he flew into his rages several times in a day. She and her daughter disappeared half a year ago, as though swallowed by the morning mist. Perhaps it was the relative calm that Angharad had brought with her that prompted me to sit by her, or perhaps I just preferred her company to my own.

"Is it done?" she asked.

I fancied that I could smell smoke, but perhaps it was just the ashes.

"It's being done now."

"It is for the good." Her voice was as empty of expression as a child learning to say a new word without understanding it.

Fury coursed through my limbs and sent me leaping to my feet.

"The good! What do you know of the good? How can Llinos be a lycanthrope?"

Angharad looked up at me with no change of expression.

"He taught her for four years, he knows…"

I stopped with my mouth still open as I realised what I was saying. If the Redeemer knew that Llinos was innocent, he was as false as she told me he was. The Redeemer couldn't be false, but Llinos couldn't be a lycanthrope. I sat down and stared at the stones of the fireplace. They were miniatures of the rocky faces of the hills that spawned them. If I concentrated on finding the best route to climb them, I was safe from the thoughts that made me want to bash my head against them. There was a perfect groove running up the side of one stone. I followed it with my eye and I could almost feel the wind in my hair as I looked down at the Sanctuary from the top of it, then looked the other way and saw…but my imagination failed me as I tried to think about what might lie beyond.

Angharad's voice dragged me back into the hut. "He knows."

"He knows what?"

"He knows that she isn't a lycanthrope. He knows that evil must be crushed."

"I don't understand."

I did. I just wished I didn't.

"Only an evil woman could turn from his path. He had to crush her to protect the Redeemed from evil."

"But the dead children!"

Angharad flinched as though I'd struck her and stared back at the fire, which named the children's killer as clearly as if she'd shouted it at the top of her voice. I remembered the long stride that led us to Llinos's hut, and thought of the one man in the Redeemer's flock who could have made those prints. The thought of Gruffydd had reminded Angharad why she sat by the ashes while the damp froze on the stones. Not because she doubted the Redeemer, but because she had seen how her own life would end.

We sat, side by side on different hilltops, until the crash of the door snapped my head up to see the Redeemer standing in it. His expression was as stern as ever, but Gruffydd's grin celebrated for both of them. The Redeemer paused to glance at me, then strode to his seat at the table.

"Angharad! Why is the fire not lit?"

His voice cracked off the walls but he must have been as delighted as Gruffydd because he hadn't added a threat. Angharad didn't wait for one. She ran outside to the woodpile. The Redeemer's gaze descended on me again. A shepherd guessing which way an unruly sheep will turn.

"The smell of cooking meat has made me hungry." There was no mirth in his eyes. Only judgment.

I scooped up a handful of ashes. They blackened my fingers as they fell through them.

"Gruffydd," I said. "May I ask you a question?"

The Redeemer's eyes widened in surprise, but he answered for Gruffydd.

"Pursuit of wisdom is a noble purpose."

I looked straight at Gruffydd. He looked back with the innocence of a lamb watching an oncoming wolf.

I dug my nails into my palm to keep my voice level. "Did you kill your mother?"

Angharad dropped the wood. For a moment that felt like forever, the only sound was the scraping of branches on stone as she scrabbled on the floor. Gruffydd sank into his corner and wrapped his arms around his legs. A tremendous wail broke the calm.

The Redeemer's mouth opened and a thrill swept through me as I realised that for the first time I'd ever seen, he didn't know what to say. I had my answer.

I stood up and found myself looking down at the Redeemer. He looked half as big as when he sent Angharad out for the wood.

"Did Gruffydd kill those children so you could kill Llinos?" I asked

My father's face hardened into the granite features of the Redeemer. He slammed his fists on the table and stood up. The day before, he would have sent me cowering against the wall before he even spoke. Now I wondered why I'd never noticed that I'd grown taller than him.

"My son shall speak no evil under this roof!"

He paused to draw breath.

"What evil have I spoken?" I asked. "I merely asked questions."

"Evil questions! Evil drawn from your thrall of the evil woman whom I have delivered you from! Now prostrate yourself before your Lord and give thanks!"

His finger pointed between my eyes. One thought took hold of me and overwhelmed even the lash of fear that his Lord struck into my stomach.

"You delivered me?"

His hand returned to his side, and he was again the shepherd mastering his errant flock. "You are confused. Perhaps I ask you to understand too much. The return to the path is not easy for those who have strayed."

He stepped toward me and reached out an open hand. "The true path is the path of suffering. I know that, more than anyone."

I'd never thought the Redeemer any more capable of suffering than the crags that he ruled. Could he ever feel as I did now?

"Was this why you beat Angharad when she didn't see? The evil you were talking about was my love for Llinos, and today you made me join you in crushing her?"

His hand closed on my forearm. "You will see the path. Trust me now, and in time, you *will* see."

Another wail from Gruffydd overwhelmed him, and we faced each other. The Redeemer released my arm and I backed away, past Angharad and through the door. The slate faces of the hills regarded me from beneath a greyer sky that announced the end of our brief respite from the winter.

A hand fell on my shoulder from behind. "You will see."

I didn't move.

"You have already found the path by joining me in ridding the flock of the evil that afflicted it. Now you must purge yourself, as Gruffydd is doing now. Return to me when you have done so."

The hand patted me with the same force that I would have used to guide a sheep to the pen, firm enough to guide yet light enough not to frighten. The door closed behind me, leaving me alone with the knowledge that my father had destroyed my mother to bind me to him.

I found myself looking at the hillsides, playing the same game that I had with the stones of the fireplace. I wondered if it even occurred to the Redeemer that I might look at the tops of those crags and see a destination rather than a barrier. Another wail burst from inside the hut.

One of my feet was in front of the other before I knew I'd put it there. The fear of the Redeemer's Lord settled in the pit of my stomach while my mind struggled with the idea of there being anything beyond the walls around the Sanctuary, but the crags were getting closer and the ground was getting steeper as my feet made my choice for me.

I heard a rush of someone else's feet and looked around. I was as surprised to see that the village was already some way below me as I was to see Angharad stumble to a halt among the first snowflakes of the year. I turned back up the slope, but now Angharad's feet matched the rhythm of my own.

Soon I couldn't hear my own feet for the roaring of the gale that hurled the snow down the hillside with all the spite of the Lord I was abandoning. The village vanished into the cloud. Dusk drained the colour from the hillside, so I could only see for ten paces, then five. An occasional glimpse of a hand or the touch of something brushing past my leg told me that Angharad was still with me, but I could only think about the next patch of rock where I would place my own hands and feet. I didn't feel the triumph I anticipated when the ground began to level off because if the going became easier for us, it became easier for the wind as well.

I had to lean forward and push myself into that wind with every step, but I welcomed it. While it flayed my face, I knew that I was walking away from the Sanctuary, and that it would hide our trail from the Redeemer's flock. Yet walking was getting steadily harder. My soaked goatskins weighed me down and chafed my limbs raw. It blew right through me, carrying my strength away with the snow that it stripped off the ground to leave the treacherous ice beneath. The ground rose and fell beneath my feet, and I was further from the village than I had ever been, but I didn't know how much further I had to go or what I went to.

My feet flew from under me. The ground smashed the breath from my body. I tried to push myself back to my feet, but my arms refused to lift me. I felt as though my waterlogged clothes held me down, but the weight I couldn't lift wasn't my clothes but myself. I sank back down and Angharad tugged at my shoulder. I tried to tell her I was too tired to ever move again, but my mouth wouldn't produce recognisable words. I laid my head on my arms. It was comfortable here. I'd fallen into a slight dip, so the wind blew over the top of my back. My clothes didn't thrash my skin like icy whips if I didn't move. I closed my eyes.

Pain returned in a new place, my scalp. My head was dragged up by the hair. I found myself looking at Angharad, who was so stupid she didn't even understand I wanted her to leave me alone. Her mouth formed words that were swept away before they reached me. She pointed into the wind that was killing us by ice, as Llinos died by fire. There was no sense in battling it any longer, but Angharad wouldn't let go of my hair, so I got up. When I'd done that, I could think of nothing better to do than follow her further from the Sanctuary.

The ground sloped downward now. I nearly fell again several times. Angharad did fall, but she just got up and kept going. I was vaguely aware of the blackness around me fading to grey. The wind dropped as we moved into the shelter of higher ground ahead of us.

The cloud fell back before us, and we looked down from the side of a long valley in the twilight. Angharad looked back at me and pointed at a collection of humps that weren't rocks as I first thought, but huts. A flare of orange in one of them showed where an unredeemed villager greeted the morning with a fire.

I had never seen Angharad smile before.

Rainfire by Night

The women's voices filled the room as they sang praises to the naked goddess. Rainfire sang with them and despised them. She hated hearing her voice swallowed by voices that never spoke a kind word to her. She watched the women nearest the fire sway with their eyes closed and vowed to die before she gave up her own thoughts like that. She had already found that she preferred having warriors wanting to beat her than to marry her. Her fifteen winters made her the oldest unmarried woman in Doune.

Yet she had been waiting for those closed eyes because they showed her that the women were absorbed by their songs and not paying attention to each other. She edged back to the wall, where the shadows of the singing women became one with each other. No one was guarding the doorway because not even Rainfire had ever dared leave the keep while the men were in council. *But I am Rainfire and I do as I please.* She could barely sit because of a beating from a warrior who saw her watching him with his new bride two days ago, but her father's short temper over the last few days told her something would happen in this council that she wanted to see.

The voices faded as she ran up the stone staircase to the top of the keep. She heard men shouting and knew that whatever her father had anticipated was happening, but she could not see it because the only window looked along the crenulated wall that surrounded the courtyard, rather than into the courtyard itself. The single light was from the fire in the courtyard, so no one down there could see her slip through the window and huddle against the wall of the keep. A cold wind bit through her shift, but Rainfire was ready to endure far worse to see her father,

Keenblade, in council.

Keenblade sat on a steel throne that was slightly inclined toward that of the Director. Their backs were taut, as though they were about to leap to their feet. The fifty-two warriors of Doune sat on the ground on the other side of the fire from them, looking equally tense.

The Director was yelling, "You're a fool, Keenblade! You'll get us all killed and still give Doune to the enemy!"

"A fool?" Keenblade spoke quietly, but Rainfire heard more menace than if he had bellowed.

"Yes, a fool! Only a senseless fool would think we can stay here and live!"

Rainfire held her breath for the moment of silence that followed. She released it when her father stood up. She might not have witnessed a council before, but she knew there was only one reason for a man to stand.

"Then I speak for all the *fools* among us." Keenblade shrugged off his cloak.

The Director hesitated, then stood. "It's taken you long enough to find the courage."

Rainfire heard the waver in the sneer he tried to put into his voice. Keenblade had earned his warrior name several times over.

The Director's sword scraped from his scabbard and sliced at Keenblade. Keenblade's sword swung into a parry. A clash of metal echoed around the castle walls. Rainfire clapped her hand over her mouth to stop herself screaming at her father to stop before he was killed.

The heavy, two-handed swords glinted in the firelight as they hacked at each other. The blades were crudely battered out of the detritus of Before, and Rainfire knew that handling them was more a matter of strength than skill, but a well-placed blow would smash bone.

The Director stepped back to avoid a blow rather than parrying it, shifted a hand in front of his hilt and lunged while Keenblade was still on the backswing. Rainfire screamed aloud, her voice lost in a great sigh from the watching warriors. Keenblade stepped to one side, parried with impossible speed and smashed the Director's fingers against his own hilt. The Director wailed, his manhood deserting him. His point dropped to the ground. Keenblade pulled his sword back and drove its point so deeply into the Director's throat that it nearly severed his head.

After the blow, Keenblade thrust his sword into the ground in front of him, angled so its edge faced the two Peoples, as did the insignia of a three pointed star enclosed in a circle that was welded to the back of the guard. His gaze raked the now silent warriors. "I, Keenblade of the People of the Mercedes, claim the Directorship of the Two Peoples of Doune by right of combat. Does anyone else claim the same right?"

Rainfire smirked at the thought of any of the warriors trying their luck while Keenblade's face was still streaked with the Director's blood.

Keenblade stepped back from the sword and smiled. All of the Peoples could see the smile, but Rainfire pretended it was for her and her alone, his way of celebrating his promotion with her. He half turned and waved at the picture presiding over the council. "Then our lady goddess has smiled on me. I hope I'll be worthy of her honour."

The naked goddess of Before smiled back. Rainfire did not know how long the Peoples had been bestowing their praises on the image, but anyone could see she was a goddess. She lay on a soft bed of Before, her glowing skin bared to the cold air that kept the Peoples wrapped in leather and wool. Her impossibly large breasts and parted legs suggested the reward a successful warrior could expect from the women he would claim.

Keenblade knelt before the goddess and kissed the scratched

plastic that covered her. He stood again and thrust the Director's sword into the ground next to his own, so that the rhombus insignia on the hilt faced the Peoples.

He sat behind his own sword. "Before we continue the Council," he said, "we must find a new Manager for the People of the Renault. I suggest Nightcloud, son of Steelfist." A murmur of surprise hummed through the Peoples, and Rainfire had to think for a moment to remember that Steelfist was the late Director's warrior name. The real surprise was the name of Nightcloud, who had yet to grow his full beard and whose warrior name referred to the dark night when he killed his only Stirling warrior to earn it. Yet nobody dared speak against the blood on the naked blade, so Nightcloud made his way to the front of the Peoples with faltering steps.

Keenblade embraced Nightcloud, leaving his tunic smeared with the blood of his father. Both men sat down on the metal thrones of the Board Members.

Keenblade spoke again. "Before we honour Steelfist, we must resolve the matter that he and I quarrelled over. Had he not insisted on leaving this castle, he would still be alive. I say that we have our herds and our homes here and cannot leave because we've lost a few skirmishes to the enemy of Stirling, whom we outnumber. What do you say, Nightcloud of the Renault?"

Nightcloud looked around as though he thought the question was directed at someone else. Rainfire smiled at her father's wisdom. He had pushed the boy into the only position from which a Director could be challenged. *My father*, she thought, *the greatest man in Doune*.

Nightcloud found his voice at last, and spoke as though he were reciting one of his childhood lessons. "We can't fight them, because their arrows kill us before we're close enough to use our swords."

Keenblade regarded him in silence. Nightcloud glanced at his father's body. "Director."

Keenblade nodded. "It's true that our swords and slings can't match their bows on *open ground*, in *daylight*." He swept his gaze across the Peoples to remind them that he had fought their enemies when Nightcloud was waving his wooden sword and bragging to his mother of the great warrior he would be. Did her father's eyes flick toward Rainfire, or did she just wish they had? "There are other ways of fighting them, ways that will make us masters of the valley rather than refugees from it, as Steelfist wished."

Rainfire's imagination filled with ways by which she herself could fight the enemy. She would serve her father as he had never been served before, if only he would let her. She sighed. What use would a warrior have for a girl? The moment ended. "Now we must honour Steelfist. Call his wives to prepare him for the feast. Let my own wives prepare the fires to cook it. Steelfist has led us long and wisely, and let us pray to the goddess that he may pass some of his strength and wisdom to us, along with his flesh."

Someone ran to call the Director's wives. They huddled together at the door of the keep when they saw their husband's corpse.

"Don't be afraid," said Keenblade. "Come to him."

Steelfist's senior wife broke away from the huddle and strode across the courtyard. The four co-wives held each other as they followed. The senior wife took Steelfist's broadsword and crouched by his head. She closed his eyes and kissed his lips. Her hand lingered on his cheek.

"Don't delay," barked Keenblade. "His spirit needs release."

The senior wife stood up and thrust the broadsword into Steelfist's heart. It was only then that Rainfire realised that the decision to stay in Doune had been taken without any discussion at all.

~~~~~

Rainfire dipped her horsehair brush in blue dye and touched it to the Mercedes she was painting on the wall. A sound startled her and she spun around to see Keenblade standing behind her. "Father! How long have you been there?"

"A while. I like to watch you paint."

Rainfire felt her cheeks flush. She wanted to tell him how she treasured such words, but she could not find words of her own.

Keenblade stepped forward. "I see these are the warriors of the Peoples with swords, and these are the enemy of Stirling lying dead with their bows. But what are these beasts that our warriors are riding?"

Rainfire flushed again when she saw the streak of blue she had made when he startled her. "They're Mercedes, father. The legends say they used to travel faster than any horse. When you said you could find a way to rule the valley, I thought. . . ." Her voice died as she realised how foolish she sounded. The Mercedes were just hulks of metal like the Renaults and Volkswagens and all the others. Whatever the legends said they once had been, they were only good for feeding the smiths' forges now.

Keenblade did not look as though he thought she was foolish. He nodded. "Good idea. But where are their wheels?"

"Wheels father? I've never seen one with wheels."

"That's because we've used them all for our wagons, but they had wheels once. The question is what animal they used to pull them so fast. We'd have to ask the goddess about that."

"So you can't use them against Stirling?"

"Not unless the goddess answers, which she never does.

But she's given us an easier way to beat them. Not a way for a warrior, but a way for a woman. A young woman anyway." He looked straight at Rainfire.

Rainfire could not hide her amazement. He was actually asking her for something. "A woman like me?"

"Exactly like you, Rainfire."

Rainfire backed up to a doorless cupboard. The day after her father had become the greatest man in Doune, he had come to compliment her painting and ask for her help. His smile really was only for her, because they were alone. Was she worthy of what he wanted of her? The thought slapped the smile from her face. "What do you want me to do, father?"

He became serious. "You know where Stirling's power comes from?"

"From their warriors' bows?"

"Their fighting power comes from their bows, yes. But we don't know how they learned to make them. We've tried it and we can't make anything throw an arrow more than ten paces. Their arrows are deadly at a hundred. So what should we be asking?"

Rainfire quailed. If she didn't know the answer, she was inadequate for the task he was going to give her. She clawed for a reply. "How do they know how to make the bows?"

She hated herself for showing her foolishness with such a question, but Keenblade nodded. "Exactly. And now we know how."

"We do?"

"We got it out of one of their women. She seemed anxious to help us when we offered her a quick death." His smile invited Rainfire to share the joke.

She smiled back. "I hope you didn't give it to her."

"We did. Eventually."

Rainfire savoured the joy of sharing laughter with her father.

"But she had a lot to tell us first," said Keenblade. "They have some very strange customs in Stirling, but the most important thing is the Cedrom."

Rainfire tried the word. "Cedrom?"

"Their chief advisor keeps it in the castle. It's the source of their knowledge."

"What is it?"

"It's not much in itself. A disc small enough for any child to throw. It's what it contains that's important. The knowledge of Before."

Rainfire drew breath slowly. So she was not only to beat the enemy of Stirling; she was to secure the knowledge of Before for her father. "How can I get it for you?"

"By joining the enemy and taking advantage of their strange customs."

Rainfire's fingers tightened on the top of the cupboard.

She felt as though he had asked her to cut off a limb. "I must leave you, father?"

"Just for a day. If you can't do it by then, you won't be able to do it at all. But when you come back with the Cedrom, all of the Peoples will fall at your feet."

Rainfire found herself reliving a memory of two winters ago. One of Keenblade's wives had tired of her disobedience and accused her of stealing food from her children, and Rainfire's own mother was dead, so there was nobody to speak for her. She had not heard a kind word for a year, but the worst of it was that Keenblade himself had pretended she ceased to exist. Even a day among the enemy would be worse than that year. At least she had been able to see Keenblade then. She looked up to see him cut off a few strands of his brown hair with his sword.

"Show me your ankle," he said.

Rainfire knelt and rolled the hide of her left boot down. Keenblade knelt in front of her to tie the hair around her ankle. The touch of his fingers sent a thrill singing up her leg. Keenblade drew back. "Now I'll be with you all the time, and they won't see me under your boot."

"Yes, father." Something in Keenblade's eyes told her she hadn't sounded as brave as she hoped.

"Here's something we can ask the goddess about. Let's see how many ravens she's sent to bless our plans."

Keenblade took Rainfire's hand and led her through the rotting doorframe. A raven was sitting on the house opposite them and cocked its head to watch them. Rainfire looked around her. "I can only see one raven." Keenblade pointed upward. "There are several up there, watching us. See?"

Rainfire squinted into the grey sky. "I can't see them. Your eyes are so much sharper than mine."

Keenblade squeezed her hand. "Now that we have the goddess's blessing, let's talk of what we must do with it."

~~~~~

The movement of Keenblade's back against Rainfire's arm stilled as he reined in his horse.

"From here we walk," he said.

Rainfire, who was riding sidesaddle, slid straight off.

Nightcloud climbed off his own horse and tethered it beside Keenblade's. He turned to the warriors who would guard them. "You look after them properly unless you want to lose a few teeth."

Rainfire sighed loudly, and he glared. He had only been a Manager for a couple of days and he was already so full of his own importance that Rainfire wondered where he put his food. Taunting him was a privilege of the Director's daughter, and one she had learned to enjoy.

Nightcloud's bombast left him as he followed Rainfire and Keenblade up a streambed that led into the pine forest above the trail. "I don't know why we had to meet them in here."

"That's because you've never seen what their longbows can do on open ground," said Keenblade.

Rainfire cast a mocking smile over her shoulder, and Nightcloud's crestfallen expression made her laugh aloud. He had not recovered before Rainfire saw gaps between the branches ahead, where the stream flowed out of a clearing. Keenblade turned and placed a hand on Rainfire's arm. "Are you ready, daughter?"

Fear crushed Rainfire's heart. She didn't know whether she was more afraid of failure or of success. She made herself smile. "Yes, Father."

She unlaced her cape, and it fell open to reveal the thin white shirt beneath. It was a relic of Before, made of a single strip of cloth that swept down from her shoulders to cover her torso while hiding very little of it. The shirt showed its age in places, but nothing that the Peoples' weavers could make came close to matching it. Rainfire felt like a demigoddess of Before, who could show her skin to a friendly sun whenever she wished. Keenblade had told her she could not fail with the power of such a relic to aid her, and she knew he was right when she saw Nightcloud's gaze. She didn't know what it was about breasts that so obsessed men, but she had seen the effect that they had. Usually without being noticed herself.

"Nightcloud." Keenblade frowned at him. "Come in front with me. Remember, keep your mouth shut and don't look surprised at anything."

He saw no need to give Rainfire any last minute advice.

Her step was confident as she followed the men into the clearing. She saw two enemies stand to greet Keenblade and Nightcloud. She had never been this close to the enemy before and was surprised at how ordinary they looked. One had a full head of grey hair, and his gait was awkward. Rainfire wondered how he defended his position, as he did not look like a dangerous swordsman. The other was only a few years older than Nightcloud, with broad shoulders and a red beard. He was the Director whom Keenblade had described, and she had to suppress a smile when she saw him already looking at her. She met his gaze and lifted her chin as she knelt in the coarse bracken.

Keenblade rapped out his introduction. "I am Keenblade, Director of Doune and Manager of the People of the Mercedes. This is Nightcloud, Deputy Director and Manager of the People of the Renault. May the sun shine on our meeting."

The red-bearded enemy was still looking at Rainfire. Rainfire allowed a smile to creep across her lips. Some instinct warned her not to smile too openly. The greybeard coughed, and the redbeard's gaze snapped to Keenblade. Neither of the enemy spared Nightcloud a second glance.

"I am Rannoch, Chief Elect of Stirling. May the sun shine on you," said the redbeard.

"I am Gealag, Advisor to the Chief Elect. May the sun shine on you," said the greybeard.

They sounded as portentous as men always did, but Rainfire

knew she had already stolen the redbeard's attention. She wondered why he called himself a Chief Elect, whatever that was.

The four men sat down on logs that had been arranged to face each other. Rainfire saw Gealag the greybeard staring at her pointedly. She could not resist smiling back.

Keenblade spoke first. "We're here to discuss the depredations that you have carried out against us. You've stolen our sheep and cattle, leaving our larders bare, and killed several of the People in the process."

Rannoch the redbeard's eyes stole back to Rainfire. She met them and held them while her father spoke on. Fingers of cold found their way through her shirt and stroked her breasts, but she ignored them and allowed the cape to slip back and reveal her shoulders.

Keenblade's voice fell silent. Rainfire had to struggle to contain her smile of triumph when she realised Rannoch had not heard a word Keenblade said.

Rannoch jerked his attention back to Keenblade, and he didn't look like the warrior who had driven her people behind the walls of Doune, but a youth caught picking his nose during sword practice. "Yes I hear your words, Keenblade, but we—I— must consider that, er. . . ."

Gealag leaned forward and spoke in a deep voice that belied his feeble body. "What the Chief Elect wishes to say is that we attacked your people to recover goods that you stole from us. If your warriors were killed, they shouldn't have tried to stop us taking what is ours."

Rainfire watched Rannoch edge away from Gealag. His hands knotted in his lap. He looked like Nightcloud when she laughed at him, and she suddenly felt she knew Rannoch. He was no longer the enemy Director, but another warrior boy who could never match her father.

Gealag was still speaking. "You've made it very clear by your constant theft of our cattle and sheep that we won't be safe until you're out of our way. We're quite willing to annihilate you in battle if you wish. If not, we'll allow you to move south of the River Forth, where you may do as you please."

Rainfire kept the slight smile on her lips while she seethed. She was angered less by the outrageous demand than by Gealag's tone. Steelfist had died for speaking to her father like that.

Keenblade spoke to Rannoch as though he didn't take Gealag seriously. "Of course we can't leave our homes to cross the Forth. Doune Castle has belonged to us since Before and we can't abandon it now. However, we would be happy to confine ourselves to, say, a quarter of the distance between Doune and Stirling."

Gealag snorted, and Rainfire twitched her shoulders to throw the cape even further back. She saw Rannoch's eyes flick toward her, and Gealag looked at her as well. Rainfire delighted to see not only hatred in his eyes, but a touch of fear as he recognised what she was doing to Rannoch. She had seen how obviously men wore their feelings many times, but never realised how easy those feelings were to control.

Rannoch was struggling for words again. "I, well, perhaps we should consider…"

Gealag leaned forward. "What the Chief Elect means is that your suggestion is ridiculous. You dare not graze your animals this side of Doune as it is, so why should we accept a guarantee of what we already have? Your choice is simple. Leave Doune or we'll throw you out."

Rannoch's hands clenched in fury at his advisor rather than his enemy. He looked at her again. She smiled back and allowed her tongue to slide between her lips.

Keenblade spoke as though Gealag's threats meant nothing to him. "Of course we won't ask you to accept a guarantee without a pledge. That's why I brought my daughter, Rainfire." He waved a hand at her. "I offer her to you as a wife. So that you'll know we're sincere."

Gealag and Rannoch both looked at her and Rainfire saw the desire in the way that Rannoch's whole body shifted in her direction. Gealag must have seen it too, because what she saw in his eyes was near to panic. He started to speak, but Rannoch cut him off. "Your offer is acceptable, and I accept your — your pledge."

Gealag ran a hand across his face, which had lost all of its keen intelligence and just looked old. He swayed as he stood up. Rannoch's eyes never left Rainfire for more than a moment at a time. Keenblade turned and held his hand to her. She stood up. Her joy at her success vanished as she realised what it meant. She would have to leave with the man whose eyes probed where his hands would surely follow, and the man who would kill her if she gave him the chance. She found she could ignore the cold no more and pulled her cape around her. Keenblade guided her hand into Rannoch's, and she shuddered at the calluses on his fingers from drawing his longbow.

Her father had asked it of her, so she let Rannoch lead her away from him. She would not look back. *She would not look back.* But when she did, Keenblade had already been swallowed by the pines.

~~~~~~

Rainfire laid her head against Rannoch's shoulder and watched Stirling Castle loom over his chariot. It was huge, several times larger than Doune, and built on a high cliff that no man could climb. She could not imagine how even Keenblade could hope to attack it. Except with her help. She smiled to herself and nestled closer to Rannoch, who took it for affection and put an arm around her without letting go of the reins. Rainfire thought about what to say to make Rannoch even more devoted to her. "How many wives do you already have, sir?"

Rannoch pulled away so he could look at her, and his gaping mouth made Rainfire wonder what she had said wrong. He threw back his head and laughed. "You don't know much about us do you? In Stirling, we only take one wife."

"But what do you do when she gets old?"

"It's simple. We love her. As I love you."

In Doune, only women pledged a lifetime with the word 'love'. Rainfire was astonished to hear the enemy Director talking like a woman.

Rannoch took a hand off the reins and placed it on hers.

"And when we love someone, we like to hear our name on their tongue. I'm called Rannoch, not Sir."

Rainfire's world lurched with the chariot. She had spent her life giving her love to her father, and neither asked nor received more than an occasional kind word or touch in return. Now the enemy was offering more than she would ever get from her father or anyone else in Doune.

Rannoch smiled at her bewildered look. "I know it's a bit different to what your people do, but believe me, it saves a lot of blood. While your men were fighting over your women, we were working on these." He patted his unstrung bow. "It took years to work out how to make them and use them, and we'd have given up before we started if we'd had to watch to see who was slipping back to someone else's women. Like you do in Doune."

Rainfire remembered her father telling her about the Peoples' efforts to make bows. Was Rannoch saying their failure was due to the Peoples' marriage system? And if a man of Stirling had to behave like a woman in a marriage, how did a woman behave? She tried asking a question as directly as a man would. "How do you know so much about us?"

She half-closed her eyes for the blow she would have received in Doune, but Rannoch just nodded. "You're not the first woman to prefer us to your own people."

Rainfire remembered what her father had said about the enemy having strange customs. She fell silent as she absorbed how truly strange they were.

Rannoch's chariot led Gealag's around the castle's hill, then up a steep road through the broken down houses of Before that had once been the town of Stirling. The horses strained at the climb until the road levelled out. The grey stone of the castle itself blocked their way, pierced by the open drawbridge beneath the gatehouse towers. If the drawbridge was closed, the walls would be as unassailable as a father's decision. She shuddered at the idea of her father leading the Peoples against those walls. She must not fail.

Rannoch stood and lifted his bow over his head as they crossed the drawbridge. "Prepare a feast, sons and daughters of Stirling! Rannoch Longbow has found a wife!"

Rainfire looked up and saw a towering warrior. Rannoch had shed all resemblance to the petulant youth who stammered his way through the meeting. The black bow reminded her of why she was here. Cheering people swarmed in the gateway and leaned over the battlements. Rainfire remembered when some of those happy young men had sent a shower of arrows over the walls of Doune Castle, picked off the warriors who rode to meet them and galloped away. The memory made her want something solid and friendly to hold onto, and Rannoch at least offered that.

She wrapped her arms round his waist as the enemy jostled around him to slap his back and shake his hand. Rannoch took Rainfire's hand and helped her down. He led her to stand beside Gealag, who was sitting in his chariot and scowling. "Our valued advisor disapproves," declaimed Rannoch. He dropped his voice and spoke seriously. "Tell us what's wrong, wise Gealag."

Gealag looked startled. "This is hardly the place."

Rannoch laid a hand on Gealag's arm. "You've been my friend and advisor since I was a child, and I want you to be happy today. Please tell me your thoughts."

Gealag sighed. "As you insist. Keenblade sent this girl to distract you, and he succeeded. He got you to agree to far less than we planned to demand and left us no stronger than we were yesterday. It doesn't put me in the mood for celebration."

The enemy surrounding them looked less happy, and angry looks sent Rainfire shrinking closer to Rannoch. His arm slipped around her, but his smile did not slip. "You're probably right. I was certainly distracted, but what of that? I've found my bride, so I don't complain. As for allowing them to keep a quarter of the land between here and Doune," he held up his free hand to still the muttering. "If they won't keep that bargain, they wouldn't have stopped attacking us from across the river. The difference is that now we know where they are, and we don't have to cross the river to counterattack. I'm sorry, Gealag, I know you want peace, but I want them where they are if we're going to have to finish them off."

Gealag's face softened a little. "Maybe you're right. You're a better battlechief than any other I've known."

Rainfire felt cold again. She had made a mistake to compare Rannoch to Nightcloud. The look that Gealag shot at her as he climbed off his chariot did nothing to make her feel better.

Rannoch raised his voice again. "Now we must show my bride that the feasts of Stirling are as unsurpassed as our archery!"

A cheer answered him and the enemy dispersed, laughing and talking. Rannoch turned to Rainfire. His breath warmed her forehead. She didn't want to look at his face, but his finger nudged her chin upward and she didn't dare resist. She tried to control his smiling blue eyes as she had at the meeting in the bracken, but she could not even control her own feelings. These eyes belonged to the man who could destroy Keenblade, and to a man who had already given her more than Keenblade ever would. Confusion blocked her throat and stung her eyes. She was horrified to find herself assailed by weakness now that she was where her father intended her to be. Rannoch pressed his lips to her forehead. She found she could fight the weakness that those eyes brought when she could not see them. She dropped her gaze so that when he pulled back, she saw nothing but her feet.

"I'm sorry," he said. "I couldn't help myself."

He seemed to be waiting for something, so she took one of his hands in both of hers. He squeezed gently. "Come on, let me show you Stirling Castle."

He kept hold of her hand while he led her over the towers and battlements, and she looked for anything that might be useful to Keenblade. It was not difficult as long as she avoided looking at Rannoch's face, though she could not be as resentful as she wanted to be when she compared the large rooms that the warriors of Stirling enjoyed with the damp dormitories of Doune.

She noted the ease with which the enemy could watch their herds half way to Doune, or send their chariots to sweep down on any marauders. Yet she noticed that although ground immediately beyond the drawbridge was open, the remains of the town sprawled for thousands of paces beyond it. There were hiding places for hundreds of warriors in there, and Rainfire saw why the drawbridge was only lowered when it was necessary. She hid a smile at the thought of how seriously men took themselves when it was so easy to think like a warrior.

"But I haven't shown you our best," said Rannoch.

He led her inside the castle to a door guarded by two warriors with short swords strapped to their belts. Both men embraced Rannoch. "We heard the news," said one of them.

"Just our luck to be on Cedrom duty at the great moment."

The word 'Cedrom' cleared the clouds from Rainfire's head. She noted the heavy wooden door, with its lack of bolts.

"Don't worry, you'll be off in time for the feast," Rannoch said to the guard. "Just a pity for whoever's stuck here."

Two guards outside this door tonight, thought Rainfire.

Rannoch took a large key from a pouch on his belt and opened the door. "Our smiths spent ages making the parts for a proper lock," he said.

Rainfire studied the lock as Rannoch lifted a burning candle from the wall in the corridor. The Peoples' smiths had given up on making working locks.

Candlelight flickered on stone walls and over something on a table in the middle of the room. Rainfire caught her breath, then saw it was an ordinary metal box. Rannoch put the candle in a holder on the wall of the Cedrom room and undid a clasp on the box, opening it. He reached in, and Rainfire gasped. Blades of red and green and blue chased each other around a silver disc Rannoch's held up. He turned it over, showing the other side coated in indecipherable runes. Rannoch held it out to her. She moistened her lips and took it between the tips of her finger and thumb.

The smooth texture of the disc set her whole body trembling. Here was the reason for leaving her father and coming to Stirling. If only she could run, and keep running until the gate of Doune closed behind her, and never have to fight the dangerous thoughts that chipped at her resolve. She would never get past the door, but she wanted to try so much that her knees nearly folded with the effort of keeping herself upright.

"I can see you've heard of our Cedrom," said Rannoch.

Rainfire ordered herself to think and act as Keenblade's daughter. "Is it true that this is the wisdom of Before?"

Rannoch sighed. "We think so, but we don't know for sure."

Rainfire turned it over to watch the dance of the colours.

"It came to us a long time ago," said Rannoch, "in my grandfather's time. There were still a few who could speak the runes then, and they said these runes say the word 'Britannica.' I don't know what that means, but they said it's some sort of store of knowledge."

"How does it tell you the knowledge?"

"It doesn't, and we don't know how to make it. Perhaps it's a key, but we don't know where to find the lock it goes into. Perhaps it needs a key of its own, to go through the hole in the middle, but we don't know how to make one."

"So you have the knowledge of Before, but you don't know how to get at it?" Rainfire didn't know how she kept her disappointment out of her voice.

"No, and I'm not sure that's such a bad thing. For all we know, the knowledge of Before may not be any help to us now. It didn't do the people of Before much good. We should be thinking about what to do with the future, not what was done with the past." He took the Cedrom and returned it to its box. "We didn't need it to make our longbows, and we should be thinking of what else *we* can do instead of what it might do. I'm sorry to say this, my love, but your people's problem is that they worship Before to avoid thinking about now. If I wouldn't lose my head, I'd throw that box into the River Forth before we make the same mistake." He snorted with laughter. "Sorry, my tongue runs away with me in here. Let's go before the feast starts without us."

He took her hand and led her out of the room. Rainfire felt she had left something behind when he locked the door.

~~~~~

She was losing a battle with her own weakness. Every mouthful of sharp wine made his hand on her waist more pleasurable. Rainfire even enjoyed being whirled around the courtyard in a dance that made her feel foolish until she found herself laughing. In Doune only the men drank and danced. Keenblade had warned her about their strange customs, but she had expected to endure them rather than enjoy them.

Rainfire tried to concentrate on the voice in her mind telling her that with half of Stirling's warriors unable to stand and the rest soon to join them, the enemy would never be so weak. She tried to see Keenblade and his warriors making their way through the cover of the ruined town, but it was so easy to lay her head on Rannoch's shoulder and pretend that all was as he thought it was. A faint glow rose over the battlements and a few threads of moonlight forced their way through the ever present cloud. Time to act. She didn't want to act. She wanted to stay here, marooned on this island of warmth and calm. She closed her eyes.

Rannoch's voice was muffled by her hair. "Are you tired? Shall we go to my chamber?"

Rainfire's stomach tightened. She silently shouted that she didn't want to go anywhere ever again. She found herself nodding and allowing herself to be taken by the hand. Cheers and laughter washed over her, and she felt she was watching from outside herself, curious to see whether Rannoch or Keenblade would prove the stronger.

She watched herself standing beside Rannoch's bed as he bolted the door, and watched while his mouth engulfed hers. He was breathing fast. "I've waited all my life for this." Rainfire watched her own surprise at his uncertain eyes and shaking hands. Had this man become a Director without ever having had a woman? The marriage system of Stirling must be more strongly observed than she had imagined.

She giggled at her own blank expression at his nakedness. She had seen an enemy, a warrior and a husband in him today, but naked and panting, he looked as absurd as any of the young warriors of Doune fumbling with their first woman.

She was naked now, and his chest hair tickled her as he laid her down on the bed and climbed on top of her. Gusts of breath blew across her face, and his weight pressed on her own breathing. His leg brushed the bracelet of hair on her ankle, and she was not watching anymore because he grated into her and hauled her back into her half-stifled body. His weight crushed her and stopped her from crying out as he rocked back and forth. She felt her nails dig into the hard mass of his shoulder, and she tried to match her breathing to the rhythm so she could get some air into her lungs. The grunting crescendoed into a groan and the weight rolled aside. She pressed her legs together.

A hand closed around hers and a voice breathed, "I love you."

"I love you." She was lying by any meaning of the word.

She turned her head to see the stone walls and ceiling that enclosed her. She thought of herself surrounded by layer upon layer of stone until she came to the outer ramparts and the closed drawbridge. Then she saw her father and his warriors hidden among the ruins. She was Keenblade's daughter. She was Rainfire.

She waited until she heard snores from the enemy beside her. She swung her legs off the bed. She winced at the soreness between them, but pulled on her shirt, skirt and cape. She found the key in Rannoch's belt and pulled an arrow from the leather bag beside his bow. The rough feel of the shaft made her stand up straight and look down at Rannoch. She could ignore her soreness when she thought how helpless he was before her. She held the arrow with her thumb along the shaft, the way Keenblade had shown her how to hold a dagger, and looked down the point to Rannoch's open mouth. She imagined thrusting it home, putting an end to her father's enemy forever.

She imagined the grate of steel on bone, and the blue eyes that would fly open for one last look at her. Perhaps it was not time to kill Rannoch. She would not be able to move freely through the castle if she were soaked in blood too soon. And he might scream. She was still thinking of reasons when she tucked the arrow under her cape and closed the door behind her. She pulled the hood up to hide her face. She didn't want anyone to recognise her and wonder why she was roaming the castle.

She jogged through the candlelit corridors, but at first she could not find the way to the Cedrom room. She imagined the moon taking its light back below the horizon while she scampered through the stone maze. She stepped out of a flight of stairs to find herself ten paces from the Cedrom guards, sitting on the floor with their backs against the wall. She nearly ducked back into the staircase, but one of them was already looking up. She angled her body toward the hand holding the arrow, so her face was in shadow and she looked as though she were clutching a wound. "Help me! Help me!"

A young guard started toward her. She found her eyes focusing on the wispy beard that lightly covered his chin. "There was a man! A warrior! I found him with a dead man, and he's right behind me!"

The beard turned as the guard looked back to his companion, who nodded. Rainfire heard a blade leaving a scabbard, and the warrior with the lightly covered chin was gone. She wished she had learned how easy it was to control men years ago. She staggered toward the older guard, seeing alert eyes darting around him beneath grey-streaked hair. He may as well be blind drunk if he can look straight at his enemy without seeing her, she thought. She sank to one knee with a groan. The guard leant over her, mouth open in concern. The part of the throat that Keenblade had told her about was straight over the arrowhead. All she had to do was flick back the cape, jam the arrow upward and back away from the warm blood splashing her face.

She stood up and savoured a power she had never imagined. Power to make a man who had defeated the best warriors of the Peoples drum his heels on the floor and spray the wall with blood. Power to light fires of impotent rage in his eyes when she showed him the key. Power to smear the Cedrom itself with bloody fingertips and slide it under her cape.

She knelt beside the dying man and sent a scream echoing through the castle. She made sure her face was smeared with enough blood that she wouldn't be recognised unless anyone looked closely and screamed again, summoning the lightly covered chin back, hunting for an enemy to run his sword through. "He was here," she sobbed. "He's got the Cedrom!"

Now was the time for the man to ask a question, if he would only stop gaping at the open door and ask it. Wasn't there any way of willing him to use his brain? "Where did he go?" he asked at last.

Rainfire stared at him as though the thought had never occurred to her, then scrambled to her feet and ran back up the stairs. "This way!"

The lightly covered chin panted after her, but could not get past her until they were standing in the empty corridor above. Her hood fell back, but she could taste the blood that disguised her face. The chin showed no sign of recognition.

"Did you hear that?" asked Rainfire.

"What?"

Rainfire was already running up another flight of stairs and hoping hoping hoping that she was where she thought she was. She shouted with relief when she emerged on to the battlements.

"What?" The chin was still on the stairs.

"There he is! Stop him!"

She pointed at the tower at the end of the wall.

"Who's there?" A guard on the wall.

"Where is he?" The chin.

"He's gone! Over the wall!" Rainfire led the chin along the wall. "Here! He went over here!"

The chin leaned over the wall. "Can't see anyone. But then I could disappear in this light too." He turned to the guard running along the wall. "Alarm! Call the Chief Elect! The Cedrom's been stolen!"

Rainfire felt a surge of elation. The chin was standing next to Keenblade's daughter, yet he had convinced himself that he had seen a non-existent thief because it had not occurred to him that a girl could have killed his companion. He crouched by one of the battlements. "Nothing here. He must have doubled his rope around it. Then he could take it with him and we'd never know how he got out."

Rainfire put a hand over her face to hide her smile. She had been ready with that explanation, but the chin was telling her lie to himself.

The chin seemed to come back to himself. "We'd better get to the courtyard. We'll have to get after him before he gets too far."

He grabbed her arm and pulled her down the stairs.

Rainfire cursed to herself. She had hoped to slip away and leave the enemy to confuse themselves, but there was no slipping out of that grip. She used her free hand to pull her hood up. Men were running around the courtyard like ants whose nest Rainfire had poked with a stick. Here was a man hopping up and down as he fastened a boot while his wife tried to buckle on his sword. There was a man shaking a comrade who was still unconscious from the feast. Was this the enemy her father was so afraid of?

Rannoch forced his way through the crowd and seized her hands. Rainfire's stomach tightened. She had still hoped she could avoid being recognised until she could disappear.

"Rainfire, my love, you're covered in blood! Are you hurt?"

Rainfire faced the power behind those eyes. She would need everything she had learned today to beat it. She allowed her jaw to tremble. "Hurt? No, I. . . ." She broke off with a sniff and fell into his arms.

She heard his voice echo through his chest as he spoke to the chin. "What happened?"

The chin hung in astonishment as the young warrior realised who Rainfire was, but he pulled himself together at Rannoch's question. "Somebody chased her through the castle, Chief Elect. Lucky for her she ran into me and Iolair guarding the Cedrom. I went after him, but he got round me, and I found Iolair with an arrow in his throat and the Cedrom gone."

Rainfire decided she could not have picked a better man.

"The Cedrom? Then what?" Rainfire felt Rannoch's grip tighten on her arm.

"We chased him up to the battlements of the west wall, and he got over the side. Must have had a rope. That was when I called the alarm."

"You said Iolair was killed by an arrow?" Rainfire recognised Gealag's deep voice, and sounded as though he had not been drinking. "Was he one of our own?"

"I didn't get a good look at him," said the chin. "She—the Chief Elect's wife might have done."

Rainfire clung to Rannoch even harder now that the moment when she would have to speak bore down on her. She would not fail. She was Rainfire.

"Rainfire?" Rannoch's hand felt slimy in her bloodsoaked hair. She allowed him to tip her head back.

"What did you see?" Rainfire turned to meet Gealag's glare. "What exactly?"

Gealag's hand hovered over his sword, and she knew he would never believe her. She had to make the enemy act before Gealag could make them think.

She swallowed and remembered Keenblade's voice. "Don't answer them directly if you have to lie. Don't try to make up a story they can trip you up on. Be frightened and confused, and let them work it out for themselves."

"I don't know!" she wailed. Gealag rolled his eyes.

"There was a man! He ran after me! He killed him in front of me! He took the Cedrom!"

Gealag's voice was drowned by a surge of questions.

"Someone's taken the Cedrom?"

"Iolair's dead?"

"My platoon's ready to get after him, Chief Elect!"

"The Cedrom?"

Rannoch lifted his arm from Rainfire, and she could feel him waving for silence. Warriors hunched forward for answers. Their eyes saw straight through her to Rannoch. Only Gealag realised they were doing her bidding, but they would work it out quickly enough if Rannoch made them wait long enough to think. She gripped Rannoch's cloak and drew a sobbing breath. Every muscle urged him to take action before it was too late, and she knew the warriors around them would see it. She forced words out of her mouth, praying to the naked goddess that they would infect the enemy with their urgency. *"He killed Iolair and took the Cedrom!"*

"Let's get after him," shouted someone.

"We'll lose the moon if we don't get out there now!"

"He'll be half way to Kildeen!"

Rainfire felt Rannoch's fists crumple her cape and she felt Rannoch being torn between Gealag's sense and his warriors' will, and still he did not see the power of Rainfire's presence as she clung to him and sobbed. Rannoch stepped away from her, shedding his indecision like an ill-fitting cloak. He organised his men into groups and gave each a part of Stirling to search. Rainfire saw why Keenblade feared Rannoch even as he led his men where she had sent him.

The malice in Gealag's eyes burned into her, but it was the malice of a man caught in a flood, unable to stem the tide that would wash him away. Rannoch ordered him to take command of the castle guard and his eyes dropped away from her. Rainfire slipped into the keep and found a window where she could watch the drawbridge. She saw the enemy find their discipline as warriors gathered in their platoons.

The moon would give enough light for swords, but not bows, Keenblade had told her. "And we know who the best swordsmen are, don't we, daughter?"

Her fingers tightened on the sill when the drawbridge clanked down. Enemy warriors jogged across it and disappeared. Rainfire's breathing sang in her ears.

Keenblade murdered the silence with yells and clashes of metal. Any moment now, the picked men he had told her about would sprint round the main battle to seize the gatehouse, and she would be Keenblade's daughter again. She waited for the joy the thought should bring. Tried to imagine the pointless orders she would use to torment the women who had spat on her, but it all seemed as drab as the winter sky compared to this moment. The last moment of the enemy whom she had sent to their deaths.

Movement on the drawbridge. Silhouettes tumbled into the gatehouse. Arrows blurred down from the battlements. Smashing swords flooded into the courtyard. Rainfire felt like the hidden girl at the Doune council again, watching the men make the decisions. The last Stirling warrior in the courtyard fell. She heard screams inside the castle. Larger objects than arrows were tumbling from above her. Clothes. Furniture. A child. A man crashed into the room. Bared teeth and bared sword glinted in candlelight. Rainfire shrank away even as she recognised Fleetfoot of the Mercedes. One hand grabbed her hair and the hand holding the sword tore her cape aside.

"Fleetfoot!" she screamed as he ripped the shirt of Before to her waist. "Fleetfoot! It's me! Rainfire!"

He looked at her face, seeing her clearly for the first time, and hauled her outside. She wrapped her cape around herself.

Keenblade was directing a small group of warriors in the gatehouse, checking that the warriors coming in were all of the Peoples. Seeing him again was like a cloudburst that washed away a painting before it dried.

"Director," called Fleetfoot, "I have your daughter."

Keenblade looked round, and back again at a cheer from his men. Nightcloud ran into the gatehouse, dangling Rannoch's head by the hair. "Their Director's head!"

Rainfire looked at the head and knew she had crushed her weakness when she felt nothing. She looked at Nightcloud more closely. The challenge in the way he brandished the head at Keenblade showed that someone else had learned to see the world differently today.

Keenblade clapped Nightcloud's shoulder, a benevolent Director praising good service. "A fine trophy, Nightcloud. We'll sing your courage tonight, as we'll sing the cunning of my daughter who gave us Stirling castle."

"Your daughter!" Nightcloud held up Rannoch's head beside his own. "Your daughter who you gave to be defiled by this half-man!"

Rainfire stepped forward and took the Cedrom out of her cape. It captured every eye in the gatehouse, glinting in the light of a fire that had started in the keep. Rainfire gave it to Keenblade without taking her gaze off Nightcloud. Nightcloud's head jerked toward her as though he never wanted to look at anything else again. Rannoch's head sank to the level of Nightcloud's waist.

Rainfire thought proudly that none of these strutting warriors could have got their hands on the Cedrom, but then she felt a stab of dismay at the thought of telling Keenblade that the enemy had not known how to take the knowledge that the Cedrom carried. With every eye on the Cedrom, she raised her gaze to Keenblade's face as he took it. Keenblade was not looking at the Cedrom but at Nightcloud, and she saw a shadow of a smile through Keenblade's beard. Her breath sighed through her lips. Keenblade's thoughts were as obvious as any other man's. He cared no more for the knowledge of Before than Rannoch had. He had only cared that the enemy's reverence for the Cedrom could be used to force them into a foolish decision, just as he only cared about her reverence for him because it made her the only woman he could send into Stirling who would not be seduced by the enemy's kindness. She had seen and learned so much that she felt as though she had been blind and deaf a day earlier.

"Don't be so quick to judge, Nightcloud," said Keenblade. "A warrior must use all his weapons, don't you agree?"

Rainfire painted a look of adoration on her face and revelled in her new freedom of thought. *You want me to be the weapon that will cripple Nightcloud as I did Rannoch, don't you, Father? You think that with me in his bed, he'll be under your control and won't challenge you until you want him to. Well, you go on thinking that, Father, because I'll be in his bed before long. But you'll trust me as much as he will. And we know what happens to men who trust me. Don't we, Father?*

Author's notes

Cassandra's Cargo

Most of my stories stem from more than one idea, and I can trace this one back to two distinct inspirations. The first was an article in *New Scientist* about 'Waterloo teeth'. In the early 19th century, the English enthusiasm for sugar combined with poor dental hygiene to generate rampant tooth decay in the upper and middle classes. Replacements of various materials were tried, including ivory and hippo bone, but by far the best option was another set of human teeth. The preferred sources were executed criminals and soldiers killed in action, preferably those young enough not to have worn out their teeth and poor enough that they couldn't afford sugar. The bloodbath of the Battle of Waterloo in 1815 flooded the European market in replacement teeth. Wealthy recipients would pay a premium for a set of genuine Waterloo teeth, and the confidence that they weren't coming from someone who died of a disease they might inherit.

The history of Waterloo teeth was so macabre it begged to be used in a story, but I had no more than an idea until I had a lengthy discussion with a writer friend about how and how not to make use of dreams in fiction. At the time, I was beginning to get interested in the history of the transatlantic slave trade and the Royal Navy's anti-slavery squadron that operated off West Africa in the early 19th Century. It all came together to produce *Cassandra's Cargo*.

Something must have worked because I felt, and still feel, that *Cassandra's Cargo* hit a level above the stories I'd written before it.

For anyone taken with the idea of Waterloo teeth, there are several sets in the Hunterian Museum in London.

The Endocrine Tyranny

I carried the central idea for this one around for years before I worked out how to make it work. The idea of reducing emotions to increase intellect is hardly a new one and I imagined all sorts of stories that felt flat before I even began to write them. From the beginning, I'd imagined a treatment that would make the exchange a permanent one. It was only when it occurred to me to adjust the idea that I was able to develop a sensible story. If the process could be reversed, I had a conflict to build a story around.

For the conflict to work, I needed a character who would fight against the return of emotion and a character who would be strongly motivated to force its return. Mary and Gareth grew into those roles. Somewhere in the process, I found I liked the idea of a character who would do something as appalling as kidnapping his ex-girlfriend and handcuffing her to a bed, but do it for very good reasons. That was when I knew I had to start filling sheets of paper.

Coldwater Cottage

This was perhaps one of my simpler stories, at least in conception. I was keen to explore the way I used descriptions of sensation in stories, and the best way to do that seemed to be to place a character in a situation where sensation is seriously limited. At least, that made sense to me at the time. I'm fairly sure I was sober.

Enclosing my protagonist in neoprene and dropping him into the English Channel seemed to be as good a way as any, so then I needed something for him to do down there. I'm not sure quite how I got the idea of a haunted house story, but once I did, the idea of placing a structure as familiar as a house in an environment as unfamiliar as the bottom of the sea was irresistible.

Perchance to Dream

This is the only straightforward humour story I've ever written, or even conceived. It was driven less by any particular inspiration than the fact that I'd just started a new job after nearly a year of unemployment, and was frantically trying to bring myself up to assimilate the knowledge I needed to do the job and keep up with colleagues who seemed to be so far ahead of me as to be over the intellectual horizon. The elation at being employed again and the sense of being overwhelmed by the job itself combined in a way that I could only describe through the story itself.

Looking back at it, what strikes me is the eclectic mix of information I threw into the story. I can remember startling myself with what I remembered of Greek mythology and then having to check my facts and make a few alterations. I can remember using an old joke I'd never thought was that funny – you'll know it when you see it – though not when and why I thought it was a good idea.

The question that really tortures me is whether it's actually funny, but that's not for me to say.

Seeking Kailash

Some years ago, I was driving around Mindanao, buying fish from markets and collecting blood samples from them. Suffice it to say that it was all for science. If I convinced the dozens of people who crowded round to watch me take blood out of a fish that foreigners are even more crazy than they had previously thought, it was entirely unintentional.

One of my lasting impressions of that escapade was of how lost I would have been without my colleagues in the Philippines Bureau of Fisheries and Aquatic Resources. When the initial study site proved unsuitable, they suggested an alternative and how to relocate the study there. When I needed samples from locations that met certain criteria, they named the locations. When I needed to get there, they arranged the transport through routes that avoided areas occupied by insurgents. Without their help, I would never have been able to complete the study I was doing within the limited time and budget I had available.

Around the idea the story was germinating, I saw the film *Himalaya*, and the sweeping vistas of the place reminded me of my own visit to the Annapurna region some time before that. I had a theme and I had a location. For once, the rest followed fairly easily.

Foreclosure

This story was my re-entry into writing after a hiatus for health reasons, which might be why it had a more straightforward starting point than many that I've written. As the title implies, it's very much rooted in the recession of the last few years in which so many people have discovered they are not as financially secure as they thought. We've seen banks taking the roofs from over peoples' heads as a result, even though the banks were involved in the decisions that led people to buy homes they later found they could not afford. While the decisions were shared between the bank and their clients, the consequences were not. The clients lost their homes while the banks were bailed out by our governments.

The joy of science fiction is the opportunity to push ideas, so I found myself wondering what else the banks could take to cover themselves. How far are we from the day when the banks will demand our first born children as security for a loan?

Summer Holidays

I worked my way through my undergraduate degree by teaching outdoor sports to children of various ages. After several summers of it, I made the mistake of signing up as a summer camp counsellor. I can't speak for the summer camps in general but I can say that I was not a little horrified by how much time I spent trying to limit bullying. I say 'limit' because preventing it altogether would have been a labour beyond Hercules, and it was certainly beyond me. I left the business with a view of childhood that was much more *Lord of the Flies* than *Swallows and Amazons*.

A few years later, I was living in a caravan on the West Coast of Scotland, which gave me a fairly detached perspective on a moral panic sweeping the press. Robert Thompson and Jon Venables, infamous as the ten year olds who had murdered the toddler James Bulger, had been released from prison. What struck me about the wave of hysteria was that a lot of the commentators seemed to be almost desperate to paint Thompson and Venables as monsters. I began to see that they were less concerned with any harm Thompson and Venables might do than with protecting their image of childhood. If they wanted to continue to conceive of children as harmless and wholesome, it was necessary to categorise Thompson and Venables as something other than children.

It was a view my experience prevented me from agreeing with. That's not to say that most children would go around murdering each other given the opportunity. The vast majority of the ten year olds I taught would have reacted to a lost toddler by helping him look for his parents. However, I also saw the cruelty of a significant minority. I like to think that the lack of compassion of the bullies I'd encountered stemmed from an underdeveloped sense of empathy, which they would grow into later. It's equally possible that they are still holy terrors to the people around them to this day. What I am sure is that if any two of them were trying to prove themselves to each other, I would not want an unattended toddler anywhere near them.

The story moved some distance from conception to completion, largely as the protagonist's capacity for violence was directed mainly against himself. I was trying to tell a story, not comment on society.

Something must have worked, because this was the first story I wrote that didn't need extensive rewriting. Consequently it became my first story to be accepted, although several stories I'd written earlier were published after later rewrites.

Steel in the Morning

The idea for this story germinated when I read Richard Cohen's *By the Sword*, a superbly readable history of swords and swordsmanship from mediaeval trial by combat to the modern sport of fencing. The book is filled with characters who are so improbable that they would never work in fiction, but the one who stood out was Joseph Boulogne, Le Chevalier de St George. Boulogne was the illegitimate but acknowledged son of a French plantation owner and one of his slaves who became celebrated across Europe for his prowess as an athlete, fencer, horseman and musician. I was particularly fascinated by the way he was trapped between classes. His father allowed him to become an intimate of the upper classes while his mother prevented him being one of them. When the revolution came, he embraced its promise to sweep away the concept of class altogether, but his paternity caught up with him and saw him imprisoned and impoverished.

At about the same time, I became interested in how best to write fast-moving action. Swordplay lent itself as it involves technical movements that take less time than it takes to read a description of them. I wanted a story that would revolve around descriptions of swordplay, so then I needed a reason for the steel to be bared in the first place.

Perhaps bizarrely, the answer came out of a conversation about *Pride and Prejudice*. What's stuck in my mind was not the much celebrated romance between Darcy and Elizabeth, but the Bennett family's treatment of Lydia. Rather than forgiving her youthful indiscretion with the 'worthless' Wickham, Darcy and the Bennett family force her to marry him and then shun the pair of them. The Regency middle classes could be a brutal lot, which gave my Boulogne-inspired character something to draw his sword over.

I moved my Boulogne-inspired character to London by making him a bit younger at the time of the Revolution and his father enough of an aristocrat to put him on the wrong side of the Terror. Le Méridian was born.

Newgate Jig

My stories rarely start with a character, but I was so taken with the character of Le Méridian that he demanded to be used a second time. The idea for the story came from a visit to London – I was living overseas at the time – just after I read *London's Underworld* by Fergus Linnane, with its description of law breaking and law enforcement in London through the centuries, and the often rather blurred line between them. I found myself standing in Old Bailey Street, looking up at what is now the Central Criminal Court. I tried to imagine what it must have been like when the building was Newgate Prison and the street I was standing in was packed with a crowd baying for the lives of men and women twitching on the gallows in front of where I was standing.

In spite of the well-dressed lawyers tucking into coffee and sandwiches from the concessions behind me, it was disturbingly easy to do.

Virulence

I wrote the first draft of this story in 1999, after reading a few articles about a few cases of avian influenza in Hong Kong. At the time, the idea of influenza as a serious threat was so far from public consciousness that several critiques of the first draft struggled with the concept because infectious disease pandemics don't happen anymore. I thought it was an odd statement at a time when HIV was giving the world its worst pandemic since the Black Death but it didn't occur to me to challenge the obscurity of influenza as a global threat.

Through multiple rewrites, the story progressed along with my writing ability and the world progressed with it. By the time it was published in the much lamented *Æon* magazine, its original title of *Pandemic* had to be changed because the word had ceased to be an obscure technical term and become such a household word that it sounded bland. Meanwhile, 'bird flu' was discussed as the pending apocalypse.

I was working in Mindanao at the time so that was where I set the story, and there it stayed through multiple rewrites. I think the choice of setting was the wisest choice I made about the first draft, and one of very few things that didn't get changed.

The Redeemed

Taken from when I wrote the first draft, this is the oldest story I allow to show its face in public. I wrote most of it in a gatehouse in the Isle of Wight, guarding a gate that nobody had any interest in going through. The first draft was so awful it was worse than I was capable of understanding at the time. Several rounds of critiquing and rewriting not only improved the story but pushed me up a very steep learning curve. In a way, this story was an apprenticeship for me.

Reading it now, it still seems rough around the edges and suffused with the hysteria that I used to mistake for pathos. For all that, I decided the final version deserves a little more exposure and included it in this collection.

Rainfire by Night

The first version of this one was one of the first stories I wrote. My original concept was to tell the story around Mitochondrial Eve, the woman who all living humans are descended from. She must have been fairly prominent in her society to give her gene line the sort of head start it must have needed to squeeze out all the others, and I started from the assumption that prehistoric politics was as dishonest as modern politics, albeit with a bit more head splitting. To emphasise the point, I put her in an oppressively patriarchal society that she would have to deceive and manipulate her way to the top of.

I don't think the concept was terrible, but the story was. I can only thank my lucky stars that I realised how awful before showing it to too many people. I left the story to sink into the obscurity it deserved, but the character I'd drawn up for Eve wouldn't let me go. It must have been two or three years after I'd first given up on her that a post-apocalyptic novel stirred the thoughts I needed to bring her back into the light. I think it may have been David Brin's *The Postman* but I'm not sure.

I was living in Scotland at the time and as I looked around, I saw a much better setting for a post-apocalyptic society than anywhere to be found in the USA. The countryside was littered with castles and forts built for the sort of tribal squabbling that forms the basis of so much post-apocalyptic fiction. I don't mean post-apocalyptic fiction set in Scotland is automatically superior to post-apocalyptic fiction anywhere else, just that the environment was already shaped for the needs of the hostile tribes that populate so much post-apocalyptic fiction.

Eve was reborn into a future where, instead of becoming the ancestor of humanity on the rise, she joined humanity in terminal decline.

Of the other ideas went into the story, one that sticks in mind was a comment by a friend on a picture of a Celtic engraving of a woman holding her vagina open. It was captioned as a fertility goddess. My friend said one day, archaeologists will excavate a stack of pornographic magazines and being unable to read the captions, conclude that they were the artefacts of a fertility cult. It was such a pertinent observation that I had to use it.

18396804R00151

Printed in Poland
by Amazon Fulfillment
Poland Sp. z o.o., Wrocław